COMMUNITY
215

DR. M. K. BLACK

COMMUNITY 215

ISBN-13: 978-1-959677-36-9 (Paperback)
ISBN-13: 978-1-959677-35-2 (eBook)

Published by Defiance Press & Publishing, LLC

Bulk orders of this book may be obtained by contacting Defiance Press & Publishing, LLC. www.defiancepress.com.

Public Relations Dept. – Defiance Press & Publishing, LLC
281-581-9300
pr@defiancepress.com

Defiance Press & Publishing, LLC
281-581-9300
info@defiancepress.com

This is for you, Daddy.

TABLE OF CONTENTS

CHAPTER 1
THE WAY THINGS ARE

As long as you are a part of a Community, you are safe.
As long as you are never an Outcast, you are safe.
As long as you never try to change things, you are safe.
Just never challenge the way that things are, and you are safe.

Rhea crouched next to the puddle and poked happily at the water, watching the mud turn the surface murky and cloudy before it slowly receded, leaving the puddle clear once more. Rhea was safe as long as she did not cross the Wall surrounding the Community. Leaving the Community would mean danger, and almost certainly death. She knew this, even though she was only eleven. She had been told this undeniable truth since she was an infant. On occasion she had been caught trying to peek through holes in the log barrier, or hastily making a climb for the top with friends cheering her on and her grubby feet scrabbling on the wood, catching splinters along the way. Father himself had climbed up after her, snatching her from the Wall with uncharacteristic roughness, and hurled her back onto the ground. Her breath had rushed from her lungs the second she hit the earth, and she had stared up at Father with newfound respect and fear.

She had not tried to climb the Wall since then.

But still she found her eyes slinking toward the Wall ever so carefully, so as to not draw any attention to her curiosity.

The Wall, in many ways, provided all life for the Community. It kept out Outcasts and other Communities that were not as friendly as hers. But sometimes, it felt as though the Wall was only there to keep Rhea contained and controlled. She knew the rules of her Community; it was not an option not to. The Community could not exist without rules: Respect those in charge—without them, the Community would surely fall. Share everything that you have—it belongs to everyone. Do as you are told—only Outcasts do whatever they want, and it results in murder and chaos. Lastly, do not lie—the Community can only thrive if those in charge know everything about the state of the Community and the people in it.

Rhea placed her bare feet in the cold puddle. Her toes dug happily into the mud, traveling deeper and deeper into the earth. Teacher, Nurse, and various other adults often chastised her and the other hardly tamed children to wear their shoes and boots, but she happily kicked them off the second she was alone. Her eyes strayed yet again to the Wall.

Someone was climbing over.

Rhea stared, her breath catching in her throat as though she was being thrown from the Wall all over again. She was several yards away, and she strained her eyes to see more clearly.

This someone did not hesitate. They hurried to come down the other side of the Wall, their hands and feet scraping against the rough bark of the logs.

Rhea was running before she even knew what she was doing. Her arms pumped hard, and she flew full speed at the Wall.

The stranger was already almost halfway down the Wall.

Rhea stopped beneath them, her head tipped back to see more clearly, unsure what to do. "Hey!" she yelled.

Their hands and feet lost their hold in surprise, and they fell directly onto Rhea. Her arms wrapped instinctively around them and cushioned their fall into the tall grass. She quickly shoved the stranger, bigger than she was, away and scrambled to her feet. This person—him, it had to be a him—stayed on all fours. He was breathing hard as he looked up, his eyes locking onto hers.

His eyes were light blue and warm. They shone through the dirt covering his face.

"Help," he whispered. "Oh, please . . . please help me."

Rhea nodded. She quickly crossed to his side and slipped her shoulder under one of his arms. He was taller than she was, and probably a few years older, but he was thin and wiry. She pulled him onto his feet and slowly started walking with him toward the Community dwellings, her mind racing.

His feet stumbled and dragged as she led him along, his head sagging down. Maybe he heard something, maybe he sensed where she was taking him, but his head suddenly jerked up. "No," he said, "I'm not—I can't go there." Turning away from her, his skinny wrist slipped from her hand.

"Hey!" Rhea said again. She turned after him, her feet tangling with his. They collapsed together again, but this time Rhea scrambled onto his back and planted her knee firmly in it, her hands finding his wrists and pinning them to the ground.

"Get off!" he wheezed, squirming despite his apparent weakness and trying to dislodge her.

"Shut up!" she snapped. He froze. "You are in my Community. You don't belong here. Who are you? Where do you come from?"

"You don't understand," he said, his voice muffled in the earth. "If you turn me over to your leaders, they will send me out there again. I can't go back out there. They're hunting me."

"Who—" Suddenly, she was in the air; someone had grabbed her by her shoulders and hoisted her away from the boy.

"Rhea, what the hell are you doing?" It was Nurse. Her rough hands stiffened against Rhea's shoulders as she stared down at the boy, who flipped onto his back and crawled away from them, his eyes like a rabbit watching its hunter.

"Please," he pleaded. Rhea knew he was talking to her, even though his eyes were still fixated upon Nurse. "Save me."

Rhea jumped as the boy collapsed, a sleeping dart protruding from his chest. Nurse lowered her shooter from her lips and turned shakily to Rhea. "Child," she said, and Rhea could hear the fear threading her voice. "What the hell have you done?"

The boy was taken to the infirmary and given the proper medicines. The Doctors kept him asleep as they examined and washed him, looking for anything amiss. Rhea was kept shunted out of the infirmary until she resorted to pounding on the door and screaming, cursing each Doctor and every person in their families and breaking countless rules in the process, until they finally let her see him. She sat next to the boy, staring at him as the Doctors worked on him.

He had curly brown hair when they cleaned him up and dark skin. He had dirty fingernails, like hers, and tough feet, like hers. She stared at his hand a long time, wanting to take it but knowing that she shouldn't.

Father finally arrived.

"What are you doing here?" he asked. She tore her eyes away from the boy, looking up at Father. She would have usually run to him, throwing her arms around him and burying her face in his stomach, breathing in his smell of soap and pine, but she didn't move.

"I found him."

"Were you messing around with the Wall again?"

"No."

"Are you lying to me?"

"No."

He crossed the room and placed a rough hand under her chin, forcing her to look into his eyes. "Fine," he said, letting her go. "You get out of here, now."

She didn't move. "What's going to happen to him?"

"That's up to the Council."

"You control the Council."

"I do not; no one controls anyone anymore. I help to lead the Council."

"Then it's your job to save him."

"Rhea." He knelt next to her, his eyes soft. "He is an Outcast."

"You don't know that!" she screamed, shocking herself with the level of her voice. She never screamed and had only ever broken a rule once with her attempt to climb the Wall. She was a true and worthy member of the Community, yet right now she wasn't acting wisely or making any sense. The Doctors looked at each other uneasily. She was embarrassing her father, and potentially shattering precious traditions, but she somehow couldn't help herself. The boy felt too important to leave up to the typical rules and processes.

Father's face hardened as quickly as it had softened. "Out." He grabbed her by the arm and marched her to the door, then dumped her onto the dirt road. She glowered up at him, but he shut the door on her.

Rhea picked up a nearby stone and hurled it at the door, watching the wood splinter, but the door hold.

~

Rage seethed through her as she paced around outside the infirmary. The Council eventually showed up, their faces blurring past her as they hurried through the infirmary doors. She attempted to squeeze in with them to see the boy again but was quickly spotted and cast away.

Darkness had turned the Community soft and sleepy. Stars began to peek out of the inky sky, twinkly gently at first before erupting into their full bright glory.

Rhea stared at the door hopelessly. Her ears strained to hear their conversation, but it was muffled.

Nurse found her selecting another rock to throw at the door in frustration. "Don't," Nurse said, the word heavy with warning. Rhea had been clouted more than once, and she allowed the rock to fall from her limp fingers.

"Go to your dwelling." Rhea shook her head furiously in response. "Girl," Nurse started, but the door to the infirmary flung open and Father strode out.

"What's going to happen to him?" Rhea asked, her voice strained with desperation.

"It is an Outcast. We will take care of it as such."

Curses burst from between Rhea's lips as Nurse picked her up and carried her to her dwelling, ignoring her furious kicks and threats. "You can't do this! Father! Father!" she screamed and screamed. Several Residents poked their heads out of their dwellings, but most withdrew quickly when they saw it was simply Rhea.

Nurse dumped her unceremoniously into her room and slammed the door, wedging a chair under the handle to ensure her security. Rhea would usually be at an Outcast ceremony; she had already been to two, but it seemed that her tantrum had left her as a sort of outcast as well. She felt unwanted, untamed, and dangerous, just like an Outcast. *We're nearly the same,* she thought, remembering the boy. She didn't know if he had seen it or not, but when he had asked her to save him, she had nodded. That was a promise, a vow. She could feel that vow somewhere deep in her chest, a tiny spark of a fire that drew her to the boy.

She threw her window open and clambered back out onto the road.

She could already hear the drums, thundering like the singular beat of all of the Residents' hearts. They split and echoed through the silence, a *boom . . . boom . . . boom* so loud that the earth seemed to shake with the sound.

Residents were beginning to leave their dwellings. The drums drew them forward as though they were possessed, some of them carrying torches. They started the hum, deep and throbbing like the drums, drawing everyone to the gate. "*Hummm . . .*" they sang as one. "*Hummm . . .*" They had to sing as one—dissent would be chaos.

They started marching their feet to the rhythm, all flawlessly in rhythm down to the smallest children stamping their tiny feet. They didn't need to be told what to do; everyone knew that when the drums started, someone was being cast out. No one asked any questions. Mothers had cast out fathers, parents had cast out children, friends had cast out friends. Everyone knew that the Council had their reasons. It didn't need to be revealed to the Residents, as their trust in those in charge was absolute. As long as one followed the rules, of course they would not be cast out.

The most important part of casting someone out was that everyone showed they were united. The smallest sign of mercy would be devastating to the Community. They were nothing if they were not united. When someone was cast out, the Residents' faces became masks, their eyes blank and lips pursed together as they hummed, their feet carrying them forward without conscious thought. Even the youngest child became a seamless member of the Community, with blank eyes, humming lips, and tiny marching feet. A few faces might slip to show anger or excitement, but most were impenetrable masks.

Rhea shoved past the Residents, ignoring any cries of surprise or shouts of anger.

She had to hurry. The gates were already opening.

In the darkness, the glow of torches shone around the gates. Beyond their small glow, the outside world was endless darkness, the open gate looking like a hungry open mouth ready to swallow up the boy.

Rhea sprinted as though her life depended on it, the boy a singular thought in her mind. His image burned behind her eyelids each time she blinked the sweat from her vision.

Rhea shoved through the throng of humming, stomping Residents that formed a semicircle around the Council, each of whom held up a torch to light the boy's way into the darkness and, if necessary, force him into it. The boy was on his knees in the middle of the semicircle. His eyes were wild with fear, like a squirrel trapped by a dog, as his curly hair waved in the breeze. His hands stretched out in front of him, a feeble attempt at defense, as he slowly retreated on his knees and the Council advanced on him.

Rhea broke through their ranks before turning sharply to face Father, her back to the boy and her right hand held firmly in front of her, palm out, screaming *Stop!* with her body.

Rhea and Father locked eyes.

Silence crashed onto the scene as though the sound had simply been switched off.

"Rhea." Father lowered his torch an inch. "What the hell are you doing?"

Rhea didn't bother to speak. Father knew what she was doing, what it meant. She kept her eyes locked on his.

The world froze around them.

With her free hand, she reached back to the boy and he took her fingers in his. She could feel the vow in her chest, still flickering, giving her strength and courage that she had never known. Her eyes still on Father's, she pulled the boy to his feet. Keeping her body in front of his, her gaze never wavering, Rhea and the boy slowly backed out of the circle, back into the Community.

Just never challenge the way that things are, and you are safe.

And Rhea had just challenged everything.

❧

Not knowing where else to take him, she brought the boy to the treehouse—her favorite part of the Community, because it was high enough to see over the Wall.

She sat across from him, her back against one of the walls of the treehouse. She couldn't carry a torch up into the treehouse, and the only light came from the moon and stars above them. The house didn't have a roof. Really, it was more of a flat fort than a house. Even when the rain pelted her face like tiny bees, she would lie on her back and stare into the sky, wishing she could melt into it.

She didn't look into the sky now; she couldn't take her eyes off the boy. He had deep skin that contrasted starkly with his light eyes. She could see the stars reflected in those eyes as though they belonged to him. Far below them, her father was answering for her crime. She would be punished herself—she knew that. She might be thrown out of the Community, her birthright as a member disintegrating like an old leaf crumpling before it gets carried away in the wind. But there were some things worth dying for. Even as a child, Rhea knew that there were things that she would die for. That was the purpose of a Leader, to know where the lines were and to protect your people. And this boy was certainly one of her people now.

"Who are you?" she asked, tilting her head to the side to study him more closely.

He waited a moment to answer. "Brooks," he finally said. Her eyes narrowed. Everyone knew that Outcasts named themselves after things in nature, like Water or Tree. A Brook was something from nature, but Brooks wasn't. He could be anyone.

"Do you know your purpose yet?" Rhea asked.

"What is that supposed to mean?"

"Your purpose. At what age is it revealed to you?"

"I don't get it."

Rhea drew herself up, thrusting her chin forward proudly. "I am Rhea of Community 215, and my purpose will be revealed to me in exactly seven years, when I am able to take my placement and matching test. I will then begin my occupation, be joined to another Resident, and we will have children based on the population needs of our Community at that time."

The boy stared at her as though she had grown a second head, then he burst out laughing. "What the hell was that?" Rhea's eyes widened in horror as he laughed at her. She knew what to do here—she should politely re-explain herself. This boy was obviously some kind of idiot, and as a future Leader, it was her task to help him understand the ways of the world.

Instead, she launched herself at him, knocking him back onto the hard log floor of the treehouse. He continued to laugh, catching her on top of him with ease this time. She drew back her fist and he caught that, too, looking amused. "Let me go!" she commanded. "Are you stupid? You aren't allowed to touch me!"

"You attacked me, *again*!" he responded, but he let her go and his laughs died away. She scooted as far away from him as possible, wondering if she had made a horrible mistake by saving him.

"I'm sorry," he said, still smiling and shaking his head. "It's just that I have never heard of anything like that. What is a . . . matching test?"

"It is the test I will take at age seventeen that will show me who I will wed."

"What? What's 'wed'?"

"How do you not know? It is a promise that you will be partners with someone and have children with them."

"You people don't . . . just pick who you want to be with?"

"What do you mean?" She glared at him, sure that this must be some kind of joke.

"Out there"—he pointed beyond the barriers of the Community—"people pick who they want to be with and have as many children as they want."

"That is ridiculous. You just ignore the test results?"

He twisted his mouth, attempting not to laugh again. "There aren't any tests out there."

"So . . . how do you know who you are supposed to wed?"

"I guess . . . if you like someone? We don't 'wed' out there."

"So what do you do?"

"I dunno. You just pick who you want and spend time with them."

"For how long?"

"I guess until you don't wanna anymore."

"How many children can you have?"

"Uh . . . as many as you want."

"Then aren't the Outcasts overpopulated?"

"The Outcasts?"

"Yeah." She was starting to get annoyed. Didn't he know anything? "Your people."

"I don't have a 'people.' People out there live wherever they want, however they want to. And there's so much space out there that we don't care how many kids someone has."

"But who is in charge?"

"No one."

Rhea realized that she had been leaning forward, like she was hungry for more information. She sat back, composing herself. "That's not true!"

"Yeah, it is!" he shot back.

"That's not possible. Without someone in charge, everyone would fight all the time!"

"Sure, sometimes people fight."

"And without keeping track of partners and children . . . the children would have to rely solely on their parents to take care of them!"

"Sure."

"Then we need to help them! We could bring them into the Community and teach them!"

He grinned. "Rhea, didn't you just say that the Community wants to keep a handle on the population in here? How are they going to handle all the extra people outside?"

She paused, mulling this over. "They could all help. We could make the Community bigger."

He smiled wisely and sadly, a smile far beyond his years. "I don't think so, Rhea." Before she could argue further, he went on. "So here, you take a test, and they just tell you who to wed and have children with?"

"Obviously," she huffed.

"Well, that's the dumbest thing I have ever heard!" he challenged, throwing his hands into the air. "You don't choose who you are joined to?"

"No," she said, her growing impatience showing.

"But what if you don't like them?"

"What do you mean?"

"What if they're mean or ugly or stupid or—"

"That is irrelevant—how someone looks or behaves has little to do with being wed to them. The tests know who you are best suited for, and this is the only way."

"Well," he said, raising his brows at her, "that is stupid."

Anger reared its head inside of her, boiling her blood. "You don't know *anything*!" she snapped, curling her small hands into fists. "You're an Outcast, which means that you aren't even good enough to be in a Community."

His eyes bore into hers unflinchingly, not caring about the insult she had hurled at him. "Maybe," he said carefully. "But there is always another way."

She shook her head. He couldn't understand. Outcasts were savages who ate their own; they didn't have a sense of Community and family like she did. And yet . . .

"What is out there?" she asked, her eyes burning with curiosity.

"In the forest? Mostly just more forest. Until you come to the mountains."

"What's on the other side of the mountains?"

"I have no idea; I have never crossed them."

"Oh. What do you do, out there?"

Brooks shrugged. "I hunt, I eat plants. Things like that."

"But where are your people?"

"Here and there. Sometimes you have people for a long time, or you might just meet them for a little while before they wander off or die. There's not really a whole lot out there."

Rhea shook her head slowly in wonder. What would the world look like beyond the Wall? "I would love to wander out there someday."

"You can," Brooks declared.

"No, I can't. It's forbidden in my Community. I can only leave once when I come of age to prove that I can survive out there, then I come right back. And when I do, I can't just wander wherever I want. They like to keep people close to the Wall, where it's safer."

His eyes glittered like he had a secret. "You never know. Maybe someday you'll be able to wander beyond the Wall."

"Really?" Rhea's voice dripped with skepticism, but her eyes lit up.

"Really."

≈

By the time they were found in the treehouse, both children were fast asleep, their bodies curled together. There was yelling and gasps when the adults finally spotted them. Rhea was grabbed by Nurse and carried back to her dwelling before being shut into her room again. Brooks was dragged to the Community bathhouse and forced into a bath. They both went to bed worried, covered in bruises, and thinking of one another.

≈

Rhea woke to the sound of the drums again. She leapt to her feet, casting about wildly for her clothes, determined to stop them from attempting to cast Brooks out again. She stumbled around in the semi-darkness, pulling on the first things her hands fell upon. She was just stuffing her foot into a boot when her door flew open, and she instantly knew that they weren't coming for Brooks this time.

They were coming for her.

She swallowed a scream of wild fear and anger, pushed her shoulders back, and held her head high. The Defenders gazed at her through the doorway, ready to yank her from her room. Usually, people came to trial screaming and crying, knowing that their fate was already decided, that they were about to be met with a swift and severe punishment. She had seen them before—their eyes seemed to scream along with their mouths, both open wide with terror pouring out.

Rhea crossed her room to the lead Defender. "Rhea," he began, "we are to bring you to stand trial for disobedience."

She nodded, attempting to communicate calm and serenity, the way a Leader should. She finished putting her boots on and straightened up.

"Well, if you will just follow me, then," she said to the Defenders. Rhea quickly swept from her room without looking back to see their reaction to her cool indifference.

Rhea strode quickly to the arena, the Defenders hurrying to appear as though they were escorting her. The drums and the "*Hummm*" of the people weren't as loud as the night before, as though the Residents were just a little uncertain about this, but they still seemed to drill into her mind and pound from within her. She passed by people of the Community—her people, her family. She nodded and tried to look into each pair of eyes she could find as she passed them. No one met her gaze.

I am young, but I am strong, she told herself. *I know the way.*

The arena was a large semicircle of stands that rose around a stage. Like everything in the Community, it was made of logs from the surrounding forest. It was already full of people with more and more streaming in. Rhea strode to the middle of the stage, gazed up at the box that contained the leaders of the Community, and waited. The sky lightened by small degrees as she waited, the stars gently winking out, surrendering to the impending sunrise.

Her father was seated in the middle of the box. On either side of him was the rest of the Council. They offered him and the Residents advice and guidance, ensured that Residents followed the rules, and curated a curriculum for the children to learn the necessary rules of being part of a Community. Now they gazed down at her, and she gazed back.

Her father held up his hand, and the sound of the drums stopped immediately. She had somehow ceased to hear their haunting hum as well, as though it had reverberated straight from her heart.

"Rhea," her father began, his voice carrying through the silent spectators. "We have found you guilty of disobedience. You will be punished accordingly." That was how all trails went: the leaders knew best, and there was no point in hearing from a defendant. Rhea nodded, her stomach coiling into knots. Would she be Outcast? Could Brooks come with her?

"You disobeyed the laws of the Community by refusing to participate in the casting out of the boy who appeared from over the Wall yesterday," the second Council member cut in. "This is in direct defiance of the ways of the Community, as we all know that Outcasts are unwelcome here and pose an imminent threat to our lives and our Community."

"However . . ." It was the third Council member's turn now. "You are the only offspring of our Leader, as your mother failed in her attempt to provide him with the required three offspring the Community needed when she perished giving birth to you."

"Therefore . . ." the next interjected. Rhea had to stop herself from tapping her foot, wanting them to just get on with the punishment. But this was the only way; everyone on the Council had to have their voices heard. "We are unable to Outcast you." Rhea let out her breath in a long sigh of relief. She didn't understand the rationale behind being spared. Perhaps her father had more power as the Leader of the Council than he was willing to show.

"Rhea, you will instead be marked as disobedient. Effective immediately," the next member announced.

Her father nodded, gazing down at her. "Defenders, take her to the Hall of Punishment and mark her. Make sure that everyone who sees her knows that she is disobedient."

Rhea barely felt the hands of the Defenders as they closed around her like vises. Her eyes locked with Father's once again. This time, he had bested her.

The drums started again.

Rhea struggled to keep her feet under her as she was dragged to the Hall of Punishment. The arena was as far away from the hall as possible so that more people would see her on the way to her punishment and on her way back. She walked carefully, this time not meeting the eyes that gazed at her, afraid that if she did, the tears would break through the dam she had built to keep them back. As they crossed the bridge over the river, Rhea focused on the beat of the drums and the *hmmm* of the people around her. The noise buzzed and swelled, growing louder and louder as they drew closer to the hall.

They passed the crops, the infirmary, and the animals. They passed the school where all of the children stared at her, wide-eyed, gathered closely about their Teachers, likely swearing to themselves they would never make the same mistake.

The sun finally began painting the sky with red and yellow fingers. Rhea pushed the thoughts of pain from her mind. She had known the cost of saving Brooks; she was just fortunate that it had not meant her life. Of course, it apparently *would* have meant her life if Father had had any other children. In that case, he surely would have cast her out without a second thought. But there really was nothing wrong with that, she told herself. *It is the only way to ensure order. Children—all people, really—are only valued as long as they are needed.* Without that, what was really the point of them?

"Rhea!" The cry amazed her, cutting through the drums and humming like a knife. Several people fell silent, staring. Brooks was running at her, fists outstretched as though he could tear the Defenders away from her.

Someone caught him and held him fast. Rhea shook her head as though to clear it. *What is he* doing? *This is the only way.* Now more people were holding onto Brooks as he attempted to claw his way to her. *He looks as though he's sick in his mind,* Rhea thought. His light eyes were crazed, his dark curly hair flew about wildly as he fought, and his mouth was open in a yell. Defenders finally reached him and laid heavy hands on him. One forced his mouth open, pouring a soothing draught into it. Brooks choked and tried to spit it out, but the Defenders held his mouth and his nose, forcing him to swallow. Brooks became limp in their arms, and they quickly hauled him away.

What was he thinking? Rhea wondered as she continued on. The little parade of shame finally arrived in front of the Hall of Punishment. She went in through the designated "guilty" door and seated herself in the chair. The Defenders busied themselves binding her arms and legs to the chair with thick ropes. *It is for my own safety,* Rhea reminded herself. Once they come forward to begin the punishment, people always raised their hands if they were not tied down. And, if they passed out after, the ropes would ensure that they did not fall to the ground. *It is truly an act of kindness to bind the guilty party, and to bind them tightly.*

The Hall of Punishment was built in much the same fashion as the Trial Arena. There was a stage where the guilty sat that was surrounded by stands for people to watch. Rhea had to wait while more and more people flowed into the stands. The more people who saw the punishment, the more effective the punishment would be at deterring others.

There was also a firepit a few feet away from her where a small group of Defenders were already stoking large flames and placing the brand into them. There were several different brands to choose from with various designations. The first letter was a large capital letter while the rest of the word was written smaller. There was the brand for Thieves, one for those who had committed Infidelity, and so forth. Branding someone as a lesser member of the Community was the only way to keep them as a member. Everyone needed to know who they were dealing with, right?

Rhea would be getting the *Disobedience* brand.

The lead Defender entered to stand in front of her. "How are you, Rhea?" he asked pleasantly, as though they were meeting for tea. The drums and the humming seemed to subside to a low rumble, although it did not stop.

"I am well, Defender. How are you?" It was the custom for adults with occupations to go by their occupation title rather than their name, as being a part of an occupation was nobler than being an individual person. This made perfect sense to the Residents. Rhea, for instance, was the only Rhea within the Community, as names never repeated within the Walls. When she died, a new Rhea could be born. When Rhea turned seventeen, she would take her placement test that would reveal her purpose and future occupation, and once she started working at eighteen, she would drop the name Rhea and simply use her occupation as her name. Rhea felt certain that her test would show what she had always known: she was meant to lead the Community in Father's place.

"I am well. You are going to be punished today," the Defender said. Rhea nodded.

"I know that I have broken the rules," she said, her voice shaking only slightly. "I am ready and willing to take the appropriate punishment as selected by our Council." She felt brave saying these words. She understood now more than ever why they were a requirement of her punishment. When she had been taught this script years ago, she had never thought she would have to utter them in this context.

The lead Defender pulled her collar away from her throat to provide adequate room. He tipped her head hard to the left to expose the right side of her throat, under her ear.

The drumbeats changed; the hum strengthened. *Boom . . . boom . . . boom . . .* the drums beat in a driving rhythm. Sweat trickled between Rhea's shoulder blades, and her eyes followed Father as he walked toward the fire. *Hmmm . . . hmm . . . hmmmmm . . .* went the hum, deep in her people's throats. Father picked up the brand, the tiny "Disobedience" red-hot on the iron poker. He took slow and deliberate steps over to Rhea. The poker glowed with heat. The brand pointed toward Rhea like a crazed eye staring at her.

I will not scream, she swore to herself, pressing her lips together.

Boom . . . boom . . . boom . . . the drums beat. *Hmmm . . . hmm . . . hm-mmmm . . .* the throats moaned, almost sounding like they were in ecstasy now.

Father joined her eyes once more, satisfaction behind his gaze. *Perhaps she will finally learn that obedience is the only way to peace,* he thought before touching the poker against his daughter's pale throat.

Rhea screamed until darkness clouded over her eyes, providing her with sweet relief.

CHAPTER 2
BROOKS

Brooks awoke to find his head throbbing like the beat of the drums. He shot to his feet but immediately had to sink his head into his hands, groaning with pain. He raised his head again, this time much more slowly. He was in an underground pit. The walls and floor were smooth earth, and several feet above his head was a grate of branches. Brooks automatically felt for his knife before remembering he had stashed it before climbing the Wall, knowing that they would take it. His fingers itched for a weapon; it was like feeling a phantom limb.

Brooks threw back his head, his dark, wild curls tumbling over his shoulders, and screamed. "Rhea!" he bellowed. "Rhea! Rhea! Rheeeaaaaa!" A face appeared through the grate far above him.

"Shut up, boy!" someone yelled back, but Brooks only grinned and continued to scream.

"Rhea! Rhea! Rhea!" His throat felt as though it were being shredded by his screams. He stopped long enough to cough hard, then continued calling for Rhea. Suddenly, a dart emerged out of the edge of his tunic, just above his shoulder. He delicately pulled it away from his shirt, which was made of deer, and laughed. The animal's hide had kept him safe this time. "You missed me!" he taunted, waving the dart above his head and laughing like a maniac. He quickly danced around as another dart shot in his direction. "Let me up there, I'll show you how to shoot!" Brooks laughed as he spun and ducked.

"Enough!" came a stony voice from overhead. The barrage of

darts ceased immediately. "Bring him up."

A thin length of rope cascaded down into the prison. Brooks grabbed ahold of it eagerly. He had never before been confined and the earth of the prison seemed to be slowly closing in on him, as though the walls were eager to swallow him whole.

The rope drew closer to the open sky as Brooks was pulled back up. At the top of the hole, he eagerly reached out a free hand and felt strong fingers clasp it and pull him onto the lovely grass. Brooks rolled into the grass, laughing all over again, and took a moment to bury his face into the earth, soaking in the smell of the life within its roots. He rolled onto his back and grinned up at the sky.

"What's your name, boy?" the stony voice asked, and a face filled his vision. The man was rather small, with white-blond hair and dark-green eyes. He looked remarkably like Rhea.

"Brooks." Brooks smiled up at him in a winning way. His white teeth flashed against his dark skin.

"Brooks?" the man said as though it were a question. "That is not truly your name. You are an Outcast."

"I am a what?"

The man sighed. "You don't come from a Community. We know this. That makes you dangerous."

Brooks chuckled again. "It's like we don't even speak the same language, isn't it?"

The man frowned. "No. It's more like we are not even the same species, actually."

"That's fair enough," Brooks agreed. He reached out a hand and the man hesitated for a second before pulling him to his feet. They stood almost eye to eye, even though the man was much older than Brooks.

"You truly have no idea what you have done, do you?" the man asked, folding his arms in a way that he must have imagined made him look quite stern. To Brooks, it appeared as though he was cold and needed a blanket.

"Enlighten me," Brooks requested.

"There has never been anyone who came over the Wall before."

"Well, I am one of a kind," Brooks quipped, smiling even wider.

"And now my daughter, my only offspring, has been marked as disobedient."

"Now, that's a real pity," Brooks said, never guessing the scar that the man had just left on his own child. "Whoever will inherit all of this?" He spread his arms out wide to indicate the Community.

"We don't have inheritance," the man sighed. "Our leaders are selected fairly through an unbiased testing policy—the opposite of what you people do."

"Right, and why do you do things that way?"

"It keeps the Council safe. They have complete support from our Residents."

"Safe? What in the world could possibly happen to you while you hide behind these Walls?" Brooks asked, his eyes dancing with laughter.

"You don't understand anything." The man fidgeted, clearly annoyed, but not angry.

Brooks had the feeling that this man was not allowed to get angry. *Maybe that's why he was selected as a Leader.* "No," Brooks agreed, "I really don't."

"That makes you dangerous."

"I am willing and eager to learn."

"Is that so? What is it you want to know?"

"Oh, but this is a very interesting place to me," Brooks said, indicating the barrier all around them. "I wonder, do you treat people equally behind your Walls?"

"Of course we do!"

"Of course you do." Brooks's smile had turned cold, and there was wisdom in it. He knew how things worked in Communities. "Am I a member of your Community now, then?"

The man glared at him with open dislike. "I haven't decided what to do with you yet," he said through gritted teeth.

"I believe that decision was made for you by your beautiful daughter."

"She didn't know what she was doing! She is a good, obedient young person. You have no idea how you have harmed her." The man stopped to take a great breath and cast a glance around. The Defenders stood far enough away that their conversation wouldn't reach their ears, but close enough to rush to their Leader's defense if Brooks attacked him. Brooks assumed that if he attacked their Leader, there wouldn't be an "outcasting" or a "trial" this time—just a quick death. "Why are you here?" the man demanded. "What do you want from us?"

Brooks allowed a cloud to pass over his face. "You don't understand what it is like out there," he recited. "It is absolutely awful! There was a group of people . . . they were chasing me . . . I don't know what they wanted; I didn't ask. I ran straight here, saw the Wall, and I knew they wouldn't follow me over it. I need help, or they'll kill me." He waited to see how the Leader would take his little speech.

"We don't help Outcasts. We take care of our own Residents."

"I was hoping that I could become one of those Residents."

"You don't know anything about our rules. You could introduce dangerous ideas to the other young people."

"I will do whatever you say. Isn't that a quality you look for in your Residents?"

The Leader twisted his mouth, not believing Brooks for a second. Brooks seemed to teeter on the edge of something for a minute, even shifting his weight between his scarred and scabbed feet before settling on his decision.

"Look," he began, a somber look falling like a veil over his laughing features. "I didn't mean to get Rhea into trouble, okay? And I really do need to be here. The people out there . . ." He shuddered, a look of fear darkening the humor in his face. "They would kill me in an instant if I went back. It's just what they do. They don't think like I do; they do what they want. Freedom goes to their heads, and they live without any laws or consequences." He fixed the man with his bright eyes, full of unshed tears. "Please don't send me back," he pleaded. "I know I can be a part of this Community. I would do *anything* to be in this Community. I am in love with your daughter."

The man took a step back as though Brooks had struck him, his face white. "What? How . . . how would you even know that word?" he demanded, his voice released in a slow hiss. "We don't talk about . . . about . . . that *thing* in this Community." He strode forward, poking Brooks in the chest with a long pale finger, his eyes darting around as if looking for eavesdroppers. "You will learn the rules of this Community, and you will follow each one to the letter. You will never mention that vile thing within these Walls again, or I will throw you out, and Rhea be damned. You will get her killed if you don't watch yourself!"

Brooks looked down at his toes quickly before the man could read his face. "I promise," he vowed.

CHAPTER 3
THE CONSEQUENCES

Rhea's eyes fluttered open, and she immediately wished that they had not. She let out a soft, pitiful moan of pain and raised her hand to the side of her throat. She could feel the outline of her disobedience with her fingers, the flesh raised where the brand had been pressed into her skin. She gritted her teeth to fight the pain, but fresh tears trickled out of her eyes. What would her Community think of her now? Would she even still be a member? They would not cast her out, not actually expel her from the Community—but the sidelong looks, muttering, and pointing would perhaps be even worse. Rhea slowly sat up, her head spinning, and fought to keep the bile rising in her throat out of her mouth. She swung her legs off of the bed and walked to her mirror. It was a small mirror, about the width of her hand. Vanity was not tolerated in the Community; mirrors were considered only necessary for ensuring that a member was clean, decent, and ready to venture out of their dwelling.

Rhea twisted her head to get a better look at her brand. The "Disobedient" was angry and red. It was small, only about two inches long. She touched it gingerly again, wondering how long it would take for it to heal, how long until she forgot what she used to look like before she had been disobedient. Her bedroom door flew open and Nurse entered.

"Good, you're up," she said. "You need to get ready for learning."

"Yes, Nurse," Rhea mumbled, her heart beginning to pound at the thought of having to go to training already. She had just been branded that very morning; her classmates would still be buzzing about her great fall from grace. She glanced outside. It appeared to be about noon; her classmates would be eating the midday meal before return- ing to lessons. After missing morning lessons, Rhea would now have to join them. Rhea's stomach squirmed at the thought of being forced to sit among her classmates, but she didn't have the courage to argue or beg Nurse to let her stay in her dwelling. The brand was supposed to warn others of her offence, but also serve as a reminder for her. The pain was too fresh to forget, and it was about to be burned into her all over again when she faced the ridicule of her classmates.

Rhea washed her face in cold water, took her morning medicinal tea presented by Nurse, and dressed in wool pants, boots, and a light tunic. She purposely combed her shoulder-length white-blonde hair around her brand, wanting to cover it as much as she could, and hur- ried out the door without another glance at her reflection.

"Rhea!" someone shouted as soon as she left her dwelling. Lila was hurrying in her direction, an eager look on her face. Rhea slowed her pace very reluctantly, eyeing her closest friend suspiciously. They had been close since they were very young, the kind of closeness among classmates that their Teachers frowned upon, as it implied that not all of the children favored each other to the same degree. However, there was technically nothing in the rules against having a best friend. In fact, the rules encouraged camaraderie among classmates, as that would only help them grow into a stronger Community. So, Lila and Rhea had stayed close.

"Hi," Rhea said, thrusting her chin forward proudly.

"Oh my goodness, Rhea," Lila said, bounding forward gleefully. "I am so very proud of you!"

"What?" Rhea asked, taken aback.

"That Brooks," Lila breathed. "He is so beautiful!"

Rhea glared at her friend, her stomach tying itself into knots. Everyone had certain aspects of the rules that they had trouble follow- ing, Father had often confided in her. Some would prefer to change their craft, even though the one selected for them was the perfect fit to their abilities; some would envy another's dwelling, or wish that they had an extra helping at mealtimes; and although no one spoke about this shameful occurrence, some might even want a different dwelling partner. Lila struggled with vanity. She was, Rhea thought but never said, the prettiest girl in her class, with thick red-brown hair, long eyelashes, and a light smattering of freckles over her nose. She looked different from many people in the Community, where brown or black hair was usually the norm, and stood out pleasantly.

Rhea looked different, too, with her light hair contrasting with her deep-green eyes. She ran a hand absently through her shoulder-length hair and resolved to grow it out so that it would cover her brand more easily. Despite the rules and regulations of the Community, the children did often voice their preference for one Resident's appearance over another in whispered tones. Lila had often been guilty of that particular offense, and Rhea frequently scolded her but never ratted her out.

"I don't know what you mean," Rhea answered, resuming her walk down the path to the school. "He is as able-bodied as anyone else in our class."

"You know what I mean!" Lila insisted. "Do you think he will be in our class? I would love it if the tests showed we were well suited!" Rhea's stomach clenched tightly again.

"There is no point in hoping. You will be matched with whoever is the best fit to be your partner," she snapped. *Sometimes Lila can just be so stupid.*

"Who do you think you will get?" she asked, practically skipping while she walked. Lila always wanted to speculate over who the girls would be joined to—a pointless adolescent practice of hers, and one that Rhea often ignored. The tests were never wrong. She would be given the partner who was the best match for her personality and genetics. He would not be related to her, he would be able-bodied, and he would be a good match. What more was there?

"An able partner who will ensure that our dwelling is safe, and our children are cared for," Rhea sniffed.

"You sound just like the rule book. Did you memorize that thing or something?" Lila whined as the schoolhouse came into view.

"Yes, of course I did. We're all *supposed* to," Rhea said pointedly.

"Well, you didn't study it well enough to stop yourself from saving Brooks!" Lila countered, smiling as though she had just won a fight.

"That's not the same thing!" Rhea caught Lila by the arm and swung her around to glare into her light-brown eyes. "He asked me to help him. I said that I would, so I did. My word is binding."

"Yes, and so are the rules," Lila said, trying to pull her arm out of Rhea's grip and failing. "You know you did something wrong, because you let them brand your neck! Oh, it looks so awful." Lila gave a delicate little shudder.

"Thanks. What choice did I really have?" Rhea was practically spitting in Lila's face, forgetting herself, forgetting that she was out in public and should be more reserved, more obedient.

"Rhea," Lila dropped her voice to a whisper, "you could have run off with him."

"What?"

"Excuse me, girls." Teacher was looming behind Lila, and both girls jumped. "You are both expected inside now for rules review, and as you missed this morning's review, Rhea, I would highly recommend that you take this time to reacquaint yourself with the way that we do things in this Community."

Rhea followed Lila and Teacher into the schoolhouse, her mind racing. What did Lila mean she could have "run off with him"? *Run off?* No one chose to leave the Community. Being a part of a Community was an honor—it meant that you were safe. You were bound to people who loved you, part of a true family. Rhea would someday use her abilities to make great contributions to her Community. Perhaps—her stomach always gave a little leap of excitement when she thought of it—she might even lead it herself one day.

Rhea was so lost in thought she almost did not notice what she was doing until she walked into the schoolhouse and every eye turned to gaze at her. There was only one schoolhouse, so all the children between the ages of three and seventeen were seated inside. Here, they reviewed the rules each morning and after the noon meal before breaking apart into smaller groups to learn how to farm, ride, count, read, cook, or do countless other apprenticeships around the Community.

Rhea tried to draw herself up proudly as she cast her eyes at all of her classmates, but she froze. Even Teacher strode to the front of the class before turning to stare at her. Rhea flushed red with shame.

She did not know who started it, but there was a slow, rumbling "*Hmmm . . .*" that went around the classroom.

They don't think I was punished enough. She opened her mouth to protest, her eyes darting like a startled doe from one classmate to the next. Even Lila had taken her seat and set her lips together to hum.

Someone touched her arm. She whirled around to face Brooks. Her hand darted to her throat, but he caught her fingers and lowered them. He brushed her hair back away from her throat and stared at her brand, her disobedience, her shame. "What did you let them do to you?" he asked, so quietly that no one else could hear. He turned back to look at the class, and the fire blazing in his eyes stopped the hum.

Rhea put her head down and took her seat quietly, Brooks right on her heels.

Afternoon rule review droned on. Rhea sat perfectly still with her feet flat on the floor, her back straight, her hands poised in her lap, and her eyes locked on Teacher, but she could scarcely focus. How much more shame would she have to take? It wasn't like the Community would ever, or could ever, forget what she had done. The brand would always remind them, and try as she might, she could never truly hide the brand. Everyone who looked at her would see it, would know.

There were plenty of others who were branded around the Community, but all of them were grown-ups. Most crimes involved abandoning one's life partner to explore another. Rhea wondered if that happened as often beyond the Wall, where people were allowed to choose.

Teacher recited all of the 427 rules of the Community, followed by all of the potential punishments that someone could face for breaking one. Punishments ranged from being denied food for a day to being outcast. There was nothing worse than being outcast. Paper being so scarce meant that there was only one rule book. Paper took so long to make and was always in great need around exam time.

All of the children of the Community attended rule review and history together in a hot, crowded classroom filled with uncomfortable wooden benches. Teacher explained the rules one by one: do not challenge the authority of the Council, do not climb the Wall, do not steal another's partner, do not lie, do not cheat, do not argue, do not complain, do not expect, do not want, and on and on and on. Judging eyes burned holes into the back of Rhea's head, and the warm flush in her face didn't subside until it was time for history.

"A long time ago," Teacher explained, "there was simply one large Community. It was called something else; no one remembers what, but it took up a lot of space and it did not contain any Walls. The people in this Community believed that they knew the best way to do everything, so they chose their own occupations, their own daily activities, and even their own partners." A few of the students sniggered at this part, even though they had heard it a hundred times, and several shot glances at Brooks. "This savage way of living simply could not last. Of course, the people started fighting with each other. There eventually were two different ideas at war, two fundamental ways of being. The original way included people continuing to make the wrong choices, to allow each other to be destroyed with freedom, to ignore the needs of others for the desires of oneself." This was the part where Teacher always paused, her eyes focusing intently on each student. "But the right side evidently won. We were able to build the

Communities. Inside the Community, you are safe."

"Inside the Community, you are safe," the class repeated. Brooks shifted in his seat. Rhea stole a glance at him and saw that he was biting his lip, trying not to laugh. Anger and confusion bubbled up within her—he needed to know this! This history was the foundation of everything.

"The *losers*," Teacher emphasized, eyes on Brooks, "were never able to form their own society at all. Today, they are still living savagely outside of our Walls. They attack anything that moves, and their only goal is to take from others. They have absolutely no respect for society and refuse to follow leaders." The silence in the room was so loud, it hurt Rhea's ears.

"Sorry," Brooks said, the slightest trace of a smile dancing around the corners of his mouth.

Teacher twisted her lip but nodded. "Your apology, while not sufficient compared to the utter destruction that Outcasts reign, is heard and accepted." She went on, "Now, our Community is led by a Council of those who have tested the highest among us. They show a fair representation of all of the Residents. We use tests because no person has a right to select a Leader; it must be done in an unbiased way. The tests grant us all of the guidance we could ever need in our lives. We know who our partners will be, how many children to provide the Community with, and what we are meant to do with our lives. Can you even imagine not knowing, and being forced to choose?" She glared once more at Brooks. "Further, the physical tests allow us to eat the appropriate amount based on our needs so that we may never grow hungry or want for more. We then know which Residents are unable to bear children and must therefore not be bestowed with a life partner, as well as what remedies we should be given each day." Several of the students were nodding along eagerly.

"Without the tests," Teacher said, "we would not know who would be worthy of leading us in the future. And we might be cursed with a Leader who is *disobedient*."

Rhea stared straight ahead as every eye in the classroom turned toward her. She had heard this history lesson every single day since she was three and old enough to come to school, but this part was different. Her own eyes stung with unshed tears, but she would not let them fall.

That was how it was going to be, wasn't it? She had chosen her punishment; she should have been free of her crime now . . . but no. Her crime would always follow her around like some ugly, dark shadow, right behind her, never truly touching her but still tainting her. Who would *want* to be her partner? Who would *want* to have a child with her? Her dark stain on her Community's history would live on. And her father would be facing the repercussions, too, for he had saved her as much as she had saved Brooks. It was all over.

Brooks put his warm, calloused hand on top of hers. She started but did not let go, even though it was against the rules to touch another person.

"When each of you turns seventeen, you will be given the chance to take your very own test. And then, your entire purpose in life will be revealed to you," Teacher finished. "And now, let us practice our reading. I have printed several of our very most important rules onto our blackboard. Altogether, now."

After the classroom time, students broke into groups according to their age to complete their apprenticeship for the day. Rhea was an Eleven, and thus was often stuck with the most boring jobs. The older they got, the more exciting the apprenticeships would be. Instead of simply cleaning up after the sick in the infirmary, for example, they would be able to watch examinations and births, preparing for the day when it might be their turn to take over if the tests deemed them worthy.

It took numerous jobs to run the Community correctly, everything from tending the crops to picking in the orchards, feeding the chickens, and most importantly of all, taking care of the bees. Community 215 did not have access to ample resources like many of the surrounding Communities that they often heard about but never saw. Instead of wallowing in jealousy, like an Outcast would likely have done, Community 215 had started a significant bee farm. The bees were responsible for Community 215's cache of honey, honeycomb, and beeswax candles. Other Communities did not even bother to tend to bees, Rhea had heard, even though she didn't know anyone who had traveled to another Community.

Students often complained—under their breath, of course, as complaints were not permitted—about having to get near the bees. Rhea did not mind. They danced together within the long boxes containing their hives, making the sweetest sounds with their humming, music that only she could hear and understand. It was like the humming that preceded a punishment within the Community, but it turned sweet instead of harsh. Rhea carefully hid her love of the bees behind a proud expression when it was her turn to tend them, carefully opening the boxes to collect wax and comb and honey, letting the fat, fuzzy bees thicken the air around her with their song and their warm colors. If she was going to be a Leader someday, she would have to know how to do every job, and do it well, but she also had to show that the only job that was a true fit for her was leadership.

Rhea always attempted to act as though she already were the Community Leader, as though someone were watching her and would notice. Of course, she knew that observation was not even how they selected the leaders; they used tests because they were unbiased, and older Residents were forbidden to discuss the tests with the younger Residents. They must be kept a secret, it was said, or people would attempt to prepare for them, to sway their answers toward a position they believed to be more favorable instead of accepting the natural order of the tests.

Rhea would not do that . . . she believed. However, as a Leader, it was her responsibility to ensure that her Residents were given the best guidance possible in the future.

It was up to her.

The Elevens weren't attending the bees today. Instead, they were mucking out the milk stables that housed milk cows and goats. This was a particularly nasty part of their apprenticeship with the stables, one that was often grumbled about behind hands. Brooks fell into step beside Rhea as they trudged their way to the stables. She tensed, starting to wish that Brooks would leave her alone. If she was ever going to lead, how was she supposed to do it when everyone hated her for saving Brooks from her own people? The Disobedience brand on her neck burned, a consistent heat that flared up as the heat in her face rose at Brook's approach.

"What?" she asked.

"Are you okay?" he said. "I am so sorry . . . I didn't know that they would . . . what kind of people . . ." He was struggling to find words.

Maybe he's just stupid. Rhea thought. She glanced around. All of her classmates were taking turns shooting glances at her and Brooks, then quickly looking away. No one was walking anywhere near them, either, providing a wide berth around them as though they were diseased. Rhea shivered. *Being an Outcast within a Community might be even worse than being an Outcast beyond the Walls.*

"Stay away from me," she hissed to Brooks. "I saved you, I kept my word, that's it—we're done." She quickened her strides, leaving Brooks at the back of the Elevens.

Rhea attacked the filth in the stable as though it would somehow clean her soul. By the time they were dismissed for their one hour of free time, her arms were shaking, and she was covered in sweat. Brooks attempted to talk to her again as they hung up their shovels, but she turned on her heel and ran.

Rhea eventually came to a stop, her chest heaving and tears swimming in her eyes, in a clearing of trees that ran right up next to the Wall. No one ever came this close to the Wall at the back of the Community.

Rhea rubbed her hands angrily over her burning eyes, trying to squash the tears from them, but they kept on coming. She shook, falling to her knees, pressing her lips together to hide the wail of utter despair that was fighting desperately to escape from somewhere deep within her.

"Rhea?" There were suddenly strong hands on her shoulders. She turned into Brooks's chest without thinking and sobbed her sorry heart out into his shirt. "I am so sorry," he whispered a hundred times, stroking her hair with one hand and holding her tightly with the other. "They will pay," he breathed, so softly she was able to convince herself that she had not heard him properly.

They will pay.

CHAPTER 4
SEVEN YEARS LATER

Brooks grinned as he sat perfectly still, listening to the sounds around him. If you listen closely enough, sounds are visions. The soft flutter from a tree is a bird taking flight, a faint buzz is a bee landing on a flower, and the snap of a twig is a predator creeping closer. He could close his eyes and see just as much as he saw with his eyes open. Such was the beauty of living and hunting in the forest for so long; the forest itself was alive, teeming with creatures great and small waiting to be discovered. Each of the plants housed life and was life itself. Brooks kept his eyes closed, the better to listen for . . . *that!* A snap to his right.

He turned his head ever so slightly in that direction. The darkness of the sky was just starting to lift, causing the stars to pale. Each pine needle that hid his face looked sharp in the slight light, as though they would cut him. There was a rustle to his right on the ground.

Yes.

His light eyes snapped open in his dark face and he jumped. He landed just behind her and brought his staff quickly up to block her spinning blow. She thrust again, and he parried. She was more aggressive today than usual—she was energized, ready and willing to fight. Brooks blocked her swings with ease until she became frustrated, lunging out more and more wildly until she became off-balance. She fell to one knee and Brooks seized the opportunity. He knocked her staff to the right, slapped his foot on top of it, and brought his own up under her chin.

"I win," he said, grinning broadly to show his shining white teeth.

"A *coincidental* win," she snapped back. In the semidarkness, she looked more beautiful than ever. She had grown her white-blonde hair down to her waist and often pulled it into a braid on one side of her neck, the right side, to hide her brand. Her eyes were dark green and glared up at him angrily. Only he could get a rise out of her like that, making her drop all of the fake pride of the Community and act human.

"I suppose I must be exceptionally lucky to have beaten you every single time we've played," he teased, offering her a hand up. She ignored it, as she usually did. It was against the rules to touch anyone that wasn't a part of your family, after all. However, fighting was also against the rules, and they had been doing that for months now.

"There is no such thing as luck."

"No?" He smiled even more widely at her, allowing his eyes to travel over her. "I've been pretty lucky in my life." She ignored that but still blushed under his gaze. In truth, she ignored all of his advances. But he didn't care; he knew what he saw in her eyes.

She leaned against one of the pine trunks and wiped sweat from her brow.

"Are you ready for today?"

"We are all ready for today," she said, as he had known she would. "Testing day comes exactly when it is supposed to."

"Any guesses?"

"There is no point to guessing." It was cute when she sounded just like the stupid rule book, but also incredibly annoying. "We will be given what we are supposed to be given, and we will be utterly thankful for it."

"Interesting. So, let's play just a little hypothetical game."

"I don't like games," Rhea snapped. "Games don't serve a purpose and only one person can win, which creates unequal outcomes."

"I know you don't, but they're not technically against the rules."

"One person besting another *is* technically against the rules."

"That's very interesting, given your desire to learn how to fight with a staff." Her green eyes narrowed, and he could not help but smile again. Fighting with her, however he did it, was always so satisfying. But it was also important if she was ever going to understand someday.

"I do not *desire* to learn how to fight with a staff," she corrected him. "It is essential that I learn how to fight with a staff before we face our week beyond the Wall. If the Outcasts get a hold of me, they will likely use me to bait my father." She waited for him to contradict her, to remind her that Outcasts do not care about the leaders, but he did not. Instead, he reached into his knapsack and pulled out two peaches. Her eyes widened with wonder. "Where did you get those?" she demanded.

Food was one of the most sacred rules of the Community. When he had first infiltrated it, they had dragged him out from a hole in the ground they used as a prison, washed and weighed him, and asked him his age. He had not known how old Rhea was, or himself for that matter, so he guessed at her age and answered. They then informed him that he would be permitted to be in the Elevens class and would be provided with an Eleven's portion three times a day. They brought him his first one right there in the infirmary. He had laughed at the small serving of vegetables, roll of hard bread, and meager hunk of meat on his tray until he realized that they weren't joking.

When he had lived as an Outcast—damn, now he was even using the word—he had eaten until his belly was so full, it ached. Food did not come his way every day, but when it did, he gorged himself. It had taken time to adjust to the minuscule portions of the Community. The leaders, he noticed, ate a considerable amount more than the common people, but that was brushed aside through insistence that the leaders needed more sustenance and that everything was truly shared out equally according to the needs of the Residents. But Brooks knew this was a lie. He noticed that Rhea and other Residents and their children who appeared to be thought of as more important than everyone else ate larger and better portions.

He also had snuck into several of the Council member's dwellings to find cooking rooms and stores of food. Brooks regularly, but carefully, stole extra portions for himself and for a few of the smaller, sicklier children who he knew needed more. Stealing food was an offense punishable by branding, but he had always found the risk worth it. He wanted Rhea to be at ease today. Whatever she said about not caring what and who she was chosen for, she wanted to lead. All he wanted was her.

"I thought maybe you would want a treat today." He held it out to her. She reached for it with both hands, hungry from the fight. "Nu-uh," he said, pulling the peach back from her. "Only if you will answer my hypothetical question." Her mouth twisted.

"I shouldn't eat the peach anyway; you could get branded for that."

"Worth it to see a smile on your face. Do we have a deal?"

"Deal." She grabbed at the peach and bit into it, allowing the juice to flow down her chin. Fruit was often cut to be portioned to more Residents, sometimes already brown or dried out by the time it reached their mouths. Brooks bit into his own peach. It was not ripe yet—he'd had to pick it himself under the cover of darkness—but the flavor and juice still burst into his mouth and dribbled onto his chin.

"So, Rhea," he said, smiling, "hypothetically, of course, what occupation do you believe you will be selected for?"

She shook her head, chewing. "You know what I am most *suited* for." She raised her head proudly.

"I see. And hypothetically of course, who do you believe you will be most *suited* to be partnered with?"

Her mouth twisted again. She hated the topic of future partners. She was the only one in their class who actually adhered to the rule of not discussing future partners at all. Flirting was common within the Community, as it was technically unavoidable and too flimsy of an offense to be punishable. But talking about wanting to wed someone was against the rules, as the odds were that you would be disappointed in who was ultimately chosen for you. This went without being said, as the leaders and the rule book could not technically say that Residents might be disappointed in who was selected for them, so they simply created a rule that said "Don't speculate."

Rhea answered carefully, "I will be partnered with someone who is able with an appropriate temperament to my own. They will likely be from our class, although the class above us does contain more males than females, so I suppose it could be someone from that class."

"I see." He spoke carefully as well, "And if you could choose?"

She marched directly up to him and jabbed a finger, sticky with peach juice, into his chest. "You know better than to ask something like that, Brooks, hypothetical or not! You know the terrible things that choice brings!"

He smiled again, trying to ease her anger. She was a particular fool. Most of the males in their class were hoping to be partnered with her, were already speculating about her. Lila received a certain amount of attention as well; she was a very beautiful girl, but Rhea was still the most desired in the class. The "Disobedient" on the side of her throat made her mysterious and alluring.

"Okay, okay!" he relented. Rhea lowered her finger. "So, you would feel the exact same way if you were partnered with Edmond as you would with Troy?"

"Yes."

"Or Gael?"

"Yes."

"Or me?"

Her eyes flickered between his and she licked her lips. "It is almost time for the morning meal," she said. "We must sneak back to our dwellings to wash." She turned on her heel and left him in the same clearing where he had held her seven years ago, promising her that they would pay for hurting her. He smiled yet again, satisfied with her answer.

The Community had allowed two old and previously unpartnered Residents to partner so that Brooks would have a dwelling to grow up in within the Community. It had caused quite the conundrum seven years ago. His "parents" had been unpartnered because they had been deemed "not fit enough" to be permitted a partner when they were younger. People were truly only valued based on what they would bring to the Community, and few things were seen as more important than a carefully controlled population. Brooks had swallowed his disgust as much as possible over the past seven years, trying to ignore how the rules were designed to be demeaning and how the Council saw their own "Residents" as property more than people.

According to the rules, "unpartnered" people could not house a child. However, Brooks could also not inhabit a dwelling with an existing family, and children could not reside alone. Brooks was therefore given the two most malicious people in the Community to call "mom" and "dad," or any number of other names that Brooks bestowed upon them. Brooks only had to step into the house to be screamed at, spit at, or punched. But they were getting older, and both were reluctant to admit any of his rule-breaking behaviors to the Defenders. Undoubtedly, Leader had chosen them in an attempt to intimidate Brooks, but Brooks had seen far too much in his short life to be intimidated by any Residents of the Community. Outside of the Wall, rules ceased to exist. Life out there was enough to make the Residents die of fright.

Brooks did not sneak in through his bedroom window, as he knew Rhea must be doing at that very moment. He walked in through the front door to see "Mom" sitting on her sleeping bench, "Dad" on his. The houses, really more like wooden huts, were arranged so that the parents' rooms were directly through the door, and the children's rooms were through the parents'. There was no need for any other rooms, as all meals were taken together as a Community to ensure

that no one was stealing anyone else's portion, and washing was con-
ducted in the bathhouses. However, Brooks saw the difference in sizes
between the Council members' dwellings and everyone else's, and he
couldn't forget it. Residents were constantly being moved from one
hut to another depending on how big or small their family was—not
the Council members, though, of course.

"Where the hell were you?" Mom demanded.

"I was out fighting our Leader's daughter, Mommy," Brooks responded without missing a beat. The look of horror on their faces was
almost worth all of the pain the Community had caused him thus far.
Almost. Dad picked up a rock that he kept by his sleeping bench for
this purpose and flung it at Brooks. He dodged it easily and laughed.

"You watch yourself!" Dad hissed, spraying spit as he spoke. "You
go around spreading rumors like that and they will brand you and
throw you out of here!"

"Really?" Brooks asked, picking his way between them to reach
his bedroom. "Are you sure they won't be punishing my, uh . . . role
models?" He grinned and slammed his door.

Perhaps even more important than the written rules were the unspoken ones. It was an unspoken rule that Residents kept their children
in perfect order. Brooks didn't exactly do as he pleased, but he was
smart enough to take care of himself and avoid the Defenders while he
snuck around the Community, learning everything that he could about
the inconsistencies and the rule-breaking of the leaders. As long as he
didn't get caught breaking the rules, his "parents" wouldn't rat him
out for fear of facing punishment themselves.

As Brooks washed, he reflected on his day. He and the other
Seventeens had already been subjected to physical tests to deem
them well enough to be permitted to become adult members of the
Community, whatever that meant. He wondered vaguely what would
have become of him if they hadn't deemed him "fit enough" to
become an adult. It was never spoken of, but there were Residents
who sometimes fell suddenly ill or who were caught breaking rules,

though they had never shown any signs of disobedience, and had to be swiftly removed from the Community. Brooks was mildly surprised this hadn't happened to him, yet. The rules stated that physical testing was essential because the Council needed to ensure that Residents were given occupations that they were physically capable of handling. Brooks saw a different motive; the Council only valued Residents as much as they could use them to better their own lives. If someone wasn't useful, they were disposable.

Today, they would be given the written test to deduce where they would work and who they would be partnered with. Brooks assumed this was a rigged assessment and resolved to mirror his answers as closely as he could to what the Council would be hoping to see from a rule-abiding Resident. The final test was the one that excited him the most; they would be finally allowed to leave the Community.

In their arrogance, whoever had designed the Community had decided that in order to prove that Residents were superior to all Outcasts, the Seventeens would be given one week to survive outside of the Community. Most of the Seventeens hovered close to the Wall of the Community, sniveling in the cold, waiting desperately to get back in, and grudgingly foraging for leaves and bugs to stay alive. They always ran back into the "safety" of the Wall, hungry and crying for their families. Returning from the week beyond the Wall was the only time when Residents were allowed to eat as much as they wanted. Brooks supposed that this practice was designed to scare the Residents so that they would never believe that they could survive outside of the Community, reinforced by allowing them to gorge themselves to emphasize the fact that life only existed inside the wooden Walls.

This was not how this exercise would go for Brooks and Rhea. He knew exactly where he would take her, and once they arrived back at the Community, they would have the answers to all of their test results.

And then he would know whether he was going forward with the plan or leaving everything behind for her.

Rhea snuck through the semi-darkness back to her dwelling. She picked her way carefully through the Community, trying to keep her boots from rustling leaves and snapping twigs. Brooks could move soundlessly, but she always blundered her way around.

Just one more day, she told herself as she slid into her window. *Just get through today, and then tomorrow we will be out of the Community.* She frowned, thinking of a more appropriate way to say this, even just to herself. If she allowed her thoughts to slip, it would only be a matter of time before she said or did the wrong thing, and it would cost her everything. *Just one more day . . . and I will fulfill my duty to prove that I am a worthy part of this Community.* That sounded better. She poured cold water into her basin and washed quickly before toweling off to stare at her reflection in the small mirror, her fingers absentmindedly undoing her braid. She turned her head to trace the "Disobedient" brand under her right ear. It was faded pink now, nothing like the angry red mark she had acquired all those years ago. Rhea dampened her fingers and ran them through her hair to wet it, then tied it into a new braid that snaked from her left temple to just behind her right ear. It was all that she could do to hide her brand, to try to blend into the Community that she had betrayed. The shame still burned deeply, hot and uncomfortable, a heavy, sick feeling that she couldn't shake. No, she didn't want to shake that feeling—she deserved it. She was glad that Brooks had been saved, but she had committed an act of evil. She had challenged her family, her Community. It wasn't done. It wasn't right. When she was Leader . . . *if* she was Leader . . . she could not allow such things to go unpunished, either.

Nurse knocked on her door, reminding her to rise. "I'm awake," Rhea said. Nurse strode in with freshly cleaned clothes back from the laundry. Rhea pulled the leggings and linen shirt on before sitting on her cot to lace up her boots.

"Why are your old clothes so sweaty?" Nurse asked, picking up

Rhea's discarded shirt and holding it at arm's length.

"I suppose I sweat in them," Rhea responded, not looking at Nurse. She couldn't lie; the urge to break even the most minor of rules had quite literally been burned out of her.

"Are you getting into some kind of trouble again?" Nurse asked, thumb and forefinger gripping Rhea's chin and twisting her head to study the mark on her neck.

"No," Rhea whispered, eyes downcast. Fear rose quickly in her chest, spreading to her sweating palms.

"Child," Nurse said tenderly. Rhea looked up.

"I am not going to hurt you." Rhea tilted her head, unsure what to say. "I know that . . . everything changed that day . . . because of that boy," Nurse whispered.

Rhea shook her head slowly. "I don't know . . ."

"Just don't . . . don't make a fuss over how things turn out."

"What do you mean?" Rhea was listening now, a hard frown line between her eyes.

"They won't want you to be put with that boy. They won't want you running things. Not after what happened." Nurse was whispering now, leaning close. "But you can't make a fuss over that—it is what it is."

"I don't want . . . I didn't expect . . . ." Rhea was frustrated now, and angry. Why would Nurse act like someone *chose* what she would do or who she would be with? The tests chose. The tests *knew*! It was factual, unbiased, scientific. "The tests will decide," Rhea finally managed. "I trust in them." Nurse recoiled slightly, a look gleaming in her grey eyes that Rhea hadn't seen before. Was it fear? Anger?

"Yes," Nurse whispered. "Of course, the tests decide."

⌢

Gael was waiting when Rhea finally let the door to her dwelling thump shut behind her. Gael had dark hair and eyes, like almost everyone within the Community. His family had a long history of being selected as leaders, a lot longer than hers did. She supposed if they lived in a more medieval time where people were expected to wed based on mutual family interests and bloodlines, he would have been selected for her. She had spotted Gael walking a different girl to class each day for several months now. Some he walked with for a day or a week, but never more than that. Over the past few weeks, though, he had made it a habit of walking her to and from her dwelling. Rhea could not fathom why he had started doing this, but it was nice to have someone to talk to. Being around him pushed the worry and doubt from her mind, or at least distracted her from them, and his acceptance meant a lot to her. It was as though he didn't see her shame. She smoothed a hand over her braid.

"Rhea." He spoke her name as though tasting each syllable. "Are you ready for exams?"

"Yes," she said, returning his smile. She was unsure what he could possibly hope to gain from spending so much time with her. The tests would determine whether they would work together or wed, but she didn't mind his company.

"I'm a little nervous," Gael confessed as they walked side by side to breakfast, his fingers just barely brushing hers. He wasn't allowed to touch her, but she didn't comment. He wasn't *really* touching her.

"There's nothing to be nervous about," Rhea reassured him. "This is the time when we are all meant to take our exams. Everything that we have ever wondered about is about to become clear."

He smiled. "You adhere to the rules so well." His eyes slid to her braid, the weak cover over her shame.

"Are you being facetious?" Rhea demanded, planting her feet and whirling to face him. Gael raised his hands as if to ward her off.

"Of course not!" he said, still smiling. "I was being serious."

Rhea put her hand to her neck, unable to help herself.

"Rhea," Gael said, taking a step closer and closing his fingers around hers to draw her hand away from the brand. Rhea bristled but did not withdraw. "The rules state that once you are branded, you are to be forgiven. The punishment is over; everyone has forgotten about it except for you."

She lowered her eyes demurely. "I broke trust with everyone that day," she whispered.

"I know." Gael took a step closer, still holding her hand. His fingers were warm. She'd never held hands with anyone before. "But you've rebuilt it since then. You might not get everything you want, but you can still get some things." His smile widened. "Doesn't that sound good, Rhea?"

She had no idea what he meant, but she wanted to make him happy; he was being so kind to her. She looked up at him and nodded. Someone shifted across the street, and she glanced over to see Brooks watching them like a raptor poised for a hunt.

❧

Breakfast was subdued. Rhea's class was so preoccupied with the tests that they didn't talk much and simply ate their porridge quickly. Since it was a special day, each person was given a peach to themselves. Rhea looked guiltily down at her peach, her mouth watering, but Gael nudged her encouragingly and she took a bite. She didn't see Brooks at breakfast.

After breakfast, Rhea walked with Gael and Lila to the schoolhouse. It would be empty except for her class today, with all of the other classes working on apprenticeships so that the students coming of age could take their tests. Gael and Lila chatted happily as they made their way to the schoolhouse, their anticipation and excitement high. Rhea's eyes darted around, searching for Brooks. They filed into the schoolhouse and found their seats at the front. Rhea looked down at a huge stack of papers on the desk before her. The tests would take hours, and students would continue until they finished them. There was no studying for a test like this, one that covered everything from personality questions to her feelings regarding her various apprentice-ships to how she would respond to her potential future children acting up.

Brooks slipped in just before Teacher went to close the door. Rhea turned in her seat to smile at him, but Brooks didn't look at her as he threw himself into his seat and glared down at his test. His stormy face was out of character; usually he acted as though each day was to be taken as a joke.

Teacher walked to the front of the class. "Class, welcome to test-ing day. Each and every day of your lives has led up to today. The test in front of you will show you who you are as well as who you are meant to be. Today will help you to see which vocation you are best suited for in order to serve our Community and who you are most suited to be partnered with."

Rhea glanced around. Her classmates looked nervous and excited, but a few also looked skeptical. *Why do they look like that?*

"You are not to look at or copy another student's test. You are not to share any of the questions with students who have not yet com-pleted the test. You are not to share your answers to the test at any time. You will stay until your test is completed. You may not change your answers. You may begin." Teacher sat behind her own desk and settled back in her chair to watch the students.

Rhea turned over her test, her heart hammering away in her throat. Her eyes found the instructions: *Write "Almost Always," "Often," "Sometimes," "Rarely," or "Almost Never" next to each of the fol-lowing questions . . .*

Rhea's eyes traveled farther down the test to the first question. *1. I get upset when things don't go my way.*

She frowned. *How would a Leader answer this? A Leader cannot get overly upset. A Leader doesn't have their own way; there is only the way of the Community, the good of the Residents. But a Leader must use necessary force if things go wrong . . .* Rhea was sweating now, her palms damp against her pencil. *A Leader must be flexible.*

She hesitated before writing "Almost Never." *There.*

Rhea bit her lip. The people reading the test would know that she had been disobedient. She wanted to remove her answer and start over, but Teacher had said not to. She sighed and moved on to the next question.

⁓

Ten hours later, Rhea laid her pencil down. She finally looked up, her spine cracking as she stretched for the first time in hours. She was thirsty and hungry, her eyes were raw, and her back was aching. The sun had set, and beeswax candles threw long shadows into the corners of the schoolhouse. Teacher dozed in her seat, her head thrown back and her eyes closed. All of the other students' tests were piled high on Teacher's desk. Rhea quietly stepped up, about to add her test to the stack, but she noticed that Brooks's was on top of the pile. Rhea hesitated, wanting to reach for it, wanting to see what he had said. Did he get angry when things didn't go his way? Did he try to work out win-win situations when compromising? Did Brooks ever get frustrated? Did Brooks ever feel trapped?

Rhea jumped as Teacher stirred, flinging her test on top of the stack and bolting for the door. Rhea sucked in the cool night air and tipped her head back to gaze up at the millions of stars twinkling overhead.

"Rhea." She turned expecting to see Brooks, wanting to see Brooks, but it was Gael.

"Oh." Rhea automatically took a step back from him. "Good evening, Gael."

"How was your exam?" he asked, walking closer. Rhea took another step back, although she could not have said why. There was something so tense, so loaded, about the way he was looking at her, as though he was searching for something within her.

"It went well, thank you. And yours?" Rhea backed up against the side of the schoolhouse. She glanced around—there wasn't a single person in sight. Dinner would have ended hours ago. Everyone was in their dwellings, their doors shut tightly against the chill of the evening, roaring fires going in their places, families close and talking together. Just like where Rhea should have been.

"It went well." Gael kept walking casually toward her until he was right in front of her. "Is something wrong, Rhea?" He brushed a hand against her cheek. "You look worried."

Rhea fought to smooth her face over into something that resembled indifference. She was unsure what was bothering her so much; she was in her Community. She was safe. *As long as you are a part of a Community, you are safe.* She was with Gael, a good and loyal Resident. Everything was fine. She managed to smile. "No, Gael. Nothing is wrong. I am just very tired. I should go to my dwelling."

Gael kissed her.

Unnoticed by either Rhea or Gael, Teacher emerged from the schoolhouse and peered around at the two of them, her arms piled high with the tests. She sighed a little, shaking her head, before heading off for the Council office. "I guess that's all of them, then," she muttered to herself.

Rhea's eyes were wide open when Gael pulled back. He smiled. "I knew I would like you best," he whispered, his fingers finding her brand and tracing it.

"Wh–what?" Rhea whispered. "You can't . . . it's against the—"

"Rhea," Gael spoke quickly, glancing around to make sure they were truly alone. "You are a wonderful Resident, but there are things that you just don't know about rules, like how they aren't for us. Your family and mine, everyone on the Council, we aren't like the others. You got caught breaking the rules, so you got branded . . . they couldn't let everyone else find out that the rules don't apply to us. So, they had to . . . make an example out of you. It was perfect, really, so everyone would think that we're all equal. But the rules aren't for us. We govern the Residents." His eyes flickered back down to her lips. "I'll make sure that we end up together."

"No . . ." She shook her head hard, trying to dislodge his words, the reality of what he had said crashing down on her. The test . . . she had just taken her test . . . it would determine everything—not the Council, not Gael.

"Yes." The voice came from behind Gael. Gael was slammed into the wall of the schoolhouse, narrowly missing Rhea. Rhea gasped and threw herself to the side. Gael whirled around and kept his footing, throwing out swear words that Rhea hadn't heard him utter before. He threw a punch at the dark figure looming over them both, but the figure slipped to one side to avoid it before following up with his own punch that stole the breath from Gael. Gael doubled over and the figure slipped his arms around him, one around his waist and the other fastened around his throat.

"Brooks!" Rhea finally found her voice but could only whisper his name.

"Rhea," Brooks said, his voice calm. "Don't you see now? Don't you see?"

Rhea clambered to her feet, watching Gael's face turn blue in the light from the moon. "Brooks," she whispered again. "Let him go."

This time Brooks shook his head. "He's a part of it, Rhea, don't you see?" He shook Gael. Gael's wide eyes fixed on Rhea as they bulged. "The entire Council here, it doesn't follow the rules. It doesn't care about the Residents. It treats everyone like dirt, kicking them out of their houses, controlling what they learn, how much they eat, what they do with their lives, who they wed, *if* they even get to wed. And *this one*"—he shook Gael again—"gets to break the rules, browsing all of his options before picking who he wants."

"Brooks . . ." Rhea wasn't even sure he had heard her, her voice was so soft.

Brooks finally looked at her, pain in his eyes. "If I don't get to pick, why does he?" he whispered.

"Let him go, Brooks," Rhea said, her voice finding new strength. "They'll throw you out this time, and I won't be able to protect you again." She slowly walked forward like he was an animal she didn't want to spook. She laid a hand on his arm, and he finally relaxed.

Gael fell to the ground, gasping in great shuddering breaths of air. Brooks kept his eyes on Rhea's hand as it rested on his arm. She hadn't touched him since they had first met. *Whatever happened to that little girl with all of the fire?* The girl who would save his life, regardless of the consequences or the dangers. He missed her so much, it hurt.

Gael finally pushed himself to his feet, pointing at Brooks. "Don't yell," Brooks advised him. "We don't want the whole Community to know what you were doing out here with the Leader's daughter, do we?"

Gael shook his head, still wheezing and coughing. "You . . . will . . . pay . . ." he finally managed to gasp.

"Oh?" asked Brooks, finally breaking away from Rhea and stalking toward Gael like a predator.

"Stay . . . back!" Gael backed up, his hands raised in defense.

Brooks stopped, smiling at him. "You can't get everything you want, Gael."

Gael sneered up at him. "We'll just have to see," he hissed hoarsely.

"I suppose we will," Brooks replied. "Rhea, have a good night." He bent over her hand to kiss it. She looked up at him, puzzled. She'd never seen anyone do anything like that before. She had never been touched this much since she was a baby and Nurse had held her. Brooks gave Gael one last smile before departing for his dwelling.

Rhea hurried to Gael's side, questions about what he had said burning in the back of her throat. Gael collapsed into her arms, shaking.

"He's crazy," he whispered. "He's not safe. He's a liar!" He pulled back to look at her face. "Rhea," he said, "nothing that he said was true. You know that."

Rhea nodded eagerly; it was exactly what she wanted to hear. "He just doesn't know better." She grasped Gael's hands, forgetting herself. "He wasn't born in the Community, so he doesn't know."

Gael nodded solemnly. "But Rhea, that does mean that he's

dangerous."

Rhea shook her head. "Brooks wouldn't . . ." She couldn't finish—Brooks *would*. Brooks had just tried to.

"Rhea, it will be okay," Gael said soothingly.

Panic rose within her again—what did he mean? "You wouldn't . . . you're not going to tell—"

"Oh, no," Gael said, releasing her hands to massage his neck gingerly. "I just know that traits like uncontrollable anger *do* come up on the tests. I believe the perfect spot for him will be made clear very soon." Rhea gazed into his eyes, not quite believing him, but wanting to.

"Yes," she said, a little uncertainly.

"Now . . ." Gael put an arm around her. She tensed but let him. It wasn't so bad, she thought, to have someone take her hand or put an arm around her. It wasn't so bad to be kissed. If it wasn't against the rules, she might even have thought about doing it again. "Please help me to get to my dwelling. I am sure that no one will mind you helping me; I have clearly tripped on a rock and hurt my ankle, so I need to lean on you." He brushed his lips against her cheek. "And tomorrow, we have to be up early for the final test. The one that takes place away from all of this."

⁓

Brooks skulked in the shadows, one with the darkness. He crept carefully, watching as Rhea left Gael at his dwelling and ducked another kiss by turning quickly from him. Brooks smiled. It could have been because of the rules, but he knew it was really because of him. Brooks had watched Gael for weeks. He watched everyone, noticed everything. From the way that Gael selected someone new to court, it was evident to Brooks that he was browsing for a partner. None of the other girls were scandalized like Rhea. Rhea was likely the last one in the class to have had a romance; the other students sneered at the rules with a standard juvenile disregard for rules. The other girls went far away from the dwellings so as not to be caught, whispered, and giggled as they compared secrets and kisses shared under a wide, innocent sky.

All except for Rhea—and Brooks. No one even dared confide such things in Rhea for fear that her adherence to the rules would cost them dearly. Brooks didn't need to see anyone; he already knew. Nothing short of Rhea would do. Loving her was like being hungry, a natural instinct that he couldn't ignore.

Brooks sat for a few minutes outside of Rhea's dwelling, wondering what she was dreaming of, before he set off for the Council office.

If he was correct, the test results would already be in. He assumed that the Council would be up tonight—supposedly going over the tests but, in reality, discussing each student at length and mapping out their future. Brooks slowed his pace as he drew closer to the Council office, staring up at the wooden building with the flickering firelight emanating from the windows. He stayed in the shadows for a long minute, watching and listening. Finally, Gael and a larger figure Brooks assumed was his father hurried up the steps and into the building, quickly pulling the door closed behind themselves. Brooks followed, running lightly on his toes, avoiding the shafts of moonlight sliced by the trees until he reached the back of the building and eased himself into the bushes under the window. The shutters were closed, but Brooks could still hear every word.

"What happened to you, Gael?"

"Nothing. I want to talk about that Brooks."

"That is a good one to start with."

"Exactly," Gael said. "We agree to declare him physically unfit? He cannot possibly be allowed to create more Residents like himself." There was a murmur of assent.

"Well"—Brooks thought this voice might be Teacher—"there is something to be said about his having a new bloodline in the Community. I know that we are fine now, but in the future, we will need to think about expanding to other Communities."

"If that is a problem in the future," said another voice coldly, "then we shall discuss it in the future." A nervous silence followed. "I believe our future Leader is right," it eventually went on. "The best thing for the Community is for Brooks to remain as insignificant as possible within it. We will take care of him once they are all back from their week beyond the Wall and the occupations have been announced."

Brooks frowned. "Take care of him"? *What does that mean?* He had never taken the "medicinal tea" provided for him by the infirmary, not wanting to risk putting something into his body provided by a group of people who evidently loathed him or wanted him to ingest something without knowing what it was or what it would do. Would they simply change his dosage and watch for some kind of change in him? Would he disappear, without so much as a chance to say goodbye to the only person he loved? Brooks didn't think he would wait to find out. This was evidently a common practice, one that they had executed before. *It must not be that hard for a group in power people to rid themselves of opposition when they keep those they control too terrified to even raise a hand to defend themselves.* Accusations were swift and public, the punishments severe and typically permanent.

"And," Gael added, "I do not believe he should be working with the blacksmith, as we originally planned. Put him on cleanup duty for the animals. He has offended me." There was another murmur of assent. Brooks rolled his eyes. There were far worse things in life than working with animals.

"Have you selected who you would like to wed?" someone asked, and Brooks stiffened.

"I know you will all be pleased with my selection of Rhea," Gael said. "I do hope that our current Leader, in particular, is pleased with my choice."

"There is no better selection," Rhea's father agreed.

"Son"—Brooks had to assume this was Gael's father—"the girl has been disobedient."

"And that has made her the most obedient of all of the Residents. She alone understands the consequences," Rhea's father replied coolly. There were more sounds of agreement. Brooks realized he was digging his fingernails into his palm.

"What about her occupation? Aside from helping you to create a strong new line of Leaders, of course."

"Um . . ." Brooks could practically see Gael turning to Rhea's father for support.

"She likes the bees," her father offered.

"Perfect. Put her in charge of the bees. Get rid of what's-his-name and give her the head position."

"We can demote him to Bee Handler. He's getting up there in age anyway; if he gets stung enough times, it will decrease the population. One less mouth to feed."

Brooks shifted uncomfortably; a branch was digging into his back. He had heard everything that he needed to hear.

"Just be sure to look after her while you two are on the outside," Rhea's father went on.

"Yes," Gael's father agreed. "You don't want her ruined by that psychotic Outcast."

Brooks would be put in charge of mucking out stalls until his back bent with age and hard physical labor, though only if he survived whatever they planned to do to "take care of him." He would live in a one-room dwelling alone, watching Rhea and Gael's children grow up. Watching Rhea tend to the bees, her white hair that turned golden under the sunshine, her dark-green eyes that stood out starkly in her pale face, her light-brown brows, her long eyelashes. Rhea following the rules, refusing to believe that the Community she loved so much was cheating her, cheating him, cheating all of them. A life designed around a few people with unlimited power wasn't life—it was servitude. The life that they could have had together would not be possible here. Would her children look like her? Like Gael? Some monstrous combination of the two?

No.

Brooks knew why he was here, what he was supposed to do. He was supposed to have accomplished his task so very long ago, but he had held on. It would have all been worth it, if only for Rhea. He could have forgotten about real life, life outside of this prison, and gone on pretending for her. He would have. But now, that was impossible.

That meant he had one week. One week to show her that they could have a life all their own.

CHAPTER 5
PREPARING

R hea's eyes flickered open early the next day. Darkness shrouded each inch of her room. She blinked hard, trying to dislodge the images from her dream that seemed to have burned themselves onto her lids. She and Gael had been walking the Community together. He'd turned to her and said, "I make the rules here," and kissed her. She had pulled back, fear rising in her chest. What if someone saw? But when she stepped away from him, she'd seen that it was not Gael at all—it was Brooks. She rushed back forward to kiss him before pushing him away, running forward, kissing him again, and pushing him back again. Rhea was guilty, confused, her head foggy and stupid.

Nurse rapped gently on her door. "Are you awake, child?"

"Yes," Rhea said, sitting up. Of course she would need to be up early today. It was the day of the final test.

Nurse had already boiled her well water for a bath in Rhea's washroom. Rhea fit her long legs uncomfortably into the little tub. She was still lucky; most families in the Community did not have a tub and would be crowding into the bathhouse to wash before heading out into the unknown. Rhea shook her head, trying to physically dislodge that thought. Most families didn't *need* a bath in their dwelling. *The Community should never give people more than what they need.* Her father needed one—his people would want to see him clean—and Rhea needed her own as well. It wouldn't do for them to share a bathhouse with everyone else.

Rhea pulled her braid free to wash her hair, allowing the long strands to flow between her fingers, her mind back on her dream. She shook her head again and quickly finished washing herself, dried off, and headed back to her room. She chose her clothes carefully, layering on her undershirt, deerskin shirt, and bear coat, then leggings, long wool socks, and tough boots. She combed her hair with a broken comb and forced it into its usual braid, her hands shaking. She tried to compose herself, putting on a mask of confidence that a Leader would wear before stepping back into the hallway.

"Rhea?" Nurse had ambled back in from the kitchen carrying a plate of food and a large pot.

"Where did you get that?" Rhea asked, amazed, not knowing that her father had stores other Residents could only dream of.

"You should eat as much as you can before you leave today," Nurse explained.

Rhea fixed her green eyes on Nurse's grey ones. "Does everybody?"

Nurse hesitated, her gaze sliding away, and Rhea knew the truth.

Nurse sat at the small table and placed the heavy plate of food in front of Rhea's chair. Rhea plopped herself down and started eating quickly. It wasn't easy; she had never had such a large amount of food in front of her before, even though her daily portions were larger than most of her classmates at dinner. Portions were dictated by a variety of factors, including age, size, and importance to the Community. Her belly groaned in protest halfway through her breakfast, and she looked up at Nurse nervously.

"I'm getting sick," Rhea worried.

"No, child," Nurse said, tucking a strand of hair that had already worked itself free from Rhea's braid behind her ear. "It's just that you're getting full. You haven't felt a full belly in a long time. They usually just give you enough to keep you healthy, but not to stuff you."

"Oh." Rhea didn't know what else to say to this. It was true, something that she had always known, but it sounded cruel out loud. "Do you get enough to eat?"

"We get more than everyone else in your father's dwelling," Nurse said.

"Where is he?"

"He's out getting everything ready for your big day."

"Oh," Rhea said again, unsure why she was so disappointed.

"Child," Nurse said, twisting her hands in her lap. "Be careful out there."

"Oh, I know. I will."

"But I mean it."

"Yes."

"Don't go looking for trouble."

"I won't."

"And don't go off with that boy."

A crease appeared between Rhea's brows, knowing she meant Brooks. "Don't we all stay in one spot?"

"Well, there is not a rule saying you have to. You just have to make it back on the seventh day before the gates close at nightfall."

"Oh." Rhea knew she sounded stupid, but she couldn't help herself. There was too much to think about.

"You . . . your future is a good one. It will be waiting for you when you get back, but there are certain things that could . . . jeopardize it."

"What are you talking about? My future? I just took the test yesterday."

The front door banged open, and Rhea's father stood framed in it. Rhea jumped back, realizing that she had been leaning over the table toward Nurse, desperate for answers. Nurse jumped to her feet, her frightened eyes darting around the room like a trapped bird.

"Father," Rhea said, standing as well. His eyes softened when they found hers.

"Rhea, it's time," he said. "You can load that food into your pockets. No one will mind." Rhea obediently stuffed the remaining bread, cheese, and fruit into her pockets, gave Nurse a last searching look, and followed Father out of their dwelling.

The alleys were packed with people coming to watch the final test ceremony. The drums beat their rhythm along with Rhea's heart. The people hummed as they walked, but it was a lighter, more cheerful hum than the one that preceded punishment. The noise crowded into Rhea's already groggy brain, and her pulse quickened with memories of her own disobedience and the punishment that would always scar her. This time, it would be okay. This time, she would make her Community proud. Rhea lifted her head and added her own "Hmmm . . ." to those around her as she walked to the gate.

Her classmates stood closest to the gate, all looking nervous and edgy. Gael smiled widely when he saw her and beckoned her to his side.

"Are you ready?" he asked.

She nodded, her throat tight, trying to return his smile. Her eyes scanned the surrounding crowd but couldn't locate Brooks. The Residents of the Community pressed in, a suffocating presence as they hummed and stomped their feet in time with the drums. The heavy music grew to a crescendo until Rhea's father came to stand on the small balcony at the top of the gate and raised his hand. The sound immediately died, snuffed out by that one gesture.

Rhea gazed up at him. He looked larger than life up there, the man who kept them all safe. Who followed every rule. The sky behind him was lightening, the stars losing their luster as the sun crept closer.

"Today," Rhea's father said, his voice loud and strong, "we come together to bring our next group of adults to their final test: they are to survive outside of the Wall for one week." The Community was still and silent, as though each member held their breath. "This test shows our Residents the value of being a part of a Community and fills them with a desire to come back to our Community. To us." A hand slipped gently over Rhea's own.

"Good morning," Brooks whispered in her ear. "Stay close to me." Rhea kept her eyes on her father, who had stopped talking to glare down at Brooks.

"This tradition dates back to the very start of our Community,"

Rhea's father finally went on. "And it is one that each of our Residents is proud to partake in. The rules of the outside are nonexistent. There will be dangers out there, but once our young Residents here have faced them, they will be all the better for it." He turned to look at the gatekeepers on either side of him. "Prepare to open the gates." The drums and the hum started up again. This time, Rhea heard the drums more clearly than ever before as they were pounded again and again above the gate.

Boom . . . bu bu boom boom . . . boom . . . bu bu boom boom...

"I shall see you all"—her father's eyes found hers, and she felt the weight of his orders pressing on her—"in one week."

The drumming increased in speed, the gates opened, and Rhea saw the world for the first time beyond the Wall.

CHAPTER 6
BEYOND THE WALL

Brooks kept a tight grip on Rhea's hand as the gates started to open. As soon as there was a gap large enough to squeeze through, he sprinted, pulling her behind him. She gasped in surprise but hurried to keep up with him. Brooks ran flat-out, hearing cries of shock and warnings pelted at his back like stones as he fled. They would believe that he was kidnapping her—of course they would. And perhaps he was. He wasn't sure yet. His plan sat half formed in his mind like rising bread dough. *Show Rhea* was as far as he had gotten.

The forest swallowed them up quickly like a warm blanket he could finally pull around himself again. It had been years since he had trekked through the woods, but he would remember how to get there. The trees muffled the sounds of the prison that they had finally escaped until they faded away entirely. Brooks made several quick turns, dragging Rhea through a small brook, over boulders, and around countless trees, checking over his shoulder to make sure that they weren't being followed. The rules stated that members of the Community could not interfere with tests . . . which Brooks knew was untrue. But he didn't think they would be brazen enough to follow him.

He didn't *think* so, anyway.

"Brooks," Rhea wheezed, gasping for air and clutching his hand.

"I'm sorry, Rhea," he said, stopping so abruptly that she ran into him.

"Here." He helped her sit on a large boulder next to the brook, reaching down to wipe the sweaty strands of pale hair from her face. "Are you okay?"

She nodded and reached into one of her large coat pockets. She pulled out a peach and smiled at the amazed look plastered across his face.

"So, you're nicking food now?" he asked, smiling. She bristled.

"No, I would never. Nurse got it for me." She pulled it back toward her as if to protect it.

"I'm only joking," Brooks said, rolling his eyes. He plucked the peach from her fingers and took a large bite before handing it back to her. She took a bite as well before passing it to him.

"Where are we going?" she asked.

Brooks shuffled his feet, looking embarrassed. "There's a place where I used to . . . stay sometimes. It's safe—as safe as you can be out here, and I figured . . . with you being a future Leader and all, you should stay safe."

Rhea smiled. "You can't call me a future Leader. We don't have the results in."

"I mean . . ." He spread his palms. "There really aren't any rules out here, are there?"

Rhea tipped her head to the side. "No, I suppose there aren't any rules out here." Her smile widened suddenly and she threw her head back, laughing. She turned and ran into the brook, stripping off her coat as she went, and splashed into the shallow water. She fell to her knees and plunged her face in, then came up spluttering and shaking wet hair from her eyes. She flopped onto her back on the bank and stared up at the sky above her, arms spread wide as though wanting to embrace the world. Brooks laughed, following after her. The water was icy cold, but Rhea didn't seem to notice. He pulled her to her feet, amazed at her change. *This could actually work.*

"Come on," he said, taking her hand once again. "It's just this way."

He led her through the forest and she stared in awe at the things around her, marveling at how tall the wild grass grew, at a family of deer that they spooked and which went trotting gracefully away from them, at a natural beehive that hung in one of the pines, at the way the trees grew so tightly together that the sun came down in long golden rays.

They finally crested the hill and looked down at the meadow. It wasn't large, but it was covered in soft grass and wildflowers. A little blue pond sat in the middle of it, and a small grouping of rocks framed it. It was surrounded on all sides by hills, giving it the look of the bottom of a bowl. He glanced at Rhea, trying to gauge her reaction. She smiled again.

"I'll see you there," she said before she broke into a run, taking small steps to avoid falling on the hills. Races were not allowed in the Community; no competition was allowed in the Community. This would be her first.

Brooks tore after her and caught her halfway down. He flung his arms around her and pulled her to the ground, carefully breaking her fall with his own body, not wanting to hurt her. She let out a happy little cry of surprise and joy as they rolled down the hill together, Brooks keeping his arms securely fastened around Rhea, her laughter mingling with his own and filling him up, making him feel weightless. They finally came to rest in a tumble of tangled limbs at the bottom of the hill, Rhea's head on Brooks's chest. *Now,* he thought.

He rolled her onto her back and took one last hungry look into her smiling eyes. Her smile slowly slid from her face, replaced with a look of longing mingled with sadness that Brooks had never seen before. "Brooks . . ." she whispered, but he kissed her to stop the flow of words.

It was a kiss that would have happened years ago if Brooks had been allowed, or if he had believed at all that she wouldn't have beaten herself up a hundred times for it because of the rules. Though it was their first, it could easily have been their last. It would only take one witness from the Community to wander in and spot them, and their tenuous futures could be gone. It would only take one Outcast who had taken up camp while Brooks had been gone to catch sight of them and slaughter them. *But some things are worth the risk,* Brooks thought. That one kiss was worth the seven years of imprisonment he had suffered for her.

∼

They finally broke apart and sat side by side, staring across the meadow, silence stretching on and on between them. Rhea finally broke it. "Brooks," she whispered carefully, as though speaking would break the spell they were under. "We can't do this."

"Why not?" he demanded, trying to keep the harsh edge out of his voice.

"It's against . . . if we are supposed to be together, the results will say so when we go back to the Community."

Brooks pressed his lips together, looking out over the home he had finally brought her to. If he told her about Gael and the others on the Council, including her own father, she wouldn't believe him. She had too much faith in the lies she'd grown up with that had twisted her into an obedient person incapable of seeing the truth. He sighed.

"Look," he said, turning to look at her, "there aren't any rules out here. All I'm asking you for is for this one week, while we're away from it all . . . can you just . . . can we just not think about what's waiting for us back there?"

Rhea's mouth twisted, thinking. Brooks took her hand and locked his blue eyes on her green ones. "This is just going to make everything so much harder once we go back . . ." she said, dropping her gaze to her knees.

"Any harder than it's already going to be, spending a week together alone and pretending like there's nothing here?"

Rhea frowned. "It's just hormones. Teacher told us that. They eventually pass."

"Sure," Brooks lied, "but what if when we get back, everything is okay? And we can wed?"

Rhea looked back up at him, eyes full of tears and hope that hadn't been spilled yet. "I suppose it's possible." Now she was lying to him as well as to herself.

Brooks hit her with his best crooked smile. "I can't resist you any longer," he said. "You really think you can resist me for the next week?"

Rhea rolled her eyes and opened her mouth to say something smart back, but Brooks covered it with his own once more.

⤙

Miles away, the rest of the Seventeens huddled together just outside of the Community Wall. A measly fire spluttered in the middle of their circle. All day they could hear the sounds of life inside of the Walls, and even smell the tantalizing sent of cooking. Stomachs grumbled and tempers were already short, but they had eventually dropped off one by one. Gael carefully backed away from the sleeping forms of his classmates and crept around the Wall until he reached a thicket of bushes. He ducked behind them and tugged open the short, nearly invisible gate behind them. Glancing around, he quickly crawled through. He straightened up on the other side, brushing dirt and leaves from his clothes.

"Good evening, Gael," his father's servant greeted him on the other side. Technically, his job title was Assistant to the Council, but this was a man who knew his place.

"What food do you have? I haven't eaten since breakfast," Gael snapped. The servant held out a sack and Gael grabbed it greedily. The other Seventeens had to choose between eating bugs, wild grass, or mushrooms that had been growing close to the Wall or going hungry. None of those options were worthy of him. Gael pulled out a loaf of bread, a wedge of cheese, a peach, and a boiled egg. None of it was hot, but he was hungry and wolfed everything down. *Let the others adhere to the stupid tradition*, he thought; he would be in charge soon enough once his father got rid of Rhea's.

He thought the old man guessed as much at times, the way he looked at him, but he knew his place well enough. It would have looked suspicious if Gael had followed his father, who had followed his grandfather, in their line of leaders. Gael's father had made a sacrifice, choosing to be just another Council member. He had been rewarded with Gael's mother, who was as docile as she was beautiful. But Gael would have everything that he wanted.

A branch snapped. He looked up from his feast to see his father standing over him.

"You didn't last long," he sneered condescendingly.

Gael shrugged. "Why would I? They're already starting to act like animals, fighting over a handful of mushrooms."

"As a future Leader, you need to show more grit."

"Why? Once I'm Leader, they won't dare challenge me. I can get rid of any of the rules."

His father sighed heavily. "You are still such a child. What do you think your future partner will do when you burn her Community's rule book? What about your future Residents, many of which could physically best you?"

"They wouldn't dare!" Gael snapped, frustration causing his fists to curl. "I'd brand and throw out any that tried to stand against me."

"This entire Community that we have built exists only if the Residents believe that they have an appropriate amount of free will. People have to choose to be ruled. Why do you think we allow them to leave and spend a week out there? They have to *choose* to relinquish their freedom, or someday they might demand it back."

Gael yawned pointedly. "Whatever you say," he said, standing up and starting to turn toward the door to lead him back out of the Community.

"If you get caught," his father's voice brought him up short, "I will not protect you. I will not lose everything that our family has built for a spoiled little boy like you."

Gael glared angrily over his shoulder. "Careful, Father," he warned. "My test results are already in as far as your precious Council is concerned."

His father's face twisted into an angry expression before smoothing back out into arrogant calm. "Tell me, how is your future partner enjoying her first night away from her Community?"

He knows, Gael thought. *How could he know that she is missing?* He supposed that everyone had seen Brooks dragging her away from the Community. Gael straightened his posture and turned to look directly into his father's eyes. "She is hungry, but she is doing well."

"I see," his father said delicately. "Have you been able to grow closer to her during your time away from the Community? It would help with your inevitable nuptials if she was actually fond of you, particularly if you plan on running a tyranny in her dwelling."

"She is absolutely dedicated to me," Gael retorted, his hands in fists.

"And only you?" His father tipped his head to one side, a small smile playing around his mouth.

"Yes," Gael snapped.

"If you say so, future Leader." His father turned on his heel and walked calmly back toward the Community.

Gael shoved the remains of his food into his pockets, ignoring the servant's protests, and shoved open the door to the world.

He walked directly into Lila.

"Lila!" he gasped, grabbing her elbow to stop her from falling. His brain scrambled frantically, trying to sort through what she would have just overheard.

"Good evening, Gael," Lila said automatically.

"I was just . . ." Gael's brain whirred, trying to formulate an excuse.

"I heard," Lila cut him off, fixing her brown eyes on his.

Gael put on his most charming smile and fished in his pocket for the remains of his meal. He presented her with half a loaf of bread, and her eyes widened. Her hands reached greedily for it, but he pulled it back from her.

"Hold on. I'd be happy to give this to you, but you need to keep your mouth shut about everything you heard and about me getting a meal."

Lila pulled her hands back and shook her head. "Not good enough, Gael." Gael wondered if he had said Rhea's name at any point during his conversation with his father. He didn't think so.

"Look," he said, taking a step closer to Lila. He had courted her before anyone else, assuming that she would have been a good partner. She was certainly pretty enough, but she was shallow and selfish. Rhea would serve him. Lila would have demands and forget her place.

Like now.

Gael brushed his free hand over her freckled cheek and smiled. "I don't know if you heard, but the test results are in. You know that we've always had something special—"

"I don't want you." Lila looked at him condescendingly, like he was something slimy she had found under a rock.

Gael's eyes narrowed, stung. "What do you want, Lila?"

"You're going to bring me dinner every night that we're out here."

"Fine," Gael replied. Easy enough, he thought, as long as the idiot didn't get him caught.

"And," she said, blushing fiercely, "I want to be partnered with Brooks."

She really is *an idiot,* Gael thought. "Lila, that's not possible," he said, shaking his head sadly.

"Why not?" she demanded. "If the tests said I should be with someone else, you could just change them. If they think I should be with someone else, they're wrong."

"It's not that," Gael said. "Brooks has been deemed unfit."

"No . . ." Lila whispered. She shook her head hard. It was as though he had just told her Brooks was dead.

"Yes," Gael confirmed.

"I don't care!" Lila's voice rose and Gael hastily covered her mouth with his hand.

"Shut up!" he hissed. She struggled for a minute before nodding, then he released her.

"I don't care," she said, her voice lowered.

"It doesn't matter if you don't care. He can't wed. The Doctors say he isn't fit to do so."

"Is it his mind?"

"I don't know."

"Does he have dangerous ideas?"

"I don't know."

"Is he sick?" Lila continued, rattling off the reasons she had heard why the Doctors might deem someone "unfit." "Can he . . . I mean, can he not—"

"I don't know!"

"Change the rules."

"No."

"Change the rules!"

"No!"

Her chest rose and fell as tears leaked from her eyes. She looked away from him angrily.

"Look," Gael said, reaching for her hand. "Who else do you want?"

She looked at him, calculating. "If I can't have him, then I'll have you."

Gael refrained from rolling his eyes with great difficulty, pleased that he hadn't chosen Lila. "I thought you didn't want me."

"I don't. I want Brooks. But if I can't have who I want, then you can't have who *you* want."

"And who do I want?"

Lila rolled her eyes. "Oh, come on, Gael, it's Rhea. You're not exactly subtle."

"So, because Brooks is unfit, which is not my fault, you are going to punish me for the rest of my life?"

"That's up to you," Lila said, setting her feet. "You could always change the rules."

Gael grinned. "You underestimate me," he said, taking a huge bite out of the bread. Lila's mouth fell open in a comical *O*. "I would be more than happy to wed you, Lila. We have a deal. I'll be sure to bring you dinner tomorrow." He waved the bread under her nose. "You didn't say anything about tonight, though."

"But—" she started, but he turned on his heel and left her standing by the door.

It wouldn't be hard to declare Lila unfit as well. Or he could declare her incapable of taking care of herself and lock her up in the health ward, or ignore their deal and force her to marry the most unattractive male in their class. Gael wasn't worried about Lila. The trick would be to keep her quiet for the rest of the week. He would keep her underfed, and she would be desperate for more food from him. He knew that she was full of it; all of the girls he had courted absolutely adored him. Why wouldn't they? He would easily have her under his thumb with a little more control.

Control was, after all, the key to a happy Community. Like all of his other Residents, Lila didn't actually know what she wanted and would have to be told what was best for her. Gael finished the bread before strutting back into the little camp that he and the other Seventeens had made right up next to the Wall for comfort and security. Their pathetic little fire sputtered.

"Where have you been?" Sara, one of the girls that Gael had only courted so that he knew he had gotten to all of them, demanded.

"Just felt like a little walk," Gael said, grinning. Lila sidled up behind him into camp. "There you are!" he said, grabbing her hand and drawing her down next to him. He nuzzled his nose into her hair and threw an arm around her shoulders. She stiffened a little but didn't throw him off. Apparently, she was going to play along for a little while as well. *All the better,* Gael reasoned. Without Rhea here, the trip outside of the Community would be incredibly dull. "I'm starving. Aren't you, Lila?" She nodded, saying nothing.

"I'm starving!" said Sara. "I would give anything for some sausage." She turned over and fell back asleep.

Gael laid down on his side to stare at Lila. "You could still change the rules," she whispered.

"Lila." He tucked a strand of her hair behind her ear. "You know I can't do that."

"I could tell them."

"You don't want to do that." Gael raised a hand straight up, high in the air, and four Defenders melted out of the forest into the camp. Lila sat up, eyes wide, gazing at them with their knives and bows with pure fear. "As future Leader, I needed protection," Gael said, smiling. He waved them off and they folded back into the shadows silently. "It's actually a time-honored tradition to oversee the Seventeens during their week away. Ensure no one makes a poor decision."

"How . . ." Lila was staring at him with horrified eyes, the firelight dancing in them.

"I am so very glad that you wanted to get back together, Lila," Gael said with one last self-satisfied smile before drifting off to sleep, his belly full and his mind at ease.

CHAPTER 7
THE WEEK

A twig snapped loud as a scream, shattering the silence of the night. Brooks stayed still wrapped up in the darkness, a fixture of the landscape. His eyes were fixed on the entrance to the rock cropping where Rhea lay sleeping. He had settled her in, told her he would be back with firewood for the night, and had returned to find her peacefully asleep, curled up on the grassy floor. He took a long look at her, filling his mind with her image before gently dumping the firewood he had gathered by the rock outcropping and turning to go keep watch. He knew his presence would not go unnoticed. He had, after all, brought her back to his spot. He could only hope that they hadn't left someone too dangerous to keep watch over his old home.

His eyes moved methodically, waiting for the intruder to take a second step. They were hesitating, waiting to see if he had noticed the twig. After several long minutes, they took a slow, careful step forward. Brooks could see her now, just inside the fringe of trees that flanked the clearing of the meadow. It was Raven. Brooks hadn't seen her in years, but her movements were unmistakable. She was dangerous. Brooks needed to get to her before she looked inside of the rock outcropping and spotted Rhea. If she did, Raven would likely kill her on the spot.

Brooks cautiously straightened his stiff legs. It was dangerous to sit on the forest floor, and shifting your feet to stand would unsettle the underbrush, but Brooks found that if he squatted, he could keep his feet in the same spot when he rose. He very gingerly eased around

Raven, giving her a wide berth until he was directly behind her. She was almost to the entrance of the cave when he grabbed her, pinning her arms to her sides in a massive bear hug. She turned the blade in her right hand, trying to drive it into his leg despite her limited mobility, but Brooks threw her hard to the ground. She landed hard but rolled swiftly to her feet, coming up in a crouch, ready to spring in a second with her knife clutched tightly in her hand.

Brooks brought both of his hands up to shoulder height, a gesture of surrender. Raven snorted. "Like I believe you would give up that easily."

"I'm not here to kill you," Brooks said evenly, praying that Rhea would stay asleep. He had made her a cup of what he had informed her was "tea" from a familiar bush by the meadow, hoping it would be enough to keep her asleep and safe while he dealt with the dangers of their first night beyond the Wall.

"I know that." Raven straightened up and took a few steps closer to him. "If you had wanted to kill me, you wouldn't have come here."

"Glad to see you haven't gotten stupid in my absence." Brooks fixed her with one of his wide grins.

"But you have, Brook." Raven returned his smile, hers full of danger. "You vanished for seven years. Your orders were to gain entry before opening the gates as quickly as possible. Adder gave orders to kill you on sight. He thinks those idiots behind the Wall have turned you."

"Really?" Brooks shrugged in an offhand manner, nervous that she could hear his heart thundering in his chest as though looking for an escape from his body before Raven's knife found it. "Well, they haven't. There was more to be learned by sticking around a few years than by opening the gates on night one."

"Like what?" she scoffed. "What could those brain-dead idiots possibly have shown you?"

Brooks reached for his pocket and Raven advanced quickly, bringing her knife to his throat. "Easy," he said, slipping into his smile. His fingers found the paper and slowly pulled it from his pocket.

It had taken him hours to copy the map of all the Communities in the area. He had snuck into the Council office, found a spare piece of paper, and carefully copied each little walled-in Community. He knew once he left those Walls with Rhea, his life would likely be forfeit for failing his mission. He needed something, anything, to offer. This was all that he had come up with. Community 215 wasn't a danger to anyone except for their own Residents. But finding and rooting out the more dangerous ones, the ones that hunted Outcasts . . . that would be worth a seven-year delay, even to Adder. Maybe.

He smoothed out the paper and handed it to Raven. Her greedy fingers snatched it, her dark eyes searching the contents briefly before finding his. "This can't be real."

"It is," he said, his smile widening as his confidence grew.

"There . . . there aren't even as many of them as they say! There aren't over two hundred of them!" Her teeth shone greedily in the moonlight as she returned his grin. "We can take them all."

"I figured Adder would be pleased with that."

"I will take it to him." Raven stuffed the map into her pocket. "That and your death will allow me to be richly rewarded."

"Hang on," Brooks cautioned, holding up a hand to stop her. "Why still kill me?"

"He said we would be rewarded if we did." Raven shrugged. "Plus, you never did fulfill your assignment. I mean, you never opened the gates, did you?"

"After I missed the first deadline, which I *had* to miss because I was locked in an underground prison while they decided what to do with me, what was I supposed to do? Open it up any day and assume that you would all be ready?"

"Doesn't matter."

"It's not like I could have just pushed the gate open! It's always guarded. There's a reason why Adder doesn't want to try climbing that Wall or just attacking the gate himself."

"Orders are orders."

"There's more to the map."

"What?"

"You heard me. That's only half the map. Did you think I would be stupid enough to give you the whole thing?"

"You're lying."

"Are you really willing to take that risk?"

Raven licked her lips, weighing her options. Brooks seized his opportunity. "Look." He took a step closer. "I'll go back and get the rest of the map. You'll take it to Adder, be a hero, and we'll just forget about this particular order. He won't mind that I'm alive a little longer when you show him the map. Community 215 isn't even one that he cares about, but the other ones on the map should keep him busy for years."

"Why are you even here? Why did they let you out?"

"You would know if you kept an eye on those gates like you're supposed to. They let everyone who's seventeen out for a week. Shows them they can't survive on their own, so they go crying back."

"Pretty stupid idea. What if they like it out here?"

"They don't."

"But you'll go back?"

"Correct."

"And then break back out, give the map to me, and then go back and shack back up with your little girl?" Brooks stiffened. Raven's eyes flickered toward the rock outcroppings, and Rhea, before finding his again.

"I've been watching for hours, Brooks," she hissed.

"No."

"What?"

"No, I will go back into the Community and I will open the gates. Then you can storm in and get the rest of the map."

"When?"

"Day after we get back."

Raven laughed. "You're lying. Once you're behind the gates, you'll forget all about us again."

"I won't."

"Why?"

"Because I told you I won't. I haven't failed yet."

"Why don't you leave the girl with me?" Raven was practically purring now, slowly waving her knife in front of his face. "I'll take care of her until you come back with the rest of that map."

"You touch her, and I will kill you. One or both of us won't make it out of here alive." His eyes bored into hers so she could see the truth.

"Fine." Raven turned on her heel to leave him in the clearing. "Suppose I'll see you in about a week, then."

~

Rhea woke up very stiff and sore with her head pounding. The sunlight poked her hard in both eyes as she gingerly sat up, her throat raw, looking for Brooks. He wasn't in the little den where she had slept. "Brooks?" she croaked. Nothing. A shiver of fear ran through her. *What if something happened to him?* She fumbled her way out of the den and stood out in the sun, blinking hard. "Brooks!" she called, a little louder this time. Still nothing. She looked around the clearing.

Brooks was floating in the pond.

"Brooks!" Rhea screamed this time and took off running for him. She splashed into the pond, feeling the shock of the cold water and the mud at the bottom sucking at her boots. She tripped and fell, smacking her face against the water. She tried to rise but her boot was stuck, her heavy coat filled with water and pulling her down as if determined to drown her. She sucked in a lungful of water in surprise.

Strong arms reached around her and pulled her upright. Brooks kept a tight hold on her as she coughed and spluttered, tears, spit, and pond water all pouring down her face. He finally laid her to rest on the bank of the pond, turning her on her side to help her breathe.

"What the hell are you doing?" he asked, his voice shaking slightly with relieved laugher.

"I . . . you . . . were . . ." Rhea gave up until she finally got her breath back and could sit up. Her clothes were soaked. She was painfully aware that she must look like a drowned mouse in her large coat. "You were in that water! Everyone knows you don't go into deep water!"

Brooks rolled his eyes. "It's not *that* deep."

"You were floating in it!"

"It's not that hard. I can teach you how."

"No." She shook her head hard, water from her braid splattering onto him. That's when she realized most of his clothes were piled on a rock by the bank, and he was only in his undershorts. "Oh . . ." She quickly looked away. It was rude to stare at anyone in a state of undress. It was also rude to be in a state of undress.

"What?" Brooks asked, trying to turn her face to his.

"You are in a state of undress."

Brooks laughed. "Most people try to get that way before they go swimming. As you learned."

"I am not going . . . *swimming.*"

"Well, your clothes will have to dry somehow. You can do it standing out here or in the pond with me."

At that, Brooks left her side and started wading back into the pond.

"Wait!" she called after him, but he ignored her. She swore very quietly under her breath. *I suppose I could take off my coat.* She was shivering hard. She removed her coat and laid it on a large rock to dry in the sun. The sun was beating down hard already even though it was still morning. Rhea looked at her coat for a second, then peeled off her boots and socks and laid them by her coat as well. She looked down at her leggings and shirt, then over at Brooks, who was watching her with that mocking smile he always wore, as if he knew everything and she was just starting to learn.

Rhea thrust out her chin and began wading after him in the pond.

The mud still sucked at her feet, but there was something pleasant about it now. A few fish swam by, startling her backward, but she persisted until she stood next to Brooks. "Well done," he said proudly. He slipped his arms around her and kissed her. He had kissed her the day before—kisses that brought the barriers between them crashing down, flooding her with new sensations—but this somehow felt different. This was the first time Rhea realized that there was truly no one around. It was a thrilling and a terrifying thought, and she pulled away quickly. Brooks ignored this.

"Come on." He took her hand in his and started pulling her toward the center of the pond. "I'll teach you to swim."

Miles away, Gael waited impatiently for the other Seventeens to fall asleep. This day had been a bad one, as all days outside of the Community were. He had watched with disgust as several of his classmates fell to their hunger and raided bird nests for eggs, then fought over them like outcast savages. It was absolutely pitiful. He had waited until nightfall, when there were the distractions of talk around the fire to claim their attention, to sneak back to the Wall for his meal. He noticed Lila following him but ignored her. She had been avoiding him all day, and he was pleased to see that she knew enough to be wary of him. "There is a degree of instability in Leaders that is crucial to success," his father had once told him. "Yes, of course you follow every rule, but at the same time, they should never know what you are going to do. This leads to fear, and fear is the key to obedience."

Gael had taken his time with his meal before leaving the Community and giving Lila the scraps he hadn't wanted. She had whined but wolfed everything down nonetheless. She was much too whiny and demanding to make a good partner.

Gael had then taken her hand to lead her back into camp so that their classmates would think they had snuck away to be alone to-gether. There was a certain number of giggles upon their return, and he nuzzled Lila's neck for good effect. She, on the other hand, looked scared and horrified when he did so, and thus hadn't played her part well.

Now, Gael had to wait for everyone to fall asleep before he could handle his problem. Once the breathing around the fire was slow and steady, he carefully rose and walked deeper into the forest. As he snapped his fingers, the Defenders melted out of the trees the way they always did.

"What?" the head Defender, what's-his-name, asked.

Gael glared hard at him. *He should know who he's talking to, even if my status as future Leader hasn't been announced yet. They should still know.* "I have a job for you."

"We don't take orders from you."

"I will ensure that you are compensated for your troubles. What do you want?"

"Bigger dwelling. The one we got is trash."

"Done."

"Fine, what do you want?"

"Find Brooks, kill him, and bring Rhea to me."

"We could do that. Won't be too hard."

"Good." Gael turned to go but quickly turned back toward the Defenders. "Oh, and make it look like an accident—maybe something those savage Outcasts did to him. Get creative, have fun with it. But don't touch her."

"Fine."

Gael turned on his heel and found his spot around the fire circle once again. Somehow, he seemed to sleep even better out here than he usually did in his dwelling.

"A little higher."

"No."

"You're not going to get him!"

Rhea released the tension on her bow string and watched her arrow zip toward the rabbit. It stuck him in the back, and he tried to run but collapsed. She smiled smugly at Brooks, who rolled his eyes. "Lucky shot."

"More than a lucky shot!" She bounded after the rabbit and held him up high like a trophy. "I guess you don't want any dinner."

"Since I taught you to shoot, it's actually *my* kill."

"You want him? Come and take him." Rhea dropped the rabbit and her bow behind her back, bracing herself. Brooks hit her like a brick wall and sent her tumbling down. They rolled together in the long grass, laughing hard, each trying to kiss the other as many times as they could.

So much had changed in the six days that they had spent in the meadow. Rhea now only wore her light undershirt and leggings; the days were always so hot and stifling. She could swim now, hunt with a bow, throw a knife into a tree trunk, wrestle, run, jump, and even laugh—all of which had never been important before. Happiness wasn't as essential as rules behind the Wall. What did it matter if one person or a few people were happy if everyone couldn't be? Rhea had never had a word for "happiness" before, but Brooks had taught it to her, just as he had taught her countless other things.

Each day she and Brooks rose together, swam together, and ran together around the meadow. They would sit still for hours, hunting together. Sometimes they sat high in the trees to get a better spot. He had taught her to fry an egg in a fire and how to gut rabbits and fish. He had shown her which berries to eat, and which were poisonous. She had found a wild beehive, the first she had ever seen, and slowly pulled a large honeycomb from it. They had shared it together before kissing the lingering honey from each other's lips. Her skin was now bronzed, her hair lighter than ever, loose and flying about her at all times. Her tie for her hair had fallen off into the pond and she'd since let it hang loose, glittering in the sunshine. She didn't bother to hide her brand out here; it didn't matter. Brooks often kissed it, thanking her in a low whisper for saving his life. It wasn't a sign of disobedience out here—it was only a sign of what she would do for him.

Three nights into their stay in the meadow, Brooks took her high into a tree to watch the sunset. She had seen sunsets before, but had never truly watched them. Brooks sung quietly in her ear as it sank below the horizon.

"What are you doing?" she asked.

"Singing."

"Oh . . . we don't do that in the Community. It's a waste of time."

"We have nothing but time out here." And so, he taught her to sing.

At first, they had curled up on opposite sides of the den and Rhea kept her back to him. But now she lay on his chest, listening to his heart, before drifting off to sleep each night. They kissed often, each kiss feeling more and more like returning home after a long time away. He was everything to Rhea. He was life.

And now it was day six.

Tomorrow was the last day, and it was not a full day. If they didn't make it back to the gates by sundown, it would mean the end of their status as Residents at the Community. She had to get to her Community, see her test results, and then she would know. *Maybe we'll be partnered together*, she told herself a hundred times a day. Brooks never talked about going back. She was terrified he would want to stay in their meadow forever, where they were invincible, where nothing could touch them.

She knew that she had to bring up going back, and that he never would.

Rhea finally straddled Brooks and smiled down at him. "I win," she said. It was a phrase she used all the time now. There was a wonderful feeling in winning; you just had to win to finally feel it.

"I'm pretty sure I won," Brooks shot back playfully, smiling at her as though she were all that he could see. Rhea blushed and sat beside him instead.

"Brooks," she began, the way that she began all of these attempted talks. Brooks cut her off by kissing her, as he always did when he heard her tone and sensed what she wanted to talk about.

He kissed her hard now, pushing her onto the ground. She knew that she should stop him, should continue the conversation, but the kiss was too good to waste. Her hands tangled in his hair to bring him closer as he clutched at her waist.

When she finally remembered what she had wanted to talk about, she gently pushed him away. "Brooks," she started again, putting her fingers to his lips to stop the next kiss. "You know tomorrow we have to go back."

Brooks looked at her, hurt in his eyes.

She went on quickly, "I mean, our test results are in. We can finally find out if—"

"And if they *don't* let us be together?"

Rhea hesitated. It would be like ripping out her heart. "They pair us with the people we are most suited with, and I am most suited to be with you."

Brooks looked at her, the laughter that usually sat in his blue eyes muted. "Do you want to skin it, or should I?" he asked, turning to the rabbit.

The rest of the afternoon was tense, both of them treading carefully around the topic of leaving, neither wanting to bring it up for fear of ruining their last day together. When the sun finally started to set, they climbed the highest tree at the edge of the clearing to watch. Rhea leaned back against Brooks, and his arms circled her.

As the last warm glow of orange disappeared and gave way to the crushing deep blue above it, Rhea sighed. "Brooks," she whispered. "We have to go back. Everyone else will be at the gate at first light tomorrow. We should head back as soon as we wake up, just to make sure that . . ." She hesitated. In truth, she wanted to get back quickly in the hope that it would help to qualm gossip regarding what she and Brooks could have been doing alone all week. That, and would they really leave the gates open all day, just for them? Just for her? Rhea knew they would be glad if Brooks didn't come back. "That we're not late," she finished lamely.

Brooks didn't respond at first, his eyes darting around the opposite edge of the clearing. He knew that he had glimpsed movement. A rabbit? Fox? He had been waiting for someone to come for him, either from the Community or from the Outcasts, all week. He thought Raven had left satisfied, but now he was unsure. Whoever it was would probably wait until they appeared to be asleep. If he could get Rhea asleep in the rock outcroppings, he would only have to stop anyone from getting at the opening. She would be safe.

"Yes," Brooks said. "I know, we need to go back."

Rhea sighed, her body sagging against his with relief. *What if I had said no?* he thought. *Would you have chosen me?* He didn't want to know the answer. If all went well, she would choose him soon enough. There wouldn't need to be a choice once he carried out his assignment.

"Thank you," she whispered contentedly. Brooks saw the movement again, a subtle flicker among the shrubs that had nothing to do with the breeze.

"We should go to bed. We have a long walk ahead of us tomorrow."

Rhea climbed nimbly down from the tree and Brooks followed her closely, his eyes constantly scanning their surroundings.

"How about some tea?" he asked. If he could get her to sleep, he wouldn't have to worry about her during the attack.

"No, it hurts my head."

Brooks was already reaching for the hollow rock that he used as a teacup. Brooks froze. "Just a small cup?" he asked.

"No," she said firmly.

Brooks hesitated. "There's still some rabbit. Are you hungry?"

"No!" Rhea's voice rose. "How can you think about food right now?"

"What?" Brooks wondered if she knew that they were being watched.

"It's . . . what if . . . what if this is it?"

"It?"

"For *us*." Her head dropped, and her shoulders trembled as tears finally overcame her and the enormous weight of their future threatened to crush her.

Brooks gently took her by the shoulders and pulled her close. "This isn't the end," he said. "I promise, this isn't the end."

Rhea finally fell asleep against his shoulder, tears clinging to her eyelashes. He hadn't seen her cry since she had first gone to school after being branded. It wasn't tolerated within the Community, but it really wasn't all that bad. Crying had worn her out, and she had fallen asleep on her own. Brooks eased himself out from under her and crept toward the entrance of the rocks.

They had allowed the fire to burn low in the middle of the clearing, and the red glow threw dark shadows at the trees. Brooks straightened up, walking toward the fire. He crouched low, prodding it with a stick, presenting his back toward the intruders.

A hand snaked around his throat as another fastened in his hair. Brooks jabbed the burning branch into the attacker's face, and they let go with a wild yell. *Stay asleep, Rhea,* Brooks silently pleaded.

Brooks whirled to face them. He recognized three Defenders from the Community, one on his knees, clutching his burnt face. *Gael.* It was his style to send assassins. That, or Rhea's father, but Brooks doubted that. The man was too cautious.

"Gael sent you," Brooks said, a calm statement. The two still standing exchanged a glance, the only confirmation Brooks needed. "Got it." Brooks barreled into the larger of the two, knife in hand, and they went down together in a tangle.

The Defender had a sharp spear that did him no good in such close quarters. Dropping the spear, he instead fastened his hands around Brooks's throat. Brooks brought his knife up into the soft meat under the Defender's chin, and his hands fell away. Brooks whirled, looking for the last Defender standing. The lone assailant was backing away, pulling his bowstring taught as he went. Brooks quickly adjusted his grip and threw his knife. It landed satisfyingly in the Defender's gut and he fell, fingers fumbling at the red mass spreading under the knife's hilt. Brooks let out his breath, eyes darting toward the rocks where Rhea still slumbered.

Two strong arms hooked themselves around Brooks's neck. His feet scrabbled uselessly on the forest floor as he was dragged backward into the trees.

"I'm going to kill you slowly," the third Defender whispered in his ear. "Then, I'll go pay the girl a visit." Brooks dug his short nails into the Defender's arm and attempted to swing his elbows into the man's side, but he couldn't get enough momentum to break his grip. He was held too tightly.

Spots of color popped in front of his eyes as he struggled for breath. The Defender decided they were far enough from the clearing and flung Brooks against a tree. Brooks smacked his head hard and blood poured from a cut on his scalp, running swiftly into his right eye. He swept it aside with his arm and struggled to his feet, turning to look at the last Defender.

His face was badly burned, his right eye a closed mass of angry skin. "You could have died quickly," he spat as Brooks took large gasps of air that tore through his throat like fire, slightly doubled over and rubbing his neck. "I wouldn't have hurt her, but you did all of this." A small blade glimmered in his hand, red light glaring off of it. "You shouldn't have infiltrated us," he said, breathing hard. "Everything was fine before you came around . . . but I can fix that."

He lunged, slicing the knife through the air, and Brooks quickly darted to his right. The Defender swore and tried again; Brooks again deftly stepped aside. The Defender adjusted his grip and plunged a third time, but a hand found his hair and jerked his head back. The Defender stumbled back, wildly swinging his arms behind him, trying to dislodge his attacker. Rhea wrapped her legs firmly around his waist, plunged Brooks's knife into his back, and twisted.

Blood painted her face as Brooks stared. A scream burst from Rhea's lips as the Defender fell, and she withdrew her knife to stab him again. And again.

Brooks recognized the Defender. He was the one who had marched Rhea through the streets on her way to be branded.

"Rhea!" Brooks leapt forward, his hand catching her wrist. "He's done." Rhea looked up at him, her face splattered with blood, her eyes shining with a wild fury he had never seen before. Rhea dropped the knife, turned, and ran back into the clearing. She dropped to her knees and vomited. Brooks hurried to her, patting her nervously on the back.

"I . . . I didn't mean . . ." she finally started, her body shaking violently.

"It's okay, he was going to kill me. You saved me."

"He was . . . he was one of ours . . ."

"No," Brooks whispered. "Not really. He was a tool to make you behave. He branded you, came to kill me, came to . . . to take you back."

Rhea shook her head. "He was doing his job when I got branded! But . . . why would he be here?" She finally looked up at him, then around at the other two bodies. "Why would any of them come here? No one would send them away from the Community—they need to be on the Wall to protect it! And they wouldn't attack members—it's against everything they stand for!"

Brooks sighed hard. *What will she believe?* She wouldn't want to hear the truth: that Gael had sent them to kill him. "They must have been rogue."

"Rogue?"

"Yeah, think about it. They must have left the Community and . . . become Outcasts . . . and came here to capture you because you're the Leader's daughter."

Rhea looked at him, hope rekindled in her eyes. "That makes sense!" she said with relief. "Of course! We will have to tell them when we get back that we found the deserters and brought them to justice!"

"Mmm . . ." Brooks said, knowing how that conversation would go. "I don't know if that's a good idea."

"Why not? Desertion is an offense punishable by death," Rhea recited.

So, if we don't go back tomorrow, do you think your father would choose to consider it desertion and hunt us down? Or would he make an exception if we choose not to go back after we finish our week beyond the Wall? Brooks wondered but refrained from saying. Most of their rules did not make sense anyway, and asking questions or using logic was absolutely discouraged within the Community.

"Yes, it is," he agreed. "But this is not the way that they're supposed to be executed, is it?"

"No . . ." Rhea breathed, her eyes widening with fear. "Do you think . . . we will be punished?"

"No," Brooks said quickly, "not if we . . . take care of the bodies, and . . . we can't tell anyone."

Rhea leaned away from him. "I don't know . . ."

"We have to. They won't brand you this time—they'll kill you. And they'll kill me."

"My father—"

"He didn't stop them last time." Rhea twisted her mouth. "Please, Rhea," Brooks pleaded. "I don't want to lose you." Her green eyes met his blue ones, and finally she nodded. "Thank you, Rhea."

He settled her back into the rocks before returning to the bodies.

He didn't have any tools to bury them with, and their fire was too small to burn them. Brooks decided to drag them away from the clearing and cover them with branches and underbrush until they were no longer visible. Animals and bugs would eventually make them a part of the forest.

Brooks stopped at the pond and dipped his hands into the cool water, watching the dried blood turn into watery clouds and dissolve. His hands shook in the water. It had been seven years since anyone had attacked him, and he had lost that fight. Brooks splashed water onto his face and took several deep breaths. Rhea needed him now.

She was sitting up with her back against one of the larger rocks, her arms wrapped tightly around her knees. Her body rocked quickly back and forth, her eyes staring blindly at the dying fire.

Brooks squatted down in front of her and found her eyes with his. He gently took her hands in his and led her out to the pond. The fire had sputtered and burned out but the moon lit the clearing, its image reflected on the pond. He helped her out of her leggings and shirt and lowered her into a sitting position on a rock at the edge of the pond. Removing his shirt, he gently washed the blood from her face, hands, arms, and chest. She closed her eyes and tears began to leak from under her lashes. When her skin was glowing, the same shade as the light from the moon, he picked her up and carried her into the middle of the pond. She wrapped her arms around his neck and her legs around his waist, burying her face in his neck.

"Do you think we'll ever come back here?" she whispered.

"No," he said. "We're going back. Residents only ever leave once."

"Yeah, I guess so."

"But we'll be together. Like you said, we're best suited for each other, right?"

"Yeah . . ."

"The tests will show that. And you'll be our new Leader," he lied.

"Yes."

"I suppose the question is . . ." He pulled back from her so that he could see her face when he asked, "Do you choose me?"

She finally laughed. "You don't *ask* that. It's a given once someone is assigned to you."

"Even though we both know you'll be assigned to me, I would still pick you."

"I would pick you, too."

"Is that a yes?"

"Yes."

⁓

Miles away, Gael paced between the trees. Where the hell were the Defenders? They were supposed to be back with Rhea by now. This was the last night that they had away from the Community. He had selected her as his partner but was still barely acquainted with her. They could have had this entire week away from all of the rules together. She had been obedient; he had believed she would do whatever he told her. Now, who knew what Brooks could have done to her? Would he even still like her now that she had been away for so long? *What if Brooks ruined her?*

Gael was special, and thus his partner was supposed to be perfect. Gael cursed and kicked a large rock as he passed, causing him to curse all over again at the sharp pain in his toe. He could always change his mind and pick a different partner, but then he would have to eliminate Rhea's father . . . and the Defenders seemed incapable of completing that simple task when it came to Brooks. Nothing was going according to plan.

⁓

Rhea watched as the sky paled. The first rays of sunshine were starting to filter into the clearing. *That's it*, she thought. *The week's over.* She buried her face into Brooks shoulder, wishing for just one more day. But then if she got it, wouldn't she wish for just one more?

And another after that? When they got back, they would know. One way or the other, she would finally know who she would be with and what she was supposed to do.

But now, everything was different. She had just spent a week with Brooks in the clearing, in a world that was all their own. They had slept and ate and kissed when they wanted, and she had distinctly heard him whisper, "I love you." She didn't know what that meant, not really, but somehow she did. "Love" wasn't a word that she had heard before within the Community—likely because it wasn't necessary or beneficial—but when Brooks said it, she still felt like she understood what he meant, even if she couldn't define the word.

She finally sat up to look at him, and his crooked smile spread across his face. She wanted to say something, but the words were stuck in her throat. Instead, she stood up and started getting ready to return to her Community. She pulled on her boots and her coat and ran her fingers through her long hair. It was wavy when freed from her braid and fell nearly to her waist. She didn't have a band to tie it back with, so she smoothed it over her right shoulder. Brooks still lay in their soft patch of grass watching her, his blue eyes soft with sadness.

"Are you going to get up?" she asked.

"Just enjoying the view," he answered before sighing and getting to his feet.

Brooks dawdled all morning, piling mud on top of their fire and disposing of animal bones. Rhea watched anxiously at the edge of the clearing until he ran out of things to do and finally strode toward her. He pushed her against the closest tree and kissed her like it was the last time he ever would. Her body came alive and she savored the feeling, remembering him, then gently pushed him back. He smiled.

"Until later, then," he said before taking her hand and leading her back to the Wall.

Gael's eyes snapped open. The sun would be rising soon; it was almost time to go back. "Get up! Get up!" Gael yelled, kicking various classmates who were huddled around the dead fire, still sleeping. "It's time! It's time!" They scrambled to their feet, yawning widely. Gael shoved a few people out of his way and stood directly in front of the gate. "Open up!" he yelled, and his classmates quickly took up the chant.

They had all lost weight—even himself and Lila, although they had lost the least. The other students had a gaunt and haunted look, like they had been through a devastating experience. "Open up! Open up!" they screamed as loudly as they could, many voices weak and shaking. A few fists started pounding on the gate.

Finally, Gael heard the drums start up. A wild cheer went through the group of Seventeens. The gate finally started to open outward toward them. Gael quickly shoved someone out of his way and ran through the opening. The Residents cheered as he entered, swarming around him to greet and welcome him. Gael smiled happily and waved at his Residents. Someone threw a blanket over his shoulders, and someone else shoved water and a cake into his hands. Gael laughed and cheered along with everyone else, pretending to watch with concern as one of his classmates, Charles, collapsed just short of the gate entrance and lay facedown in the dirt. Gael hoped he would either get up before sundown or be left outside. If he couldn't get up, he was likely too weak to be of much use to the Community anyway.

The rest of the Seventeens stepped over or onto Charles to hurry back into the safety of the Community. Gael ate and drank, talking and laughing with the Residents, his future subjects, until a strong hand closed around his arm and turned him around. Rhea's father glared at him, his face inches from Gael's.

"Where is she?" he demanded, his lips barely moving. "Where is Rhea?"

Gael took a hasty step back, but Rhea's father kept pace with him, snarling into his face. He was usually a composed Leader who knew his place. Gael's family had created the Community, had written the rules—they were evidently responsible for it and knew how to lead it. But a rebellion the year that Gael was born had forced them to switch Leaders each generation. It was only "fair."

"I don't know," Gael said, trying to remember what he had told his own father about Rhea's week beyond the Wall. "She . . . she was around . . . and then wasn't."

"Where did she go?"

"How should I know? I took excellent care of her! She wandered off, and who knows what she could have gotten herself into?"

"If she is not back by sundown, your status within this Community will no longer exist."

"Are you threatening me?" Gael demanded.

"Yes," Rhea's father hissed before turning on his heel and stalking back to the top of the Wall to watch for his daughter. Gael shifted his weight uncomfortably and glanced around. No one seemed to have noticed the exchange; the attention of his Residents was diverted to the weaker Seventeens. What could Rhea's father have possibly meant? Perhaps it would be time to rid the Community of their current Leader sooner than he had thought. He turned and walked directly into his own father.

"How was your week?" Father asked, a light smile playing around his thin mouth.

"Fine," Gael snapped.

"And where is your intended?" he carried on, lowering his voice.

"How should I know? I haven't seen her since . . . for a few days."

"Very interesting. And I see Brooks has not yet returned. I also received a report that three of our Defenders have not reported this morning. Three Defenders who were stationed at your camp."

"So?"

"So, if you are responsible for the death of one of our own

Residents, who also happens to be our Leader's daughter, you will have sacrificed your entire future for a grudge and a crush. This is why we have the tests—so that people like you don't get above themselves. I thought, as my son, you were worthy of the prestige and power that I had to deny myself. It appears that I was wrong."

"What do you—" Gael felt panic rising in his middle. He must not have qualified to be Leader according to his test. *What does this mean?*

"This means," Father continued, answering his unasked question, "that if Rhea does not show by sundown, I will personally remove you from the Community and nominate a new future Leader to the Council."

Gael felt heat rush to his face. "I'm your son!" he snarled, the words forcing their way through his bared teeth.

"There are things more important than you in this world," his father whispered, then turned to join Rhea's father on top of the Wall. Gael glared after him, not knowing what he had meant or truly caring. So what if the Defenders had killed Rhea along with Brooks? Gael would find someone new.

Tears stung his eyes. Why was everyone hounding him, as though it was his responsibility to look after every Resident? He was barely an adult! He shook his head. His father, Rhea's father, and many others who might not support him today could be removed very easily once he was finally officially Leader. It wasn't like he needed them to run the Community; he was born to do this. It was rightfully his.

Gael shook his head to clear away all the negative thoughts, put on a wide smile, and headed for the dining hall.

CHAPTER 8
GOING BACK

The journey back to the Community seemed to take much longer than the journey away from it. Rhea reminded herself that she and Brooks had run from the Community and were now walking back in a rather resigned way. As they drew nearer, Rhea's footsteps grew more unsteady. Her hands trembled in her coat pockets. They would know that she and Brooks had spent the week alone together. What would everyone think? Would she be punished?

She glanced sideways. Brooks's face usually was alive with a kind of wild joy, a crazed laughter that she had never seen in anyone else. Now it looked cold and stoic—closed off, as though he had bundled deep inside of himself where pain could not reach him. Would he ever forgive her for choosing to go back? As though he could read her mind, Brooks flashed a quick smile at her and slipped his hand into hers.

The Wall finally came into view, looming ominously over their heads. It had grown in the years since Brooks had climbed over it, with new trees being felled from their clearing and piled on top, followed by a walkway along the top of the Wall so that Defenders could patrol it. A small cheer went up from a few of the tiny figures on top of the Wall as Rhea and Brooks came into view, and she hastily released her tight grip on his hand. He glanced at her but didn't attempt to take her hand again. The Wall loomed larger and larger before them as they crossed the large clearing around it to reach the gates.

Rhea could see her fellow Residents grouped through the gate, her father standing right on the line. A crumpled figure lay motionless on the ground just short of the gate. Rhea sped up to peer at it. It was Charles, a small and sickly boy in her class. His eyes were closed, but they opened at her touch.

"Charles?" she asked.

"Rhea," he whispered, his voice weak and raspy. "I can't seem to find the strength to carry me those last few steps." He smiled through cracked bleeding lips. "But . . . at least I finally escaped. I can die free."

Rhea shook her head, tears stinging her eyes. It was too much. Walking back with Brooks, knowing what they were likely leaving behind, knowing that the last time they had kissed would probably be the last, and now this ominous warning right at the foot of the gate.

Brooks knelt next to her. "Why won't anyone help him?"

"They . . . they can't cross the boundary . . ."

"Why didn't someone help him in when they came back?"

"They . . . you're supposed to walk across the line at the gate on your own." Brooks swore under his breath. Rhea looked up; her eyes found her father's. They were identical in shape and color to hers, mirror images of each other. It was like gazing into her own dark-green eyes.

Rhea carefully gathered Charles in her arms. He was very light, small, and sick as he was, while she was strong after working out with Brooks each day and eating better than she had in her entire life. She felt rejuvenated, alive as she had never been before.

"Rhea," a voice in the crowd before her spoke up, a final warning. "Residents are to pass the line on their own to show that they are still capable of meeting the needs of the Community."

"And Residents are to use their own abilities to help one another to the best of their ability," Brooks shot back. Rhea kept her eyes on her father's, the way that she had last time she had broken the rules in front of him. She walked carefully up to the line at the gate, keeping the toes of her boots behind it. She held out her arms, stretching so that

Charles was on the correct side of the line. Rhea's father took Charles from her, nodding slightly.

"Brooks is correct," he said, turning to face the Community. "We take care of one another to the best of our ability. It is the most important rule within this Community, far more important than requiring a sick child to cross the line on his own. He has plainly chosen to come back to us, as he made it as far as he possibly could, and we will welcome him back with open arms." He carried Charles to the stretcher lined up just inside of the gate for just this purpose, and Charles was quickly carried back to the infirmary.

Rhea smiled, stepped over the line, and hugged her father. A cheer went through the crowd, and she wrapped herself up in it. She was back. She was so happy in that moment that she forgot to look for Brooks. She quickly broke away to look back over her shoulder, but Brooks had already crossed the line and was standing with his hands in his pockets, his eyes darting around the Community with a sour look adorning his dark face. Rhea released her father and joined him, nudging him gently to get his attention. "Is everything okay?" she whispered.

"Just . . . can't believe we're back," Brooks replied lightly. He reached for her hand automatically before quickly stopping himself.

"Shall we go to the feast?" she asked tentatively.

"You go. I'm not hungry."

Rhea hesitated. "You know the ceremony will take place at sunset. You'll need to be there to receive your occupation and your . . . your partner."

"I'll be there," Brooks said before striding away into the depths of the Community. Rhea watched him melt into the dwellings, frowning slightly.

"Rhea!" She jumped and whirled, her hand going instinctively to her waist, to a knife that was no longer there. Weapons were not allowed within the Community; weapons were not needed within a Community. What would Residents possibly have to defend themselves against? They had the Defenders, after all, who enforced the rule of the Council.

Gael looked down at her hand groping for a blade that wasn't there. "Are you okay?"

"Yes," she said, quickly dropping her hand. "I'm well, thank you. And how are you?"

Gael shook his head. "Where the hell were you?" he demanded, lowering his voice. "You disappeared as soon as the gate opened! You and *him*."

Rhea brought herself up to her full height so that she and Gael were nose to nose. "I completed my week beyond the Wall, and I returned in the allotted timeframe."

"Come here," Gael said, taking her arm. He dragged her away from the crowd around the gate that still hung open. It was a requirement that the gate stay open until sundown; it would close right before the ceremony.

Gael marched her along the Wall until the noise of the Community faded behind them, his grip tight on her arm. He finally stopped behind a small copse of trees and turned to face her, still holding on tightly to her bicep. "What the hell were you thinking?"

"You will have to be more specific," she countered, amused despite herself. The red on Gael's face deepened as his anger rose.

"You disappeared. With *him*."

Rhea gazed steadily at Gael, choosing not to answer. She felt so different from who she was before her week beyond the Wall. *Perhaps I am simply growing up,* she thought, but it was more than that. The fear that had weighed so heavily on her since the day she was branded as disobedient had somehow slipped off of her.

"Where were you two this whole time?" Gael finally asked.

"We were somewhere beyond the Wall. I'm not sure where."

"What were you two doing out there?"

"Completing our week beyond the Wall."

Gael let out a snarl of frustration. "Rhea, as my future partner, there are expectations of you! You can't just go off with another man and—"

"What do you mean, 'your future partner'?" Rhea interrupted. "The tests decide who we are most suited to be with and the results have not been announced!"

"That doesn't even matter!" raged Gael. "What did you do with him?! If he touched you—"

"No!" Rhea attempted to pry Gael's hand from her arm, but he held on. "The test will decide who I am going to be with, not you! I know what the rules say. If you attempt to intervene and sway who I will be paired with, I will report you!"

"You truly are just a scared, stupid little girl, aren't you? None of this was ever real! *My family* made all of this possible, which means that I *own* you!" He grasped her other arm to hurl her to the ground, but she wrapped her ankle around his and he toppled down as well, landing hard on the earth next to her. She quickly rolled away and scrambled to her feet, poised for the fight. Gael charged, his hands outstretched as if ready to wrap them around her throat. She quickly ducked and used his momentum to flip him over her back so that he landed hard once again, behind her this time.

"Gael," she said, her voice calm and icy. "You are attacking me. I request that you stop this behavior at once and turn yourself in for evaluation of your mental state and accept punishment." This was the correct line to use if someone attacked you. Self-defense was not necessary because, naturally, any rational person would come to their senses if you said the correct words.

That was what the rules said, anyway.

However, Gael did not stop. He found his feet and slowly stood. In a few quick strides, he was before her again and raising a hand to strike her. She ducked, and his hand instead found a tree trunk. A wild yell of pain escaped him as he clutched his skinned hand. Blood seeped between the split skin of his knuckles. "Perhaps you will not stop because it is against the rules to attack me. But perhaps you will stop because you are embarrassing yourself," Rhea mused.

"What's the matter with you?! You were supposed to know your place here, as a female, as my partner. It's like you forgot everything you've been taught!"

"I did not forget," Rhea whispered. "It's like I only just started remembering."

"No!" Gael said, pointing at her. "I'll just have to teach you what it means to be a Resident after we're wed."

"If the tests will it," Rhea responded coolly. "I have very little faith that you have any influence regarding who I will be wed to. You evidently know very little about the history of our Community. Your family did not *start* it!"

Gael smiled malevolently. "You'll see," he hissed, turning on his heel and stalking back toward the open gate.

⌐

Brooks watched carefully from his hiding place in the bushes, attempting not to laugh. He could have intervened at any time, but it would have simply been wrong to take the joy of besting Gael physically away from Rhea. He wondered if she would believe him later tonight when Rhea was named to be Gael's intended. It didn't really matter, though; they wouldn't be here much longer.

Rhea picked her way to her dwelling, pushing open the door to find it deserted. Nurse and Father would both be down at the open gate for the day. Her dwelling looked much smaller than it had just a few days ago. It seemed dark and sad compared to her rock outcropping, where sunlight had streamed through little gaps between the rocks and drew yellow patterns on the green and brown of the forest floor. She poured water into the tub, not bothering to heat it first, and clambered in.

She was not as dirty as she had assumed she would be. Perhaps all of their time in the pond had kept off most of the grime. She closed her eyes, remembering every kiss and embrace. When she opened them again, her vision was blurred with tears. She quickly swiped both hands hard across her eyes before viciously scrubbing her body, face, and hair, rinsing off, and climbing laboriously out of the tub. She looked down into the slightly grey water, thinking of the pond, before pulling the drain and watching it slide down and away from her, listening to it being emptied into the yard. Rhea dressed quickly and played with her hair. She hadn't tied it back into its braid since the day they had left the Community. The braid stayed in place well and covered her brand more easily than when she wore her hair loose, but there was something so beautiful about those white-blonde curls sprawling around her face. They were spirited and messy, not following any pattern, and tended to frizz on the top, but they made her look so much more alive. She let her hair fall naturally around her face and left her dwelling.

Rhea spent the next several hours waiting for the sun to go down with the other Residents, eating and talking and staring at the open gate. It looked rather like a gaping mouth, ready to swallow them up. Everyone was eager for the naming ceremony and to see the gate closed once more. She sat in a circle with the other Seventeens around a firepit, watching the sun make its slow descent through the sky. She caught Gael's eye, mostly because he had chosen the seat directly across from her and was glaring at her and gave him a wide smile.

Lila sat on her right and chatted animatedly about her week outside of the Community. "It was so cold all of the time without blankets! And the bugs, there were bugs everywhere. I missed my dwelling so much! And I was so hungry without being able to have three meals each day!"

"Yes," Rhea lied. She had never been cold; Brooks had laid next to her, and they had piled their coats together. She hadn't been bothered by bugs; they had never tried to hurt her. People were more dangerous than bugs. She hadn't missed her dwelling at all, or ever felt hungry. When she had found the wild beehive, she was so ecstatic that she had insisted on claiming a piece of honeycomb for just her and Brooks. Brooks had protested, but she had approached slowly and carefully, letting the hum of the bees, so much sweeter than the hum of the Residents in her Community, swell around her until she was a part of them. She lifted her head and let her own little hum join theirs before reaching carefully into the hive, taking out a chunk of honeycomb, and returning to Brooks. He had been so pleased, he had laughed and swept her into his arms. Then they had shared the comb together, and Rhea had never tasted anything sweeter.

"Rhea? Are you listening?" Lila asked.

"What? Oh, yes. I apologize."

"I accept your apology," Lila answered automatically, delving into the next topic of conversation. "So, what happened with you and Brooks while you were gone?" There was a bitter edge to her voice that Rhea had never heard before.

"What? Oh, we completed our week together."

"That's not what I mean, and you know it. What did you two do?"

"We hunted and gathered. We ate and slept."

"Together?"

"We hunted and gathered together, yes."

"Why are you avoiding my questions? What did you two *do*?"

"Lila, I really don't want to talk about it."

"Did you kiss him?" Rhea opened her mouth, unsure how to respond. Lila twisted her mouth and looked away. "You don't get to have *everything*, you know," Lila snapped.

"Yes, I know . . ." Rhea said. Goodness, yes, she knew that she couldn't have everything. She would settle for just one thing that she wanted.

Lila rolled her eyes and turned her back on Rhea. The conversation around them shushed as Rhea's father stepped onto the platform at the top of the open gate. The sun sank below their sight behind him.

"Close the gates!" he said, not having to raise his voice for it to nevertheless carry. The iron hinges groaned as the gates were pushed shut by Defenders on either side. The drums started up, and the Residents began their hum. "*Hummm . . .*" echoed through the Community and seeped out into the world beyond. Rhea watched the gap between the gates shrinking, fighting a mad urge to throw herself through them and run until she found herself back in the meadow with Brooks. She balled her hands into fists on her crossed legs. The last rays of sunset streamed through the gap, filtered by the trees on the other side but still red and strong. The gates closed with a thud, and Rhea released her held breath. That was it, then. Her eyes scanned the onlookers leaning against the Wall next to the gate and found Brooks watching her. She considered trying to smile, but somehow she couldn't force the corners of her mouth up. His eyes were sad and resentful, and she supposed that she deserved that.

"Now that we are all back where we belong," her father continued, wrenching her attention back to him, "we shall begin assigning partners and occupations. This year of Seventeens offers significant talent, as their tests proved." Rhea sat up a little straighter. "First, Annabeth." Annabeth rose to her feet, visibly shaking. "You are most suited to be partnered with Jacob, and your occupation is papermaker." Annabeth smiled weakly at Jacob, who looked rather disappointed as he gazed back at her before sitting back down.

"Next, Abigail," her father continued. Rhea waited impatiently. It would take them a long time to reach the R's and announce her fate, but Brooks's would become clear much sooner. She wiped her sweaty palms on her pants.

Finally, he called out, "Brooks." Brooks stood, gazing defiantly at all of the faces turned to him, his arms folded. "Brooks arrived late to this Community and, as such, is unfit to wed. He shall not be given a life partner. He will, however, have the opportunity to prove himself to his Community by tending to our animals."

Rhea recoiled as all the breath was forced from her body. How could this have happened? Brooks being unfit was worse than any other outcome she had envisioned for him. Unfit Residents were given wide berths, the smallest portions of food, and the most demeaning jobs. Any number of things could have deemed him unfit—anything from a question regarding his ability to father children to an illness in his mind or body, or simply that his ideas were too dangerous to allow him to have a partner and a family. The population of the Community was the most essential aspect of its survival, and Residents who couldn't contribute to it were seen as lesser than everyone else. Rhea's own mother had died in childbirth, which was seen as the highest honor of any female Resident.

Brooks locked eyed with Rhea and sat back down while the ceremony droned on and on. Could she have been so mistaken to believe that she and Brooks were really well suited for each other? Who could she possibly be happier with than him? Mutinous thoughts swirled through her head, and for once she did not attempt to stem them. They should have stayed in their meadow.

Lila nudged her, and Rhea realized too late that her name had been called. She rose hastily to her feet, trying to compose her face into some semblance of eager anticipation.

"My own daughter, Rhea, is partnered with Gael. Her occupation will be that of Beekeeper."

Rhea sank down. *Gael.* The man who had accosted her, told her he would teach her what it meant to be wed to him. Gael, who had kissed her. She realized she had missed Gael's given occupation but found that she did not care. Lila was pouting next to her, gazing at Brooks, who was staring at Rhea's father with a sour look adorning his face.

The ceremony eventually ended and Residents swarmed the Seventeens to congratulate them. Some of them looked very pleased, Gael among them, who began picking his way toward Rhea. She smiled as graciously as she could, her frozen face working hard in the process. Gael would be allowed to court her openly over the next year while they were both trained in their new professions. School was now over, to be replaced by their apprenticeships. After they wed in spring of next year, they would move into their own dwelling together and be given their next assignment according to the population needs of the Community. She would have to remove herself from her duties as Beekeeper after discovering her pregnancy until her child reached the age of two and could enter school to start learning the rules of the Community. And so the process would repeat. Women were often provided less important jobs than men, but that was simply the way the results of the tests shook out, right?

Gael took her hand, smiling at the people milling around them. "I could not have hoped for a better partner as I lead our Community!" he announced, pulling her close and planting a kiss on her mouth. Kissing in public, while not against the rules now that they had been paired, was considered rude, yet cheers went up from the crowd at his bold move. Rhea's mind seemed to be working in slow motion. "*As I lead our Community*"? Everything clicked. Gael would be taking her father's place as Leader. There would be no skulking away from a single rule, even within her own dwelling. How had Gael known that he would be selected as Leader? Or that she would be picked for him? *No one ever knows in advance.*

~

Nurse and Father both walked Rhea to their dwelling, shooting each other concerned looks at the stony expression on her face. Father kept opening his mouth to say something before snapping it shut again. As soon as they made it, Rhea politely bade the other two goodnight and walked to her room, gently closing the door before flinging herself onto her bed and sobbing her heart out.

"I don't understand . . ." her father said over and over again to Nurse. "She couldn't have made a better match."

"No," Nurse agreed, staring hard at him. "You wouldn't understand."

Brooks sat outside of Rhea's window and listened to her sobs. *This is what she wants.*

CHAPTER 9
THE FIRE

Smoke. It slithered into Rhea's nostrils and down into her lungs. She hacked and tried to cough it out, but it snaked deeper into her and curled into her chest, her stomach, filling her with thick poison. Her eyes shot open and she sat up, coughing.

Something was on fire.

No, she thought desperately. *No, no, no, no, no!* Her blanket tangled around her legs and tried to keep her tied to the bed, but she struggled to her feet, throwing her hair from her face, and staring around. *Brooks.*

She threw open her bedroom door, ran down the hall, and flung open the hut door, ignoring Nurse's wail of fear as she ran. Brooks's face burned white-hot in her mind. He was all that mattered—she had to find him. She willed herself to be drawn to him as she sprinted down the road until finally, she saw it. The Hall of Punishment was aflame.

"FATHER!" Rhea screamed, throwing herself at the flames only to be thrown back by the heat. She tried again, screaming and clawing at the heat, feeling her palms blister.

"Rhea!" someone screamed. She knew it was Brooks. She shook her head, wanting to ward him off. Not now. There were things bigger than him and her to deal with now.

Father—no, all of the Leaders were likely stuck in the Hall of Punishment. Perhaps even still alive and refusing to leave, because the rules said that they were obligated to guard the hall from danger. She almost laughed. It was so pointless, so exasperating to know that at this very moment, her own father, the only thing standing between herself and orphanage, might very well have been able to find a way out and to her, but he simply wouldn't. She could envision him sitting in the Audience Chamber, nodding as they discussed current business, while the flames licked around them. She threw back her head and watched the flames dance to the top of the Hall. If he wasn't already gone, he would be at any moment.

Someone grabbed her arm. She turned as though in a dream to see a stranger. Her mind moved slowly, sluggish with shock. *A stranger?* There were no strangers in the Community. The man lifted his arm high above her before crumbling into a heap at her feet. Brooks stood behind him, pulling a knife from the stranger's back. *Where did he get a knife?* Rhea wondered vaguely. *We left the knife in our cave.* He was grabbing her hand, pulling her along behind him. Sound was finally reaching her ears as she gazed at her Community, her everything.

Everything was ablaze now. People were running in all directions, screaming for help that did not come. The Defenders were cowering as strangers—*Outcasts,* Rhea realized—bore down on them with thick clubs, long machetes, crude swords, arrows, or torches.

"The gate!" Rhea whispered, unable to truly find her voice. "Who opened the gate?"

Brooks was dragging her along to the horses, but her feet tangled themselves up against each other and she fell. He stooped quickly and scooped her into his arms, running for the horses. Somehow, no one seemed to bother them. Brooks heaved her onto the best horse, a young and strong stallion, and clambered on behind her. She watched him turn for half a second and stare at one of the Outcasts, a girl with short dark hair, who gave the tiniest nod before Brooks kicked the horse into a gallop.

They rode quickly through the gate, ignoring the screams and the hands reaching for them, begging to be taken along. Rhea wanted to turn, to stop, to help, but she was frozen, her mouth open in a silent scream.

Brooks didn't slow until they were deep in the forest and the sounds of the butchery of the Community had faded, swallowed up by the trees. He wrapped his arms tightly around her and whispered into her hair, "You're safe now."

"We have to go back" was the first thing Rhea was able to say. Her voice shook, and her cold fingers found Brooks's warm ones and squeezed them to steady herself. "Brooks, turn around."

"We can't go back," Brooks said gently. "They'll kill us."

"They'll kill *them*!" Rhea snapped. Brooks did not answer, but she felt him shift behind her as he nudged their horse into another gallop.

"Brooks?" she asked uncertainly, twisting in the saddle to stare at him. He looked away. "Brooks . . . no." He slowed the horse, still looking anywhere but at her. The forest was spinning around her, dizzying her, sucking the air from her lungs. He tried to kiss her, but she grabbed his face in both hands and threw her body off the horse, pulling him with her. They landed side by side and both rolled away from the horse as it reared nervously. Rhea tried to crawl toward it, but Brooks grabbed her ankle and held fast. She lashed out with her foot, kicking, connecting with his nose, and hearing it break under her boot. Brooks cried out, his hands flying instinctively to his face.

Rhea scrambled to her feet, sobbing, and sprinted for the horse, but it turned uncertainly away, nervous from her eagerness. Rhea caught his reins and brought the beast around, trying desperately to shove her foot into one of the stirrups. Brooks caught her by the shoulders, trying to turn her, but she elbowed him hard in the stomach and he fell back with a grunt. Rhea swung herself into the saddle and turned to send one final blazing, tear-stained look at Brooks.

"You killed them."

"I didn't start this!" Brooks bellowed, voice thick with emotion.

"You opened the gate." Rhea turned her back on him and rode

furiously into the forest.

It took Brooks a few hours to walk back into Community 215. Blood poured from his nose, and he could feel his face swelling painfully. If it hadn't been directed at him, he would have been proud of Rhea's kick. He dwelled on the pain in his nose, as it distracted him from the much deeper pain of Rhea's departure.

When he finally arrived, Raven had the remaining Residents corralled by the gate, a line of Outcasts standing between them and the open gate brandishing weapons to keep them in line. Brooks looked around. It appeared that most of the Residents were still there and still alive. "Where's Adder?" Brooks asked, coming to stand beside Raven. She snickered.

"Did you just get dumped?"

"No. Why?"

She pointed at him, grinning. "Looks like your girl can take care of herself."

"Fell off the horse."

"And she didn't come back for you?"

Brooks opened his mouth to retort, but the thud of hooves on hard earth drew his attention back to the open gate. Adder had finally arrived with his usual barrage of guards. He was a large man with long dark hair and a scar across his face. Outcasts elected their own leaders, and it was evident by the sight of him that he had been selected for his formidable looks. Adder had been a popular enough leader when Brooks left, but he was still unsure as to why he hadn't been voted out yet. The Outcasts had faith in his cruelty against the Communities, as it made them feel protected, but he wasn't loved.

Adder dismounted and embraced Brooks. Brooks suffered the embrace impatiently, trying hard not to roll his eyes.

"Welcome home, child," Adder said, holding him at arm's length to examine him. "Are you okay? Did they treat you well?"

"They accepted me well enough." Brooks wiped blood from his nose before it could reach his mouth. "They're like sheep. They don't know how to think for themselves."

Adder nodded gravely. "At first, you were to be put to death at first sight for failing to complete your mission." Brooks stared him down, refusing to look scared. What more could they possibly do it him? "But then Raven approached me to inform me of your predicament."

"What do you mean?"

"How you had fallen in love," Adder said, his voice husky. Brooks grinned through the blood, knowing he looked insane.

"She didn't feel the same way," he admitted, indicating his nose.

"Of course she did," Adder said gently. "She likely just needs time to adjust to her new life. Not to worry. We will find her." Brooks shivered, thinking of Adder's henchmen hunting Rhea and wondering if they were already on her trail.

"That's not necessary."

"Returning her to you will be your reward."

"She will not come quietly."

"She will be persuaded."

"I would like permission to find her myself."

"Nonsense, your place will be by my side! Now, to the matter at hand." He turned to the terrified Residents, who had been watching this exchange with wide eyes. "Where is my wife?" The Residents all looked at each other uncertainly.

"Adder," Raven said, taking a step closer, "maybe you should explain what's going on."

"Of course. You are all now free from your prison here. You can join my company, and I will keep you safe. We don't hide behind Walls or follow ridiculous rules. Brook"—he indicated Brooks, who had nearly forgotten his real name—"will be able to brief me further, but I already know what you people are forced to do behind these Walls. You have the freedom to choose who you want and what you want while in my company. The only rule we have is to do as I say."

Adder took a few steps closer to the Residents, who shrank back. "There is no reason to be afraid. I have been liberating prisons like this for years. You people are always thrilled to join my company. It is all due to Brook that you are all free." Accusatory eyes found Brooks.

"But there is one problem that I have," Adder continued. "My wife was taken captive into one of these Communities several years ago. I haven't found her yet, and we will not stop until I do. Where is she?"

The Residents shifted uncomfortably.

"Your first order," Adder said, his voice lowering dangerously, "is to tell me where my wife is."

Rhea's father stepped forward. Brooks hadn't noticed him before and breathed a visible sigh of relief at seeing him still alive. His blond hair was covered in soot, and he held his hands awkwardly to his chest as though they were burnt.

"We don't know who you are talking about," Rhea's father proclaimed. "We do not have any 'wife' here. We have done nothing to you, and we are not prisoners. Each person here has chosen this life over the one outside these Walls. I ask you to please leave."

Adder scanned the crowd. "I see that she is not here," he stated. "You would know if you saw her. She was the most beautiful and delicate creature." He strode up to Rhea's father but the man stood his ground defiantly, gazing up at Adder.

"Who are you?"

"I am the Leader of these people."

"No," Adder said softly. "I am your leader now. It is something that you need to get used to."

Brooks hurried forward. "This is my love's father," he said urgently. "He is a good man, and he will learn to follow." He shot a dark look at Rhea's father, watching the color rise in his face.

"Rhea is not for you!" he snarled, finally breaking after years of calm and patience. "She was never for you! She deserves more!" He raised a red blistered hand to point directly into Brooks's face. "*You* did this! You destroyed everything!"

Adder stepped quickly forward, his arms slipping around Rhea's father as though in an embrace. When he stepped back, Rhea's father stared blankly at Brooks, his eyes widening. He took a shaky step forward, his hand extended toward Brooks, his fingers just scrabbling Brooks's throat before he crumpled into the dust. Screams echoed around the Community as everyone fled from the spot where Rhea's father lay dying. Brooks knelt next to him, grasping his hand in his own. Adder had left his knife in his belly, and Brooks could see the life draining slowly from his eyes.

"I'll take care of her," Brooks whispered, hoping that Rhea's father could hear him over the screams. It suddenly dawned on him that he didn't know the man's name; he had only been known as "Rhea's father" to him and "Leader" to everyone else in the Community.

"You . . . can't," Rhea's father gasped. Brooks held his gaze until the life flittered away.

Adder waited until he was dead, then gently eased Brooks to his feet. "It's for the best. He didn't understand your love." He turned back to the panicking Residents. "As I said, the only rule is to follow orders." He ordered, "Kneel." The Residents could not have been more prepared to follow orders. The thin veil of diplomacy that they had clung to behind their Walls was not the same as independence, and they dropped to their knees as quickly as possible.

"Now you will rise," Adder declared, his arms wide, "as my children, free men and women!"

❧

Raven set Brooks's nose and sloppily mopped the blood from his face. He let her, not caring what happened to him. "How does it feel to be appointed to Adder's personal guard?" Raven asked.

"Like I finally escaped from one master to serve another." His eyes found hers. "We aren't supposed to work for our leaders. Our leaders are supposed to work for us. Are you with me on this?"

Raven shrugged. "I have always had difficulty following orders, Brook."

"It's Brooks."

CHAPTER 10
ALONE

Rhea finally slowed her horse, worried that a stray root would reach up from the forest floor to trip them up. Her wide eyes took in her surroundings. Every direction looked exactly the same, endless trees under a grey sky. She glanced behind her, but the forest had swallowed Brooks. Silence pressed hard on her from all sides, and she shivered. She hadn't bothered to put on her coat in her panic to help with the fire. It wasn't too cold now, and it would get warmer as the day wore on, but by nightfall the temperature would drop and could plunge her into hypothermia. She didn't have any food or any water, didn't know which way to turn. To go back to the Community would mean death—the Outcasts wouldn't spare her without Brooks—though death was likely what she deserved.

Rhea closed her eyes and tears began to fall from under her lashes. She had allowed Brooks to stay in the Community. It was her fault that nearly everyone she had ever known was now dead. Her father, Nurse, Teacher, Lila—everyone. What did it mean for her? Her family, her occupation, her Community, and her future partner were all gone. How would she survive? She had never in her entire life been so utterly alone. She had never had to make a decision before, no matter how trivial. She wore whatever clothes she owned that were clean, learned whatever was presented to her in school, would have wed who she was instructed to, and would have birthed the correct number of children according to what she was told. She had never had to create, debate, or even come up with an original thought. In fact, it had been actively discouraged.

Dissent was poison to Community. New ideas were a challenge to the way that things were, and proposing a new idea indicated that things were not already perfect. Furthermore, it wasn't fair if one person was better at coming up with ideas than everyone else. Fairness was everything. Even when she had completed her week beyond the Wall, Brooks had been there.

Rhea wiped her face with the back of her hand. *Brooks.* Brooks, who had planned this for years. Brooks, who had taken their food and education and hospitality and thrown it all into the wind. Brooks, who had kissed her, who had manipulated her, who had tried to force her to believe that life would ever be any different from the way it had always been. He had stolen her entire life and future away. Anger bubbled up, white-hot, and she mentally wrapped herself in it, feeling it warm her despite the chill of the air. Brooks was wrong. The only correct way to live, the only way that any of this actually worked, was to live within a Community—to do what you were told, to never question the way things were.

Rhea turned her horse around. She would go back, if she could find her way, and rebuild the Community that Brooks had burned. She would create a team of Defenders whose sole job would be to wipe out the Outcasts. There would never be any dissent again.

Rhea shook the thoughts of doubt that threatened to edge into the corners of her mind. With new resolve she wiped the tears from her face, dug her heels into her horse's side, and began her journey, completely unaware that she was going the wrong way.

CHAPTER 11
MUTINY

Camp was exactly the way that Brooks remembered it. *Brook.* His name as an Outcast was Brook. He was now an Outcast again, a child of the forest who thrived among the trees. As they approached camp, Adder pressed his horn to his lips and gave it a long, low blast followed by two short ones. The seemingly empty clearing before them slowly came to life as people began climbing down from their high perches in the trees or creeping out from the underbrush.

All of the dwellings were designed to blend in with the forest. Branches fanned over huts that were built right against trunks, leaves covered dugouts in the earth, and platforms for the highest-ranking members of camp were stationed high in the trees. Camp was designed to blend in; in fact, sophomoric Community members would often walk directly through it while looking for Outcasts to raid or while carrying trade goods and end up being raided themselves. Brooks tipped his head back and could just make out the signs of the tree dwellings in the growing gloom.

Brooks had mostly lied when he was in the Community about his life as an Outcast. He had described the Outcasts as sporadic and unorganized. However, in some ways, life outside of the Community was not all that drastically different from life within the Community. There, you were valued only as well as you and your family were connected to the origins of the Community and desired by the families in charge. Here, Adder took what and who he wanted when he wanted. He threatened, bribed, and flattered. His tactics were cold, but predictable. It had taken Brooks years to understand the complex hidden hierarchy of the Community, where they claimed none existed. There, anything you said or did could warrant deep offense or break one of the countless unspoken rules that governed. Here, the rules were simpler; you would likely be left alone as long as you never pissed off Adder and he never saw a purpose for you. As an Outcast it was at least *possible* that you could be free to make your own choices. While all Outcasts were tough and prepared for an attack on or from a Community at a moment's notice, Adder focused on the most intelligent, most cunning, and strongest to be in his guard. Anyone could select their own partner and choose when and if to have children, as long as she didn't catch Adder's eye. All children would be left to their own devices, unless Adder saw a use for them. As he had for Brooks.

Adder clamped a hand on Brooks's shoulder, pulling him out of his contemplation. Adder was smiling and calling out to camp members on all sides. He handed calculated compliments out like treats, causing many to glow under the praise. The Community members trailed at the end of their little parade, terrified looks on their faces. Brooks glanced back and found Gael's eye. He smiled maliciously, and Gael hastily looked back at his shoes.

As the sun sank, fires spurted up on all sides. Camp came to life, laughter and chatter erupting as the fires roared into being. Brooks's mouth watered as the smell of venison wafted across camp. As his status in camp had grown since he had brought down a Community, he would be given a true portion. If he was just another camp follower, he would only be permitted to eat what he caught that day. Sharing wasn't against the rules—there weren't any true rules—but followers knew how to take care of themselves and their families, and those who didn't want to hunt, garden, or gather quickly learned that it was the only way to eat. Status certainly had its perks.

Brooks sat in a place of honor next to Adder. Adder's fire was the largest, a true bonfire. Camps didn't have to hide at night when Community members were too petrified of the darkness to initiate a raid. The night belonged to them. Brooks's eyes flickered to Adder's axe and dagger on his belt before finding Raven's. Her eyes made the same journey before settling on his. She settled herself across the fire from him and promptly began talking with the men on either side of her. She was so different from Rhea, he thought; she was tough and egotistical, rude and crass. Rhea was delicate, obedient to a fault with flashes of fire.

"Brook." He started and looked up in time to take the bowl of venison stew offered to him by one of the followers. The faces around him were mostly unfamiliar, with only a few that he remembered from his childhood. Adder had a lot of turnover from deserters and mutinous members, either in reality or in his imagination.

"Brook is distracted," Adder said. "His girl is not with us tonight." He clapped a heavy hand on Brooks's shoulder again and Brooks fought to not throw it off. "But she will be soon! We will find her. As we will find the Community that took my own girls." Adder wiped his eyes. He was always quick to cry when the topic of his wife came up, even though he was the only one who ever mentioned her. Brooks had always wondered vaguely if she was simply in hiding from him. Adder was prepared to tear down each Community to find her. That wasn't love; it was a twisted obsession. Wildly different from him and Rhea.

"There is nothing more important. When it comes to my wife, I will move heaven, hell, and anything in between to reach her," Adder whispered, his voice twining through the chatter on all sides and silencing it like a bucket on a fire. Brooks nodded. He often found it wisest to remain silent while Adder rambled. "Don't worry," Adder added. "I have our best hunters searching for her."

It took Brooks a minute to understand what he had said. "What?"

"Our best hunters. They will find her."

"Your wife?"

"No, I will find my wife. They will find your girl."

Brooks's heart rate quickened. "You sent hunters after Rhea?"

"Of course! I only needed to send one. He will bring her back to you."

Brooks stood up quickly. "When does he leave?"

"He already left."

"Who did you send?"

Adder didn't respond; he just looked at Brooks with amused eyes. Brooks felt cold dread drop into his stomach. He knew the answer.

"Call him back."

Adder slowly rose to his feet. "Did you just give me an order?"

Brooks turned away, but Adder grasped his shoulder and forced him back around. "As you were instrumental in the last Community we conquered, I will give you one chance to apologize for that," he warned in his carrying whisper Brooks remembered only too well.

Brooks set his feet. "I am going after him."

"Your place is here."

"It hasn't been for the past seven years."

Adder snarled, "Your place is wherever the hell I say it is!"

"No," Brooks said, smiling lightly. "My place is with her."

Adder drew his dagger. The firelight danced across his face, throwing it into light and shadow, gleaming off of his cold eyes. "Kneel, child, and take your punishment."

The throng of camp followers began to close in, as though they could sense the potential bloodshed. Followers were expected to follow each of Adder's orders, including when he told them to kneel for death. Brooks sank to one knee.

Adder lifted his eyes to the audience. "To all of my new followers, you have never known the price of disobedience. Learn it here."

Right, Brooks thought, *they "don't know the price of disobedience" my sweet behind.*

"Adder!" Raven hurried to his side and leaned close, but Brooks could still hear her whisper, "Please, make it quick. He deserves that."

Adder nodded, shoved his dagger back into his belt, and pulled his axe. Raven stepped back to give him room. The axe was Adder's execution weapon of choice. He towered over Brooks's kneeling form and raised the blade. In an instant, Brooks flung the handful of dirt he had gathered while kneeling into Adder's eyes. Adder yelled and raised his hands to clear his eyes while Brooks sprang up from the ground, grabbing Adder around the waist and using his state of imbalance to bring him hard to the ground. His hand still clutched the axe as he fell and Brooks planted a foot firmly on his hand and stomped several times, grinding down the heel of his boot onto Adder's hand, feeling the crisp crunch of bones as they broke.

He fastened both of his hands fastened around Adder's neck. The fingers of Adder's free hand found a stone and smashed it against Brooks's head. Spots of color popped in front of Brooks's eyes as he rolled off of Adder, clutching his head. Sticky blood pooled onto his palm. Brooks blinked hard to bring Adder into focus. He was on his feet again, axe discarded, and cradling his broken hand. Brooks's eyes found the axe briefly before fastening back on Adder's face. The axe was too far.

"I don't need it," Adder said through gritted teeth. He charged and Brooks tried to dodge, but Adder caught him around the neck with one thick arm and brought him in close in a chokehold. Brooks's fingers gripped Adder's arm, scratching hard while trying to stomp on Adder's feet. Adder grunted in pain but refused to loosen his grip. Brooks choked, needing air, craving it. He tried to dig an elbow into Adder's ribs but couldn't get enough momentum to harm him.

Adder leaned in close and hissed in Brooks's ear, "You were right—I sent a hunter to kill her." Brooks wheezed and struggled harder than ever, darkness starting to close in around the edges of his vision. He was going to die; nothing had gone right at all, and he was going to die now. "Her death was meant to be your only punishment! You wasted seven years, you refused to carry out your mission, and now you are going to die, all because of her. Was she worth it?" Brooks fixed Rhea's smiling face in his mind, wanting it to be the last thing he thought of. Adder groped for his dagger with the two working fingers on his broken hand, but they came away empty.

Raven leapt onto Adder's back and wrapped her legs around his waist, plunging his own dagger into the back of his neck, right at the soft spot where his skull met his spine, and wrenching it free to plunge it in again. Adder released Brooks in an instant. Brooks fell onto all fours, gasping and choking, his throat on fire as life flooded back into him. Raven stepped coolly over Adder, grasped Brooks by the arm, and hauled him to his feet. He leaned heavily on her as she raised Adder's dagger, dripping with blood, into the air. The fire made the dagger shine like a beacon.

"Kneel before your new leaders, you bastards!" Raven yelled affectionately.

CHAPTER 12
THE HUNTER

Darkness descended around Rhea. She pushed her horse as far as she dared, still terrified that a stray root or rock would trip them as the night deepened. She looked around frantically, ears straining, wanting to hear any signs of life. She should have reached her Community a long time ago, she thought, and she found herself vigorously shaking her head to try to dislodge the doubt that ebbed into her mind: that she was hopelessly lost. What would she do out in the wilderness on her own? Rhea slid off of her horse's back, trying hard not to think about Brooks. She slipped the saddle off the horse and tied its reins to a low branch so it could reach the grass. She thought of taking its bridle off, but what if it ran off and truly left her all alone?

She glanced around cautiously. Everything looked exactly the same in every direction—trees, grass, and growing darkness. She picked a tree with a large trunk and put her back against it. She had never been alone before. There had always been the Community, and outside of the Community there had always been Brooks. But Rhea had never heard silence like this before. It pressed on her as if it were screaming, and when it was finally broken by a distant rustling, she jumped. Rhea shivered, wishing she was wearing a large coat, wishing she had a fire, wishing she could curl up in Brooks's arms. She set her chin defiantly to no one in particular. She knew how to build a fire. She was just as capable as Brooks; she didn't need him.

Rhea gathered the driest brush and old branches that she could find and piled them up against a large boulder. She scraped away the grass growing next to the boulder until she found dirt, then piled her kindling and wood carefully, the way Brooks had taught her to. She cast her eyes around the small clearing, looking for a flint rock. She knew Brooks had found flint rocks along riverbeds, but she didn't know where the nearest river was. Was it possible to find a flint rock just along the forest floor?

The snap of a twig shattered the quiet around her. She straightened up, eyes darting around desperately to find the source. The silence was complete once more; even the wind seemed to be holding its breath. Rhea stayed still as long as she dared, almost wanting there to be a clear sign of danger to end the agonizing suspense. Finally, she was forced to relax her clenched muscles. She carefully ventured away from her clearing, gingerly putting one foot in front of the other, wanting to move silently. Her foot struck something, and she looked down. Flint rocks, with ragged edges, ideal for starting a fire. Rhea whirled in a circle, raising her hands and desperately wishing that she had something, anything, to defend herself with, but saw no one. Unnerved, she collected the rocks and returned to light her fire.

Once the fire was lit and Rhea was satisfied that it would not go out, she selected a low-hanging branch from a nearby pine. She climbed up to it, stuck out her boot, and stomped repeatedly until it finally came free from the trunk and crashed to the forest floor. She climbed down after it and fashioned it into a spear by dragging a rock toward the shortest end of the stick until it became a point. It was a poor weapon, but it was something. Brooks had taught her how to fight with a stick.

Rhea angrily wiped tears from her eyes with her fingers. Her Community, and in it everything and everyone that she had ever known, was gone. It was all her fault. No—not her fault. *Brooks's* fault. But she had let him in. What was she supposed to do now? Rhea stared at the dancing flames. Everyone else might be gone, but she had to keep on going. There was nothing else that she could do. She would find another Community, and they would tell her what to do.

Rhea blinked and raised her eyes from the fire.

A man was sitting across the fire from her. He was smiling, perfectly calm. "Are you her?"

"What?" Rhea whispered. How had she missed him? How had he sat down so silently? Her eyes had been blurred from tears and raw from staring into the fire, but he should have made *some* noise. Was she imagining him? *No, of course not.* She had never been permitted to imagine.

"Sweet child," the man said, almost signing. "You are so lost, so sad, all alone out here. Where do you come from?"

"I . . ." Rhea didn't know what to say. He was obviously an Outcast. He was dangerous—he couldn't be trusted. Brooks had been an Outcast and look where that had gotten her.

"It's okay," he assured her, smiling wider. His hair and eyes were brown, and his face was gentle and kind. "You can tell me."

"My . . . my Community burned down," Rhea said all too quickly. "It was Brooks. He—he opened the gates and out—people came, and they—they killed everyone!" Rhea was shaking now. "Please . . . I need to get to the closest Community. I don't—I don't know who you are, but if you would help me, I would be very grateful."

The man nodded, his head tipped to one side, studying her. "You are her, then. It doesn't truly matter. Your fate would have been the same, but if you weren't her, I would have had to hurry you along. Now that I know who you are, I can take my time."

"Your . . . what?"

"My time. I can take my time while I kill you."

Rhea froze, one hand curled on her spear that felt like nothing more than a twig in her hand. "Please . . ." she whispered. "I haven't done anything to you."

"I do enjoy a good talk around a fire," the man said, dropping his eyes to the flames. "You did well with my flint."

Rhea couldn't sort her thoughts into any form of sense. Had she misheard him? Why would he speak so casually of murder, without any shame? "I . . . I don't know you."

"Oh, I know that. You don't know me. You haven't done anything to me, and I haven't done anything to you . . . yet."

"But . . .." Rhea wanted to believe this was some kind of cruel attempt at humor. Who would tell someone that they were going to kill them before doing it? What kind of twisted ploy was that?

"Your boyfriend, Brook, he was supposed to open those Community gates a long time ago. Seven years ago, in fact." He slowly slid a knife out from his belt and let the firelight gleam off of the blade. Rhea's eyes fastened on it. "Because he took so long to accomplish his mission, Adder—that's our leader's name, Adder—decided he needed to be punished. The best punishment Adder could think of is killing you." The man tipped his head the other way. "I wonder which part of you I should bring back to show him that you are dead? So many parts of you are very . . . distinctive."

Rhea's heart hammered against her chest as though trying to escape from her doomed body. Her hand was dripping sweat on her spear head. "Please . . ." she managed to whisper again.

"Begging is always . . . enjoyable." The man smiled. "My name is Spark, if you would like to use it." Rhea finally tore her eyes from his knife to look back into his face, but he was looking at her spear. "When prey fights . . . that can be enjoyable as well."

"You . . . you don't have to do this," Rhea said, her voice cracking. "You could—could come with me to the next Community. We could keep you safe from . . . from Adder."

"There are just so many things that you little servants just don't understand. Out here, we do what we do because we *choose* to, not because someone forces us to. Can't you see it in my eyes? How very badly I want to kill you? Why would I ever give away my freedom out here to be some idiot's lapdog in a prison?"

"It's—it's not a prison!" Rhea shouted, the anger that she had been feeling all day toward Brooks bubbling up within her.

"Oh? Please, do tell me more."

"It's a *Community*! It's a place where people take care of each other!"

"Yes, it is your place to take care of others in there. Regardless of what they ask of you or what you really want to do. You would do whatever they told you to and ask for another once you were done. What kind of life is that?"

"A kind where men like you are tossed out into the wild where you belong!"

"Oh, that's not how I came to be an Outcast. Yes, I know that's what you people call us. I escaped only after cutting the throat of each man in that Community. Then I walked out of those gates as if I owned the place, which, by that point, I did. Adder gave me a mission similar to the one that your boyfriend got, but I went above and beyond in my orders. It only took me two days to gain their trust, and a few hours to destroy it. I left the women and children for Adder. He's convinced his wife was taken by a Community and is being held somewhere. Personally, I wonder if the poor bastard finished her off himself and can't handle the reality of it."

"Brooks would never do anything like that."

"You have no idea who Brook is and what he has done. You don't even know his real name."

"You're wrong!" Rhea screamed. She hoped that someone, any-one, might hear the noise, might come and find her.

"Good!" Spark said, looking excited. "You are starting to realize that you cannot reason with me and are resorting to screaming. You can scream and scream all you want out here, but no one will hear you. No one will care."

Rhea bit her lip, her mind working furiously.

"You're thinking," Spark whispered. "I'll give you something to think about: If you do not fight me, I will kill you quickly, but if you fight, you will stay alive until morning, and you will feel every ago-nizing second of it." He turned the knife. "I can heat it in the flames, and it will melt right through you," he said, his voice dropping lower and lower. "I can cast it aside and use my hands, if you would prefer. I am the executioner, but if you would like to pick the method, I am listening."

"No," Rhea said, shaking hard. Tears stung the corners of her eyes again.

"No?"

"No, I don't want to be toyed with any longer." Rhea stood up, her spear clutched tightly in both of her hands, the point facing directly at Spark. "You won't be the first man that I've killed."

The man smiled broadly and leapt to his feet. "You are a rare specimen after all," he chuckled, wonder in his voice. "I will enjoy this."

Rhea resisted the urge to turn and run, forcing herself to face death head-on. She drew back a boot and kicked it swiftly into the fire, trying to kick up some sparks into the man's face. He dodged easily, as though he had been expecting it, and circled around the fire toward her. Her back came up against the boulder that she had been resting against just a few minutes earlier. She thrust the spear at the man, and he sliced off the tip of it with his knife. He continued to swing the knife, whittling down her spear until she let go. She tried to hurl herself to his left, away from his knife hand, but he caught her and flung her back toward the rock. The back of her head struck the rock and she crumpled to the ground, blinking hard, trying to focus her eyes on her attacker.

Spark stood over her, a sad smile playing around his mouth. "You were not half as tough as I had hoped." Rhea lifted a hand to the back of her head and felt sticky blood matting her hair. She was going to die, alone here on the ground. Her dark-green eyes found Spark's cold brown ones. He walked slowly forward, leaning almost lovingly down toward her. Rhea waited as long as she dared, slowly inching her fingers along the dark ground until Spark was kneeling over her, then she snatched a burning branch from the fire and thrust it into his face. Spark screamed, his voice ringing loudly and echoing all around her. He dropped his knife and his hands flew to his face. Rhea quickly snatched up his fallen knife and held it uncertainly in front of her.

Spark lowered his hands, focusing on the knife. "I guess you won, then," he hissed, the calm demeanor having shattered to reveal raw, animalistic rage. "You can let me go." Rhea hesitated, tears coursing down her face. Why was this her responsibility? Why wouldn't someone come along and tell her what to do? "You don't have the brains to kill me now." Spark took a slow step closer. The fire flickered across his burned and blistering visage. She had burned the entire left side of his face, from his scalp to the corner of his mouth. She felt bile rising in her throat. She felt she ought to apologize, as one does when they accidentally hurt someone else, but it wasn't an accident. It had been her or him. She felt that she needed to stop him from leaving. The knife shook in her hand.

"If you let me go now, you will never rest. I will be living in every shadow. I will be in each breath of wind. Every twig that you hear snapping will be me creeping in closer. You will never close your eyes without seeing my face. You will wait for me to take your last breath and give it to me gladly, because it will mean an end to the torment of waiting for me."

Tears spilled down Rhea's cheeks. "Why are you making me do this?" she screamed. "Why can't you just leave me alone?!"

"Because you're weak! You're pathetic! Make a decision and live with the consequences!"

Rhea lowered the knife. "No," she whispered fiercely. "You can't make me do anything. Just leave, and I'll let you live." She turned to walk back to the fire.

He was on her in a second. He pounced like a lion, the cold blade of a second knife pressing at her throat, and she realized her mistake.

Twang. Thunk.

The knife shuddered against her throat.

Twang. Thunk.

The knife fell away.

Rhea turned. Spark had keeled over onto his side, plainly dead, two arrows protruding from his side.

Brooks strode toward her, bow in hand, his lightest smile upon his lips.

CHAPTER 13
REUNION

A scream stuck in Rhea's throat as Brooks approached her. She wanted to run simultaneously in two separate directions. She wanted to throw herself at Brooks and kiss him, yet she also wanted to hit him. She settled for backing away quickly.

"I guess I don't owe you one anymore," Brooks said, his smile widening. "I missed you, Rhea."

"No . . ." Her knees gave way, and she sank onto the forest floor. It was all too much. What was she supposed to do now?

"Rhea." Brooks knelt next to her and laid his bow aside. "It's okay, he's not going to hurt you."

Rhea slapped him. Brooks reeled back, hand on his cheek, before breaking into laughter. "I suppose I deserved that, although you did already break my nose." Rhea barely remembered that but noted with some satisfaction that his face was badly bruised, and his nose now sat crookedly on his face.

"Just leave, Brooks," she said. "I can take care of myself."

"I can see that," Brooks retorted, glancing over at Spark. Rhea stood quickly and walked back to the fire. She sat down heavily and leaned back against her rock. "You're hurt," he said, following her. His hands gently touched her hair, but she pulled back.

"How long did you plan it?" she demanded, venom in her voice. Brooks winced.

"I guess it was stupid to think you would be happy to see me."

"Yes."

"How about we make a deal?"

"No."

"I'll tell you whatever you want to know if you let me treat the cut on your head."

"No."

"I'll take you to the next Community."

"I don't want the next Community! I want *my* Community!" Rhea was on her feet again, but she swayed a little and blinked hard to try to keep Brooks in focus. "You destroyed my Community—everyone I love is dead because of you. You're lucky I don't kill you!"

The smile had vanished from Brooks face. "Rhea, they're not dead," he said. "They're all fine."

Rhea's heart quickened. "What?"

"Please sit down." Brooks patted the ground next to him. Rhea shook her head, causing it to pound painfully, but Brooks caught her by the elbows and eased her to the ground. He spoke quickly, "Adder, who was the leader of my group outside the Community, he's been looking for his wife and little girl for years because he thinks someone in one of the Communities stole them, and he sent me in to open up the gates. He'd done it lots of times before, sending kids to infiltrate Communities and break through the security. I was supposed to do it after I got there, open the gates before sunrise so that no one would be prepared. They didn't want to just attack, because he was worried his wife and daughter would get hurt. Also, those Walls are hard to get over or break through, and while in the clearing, we would be exposed. But I didn't go through with the mission . . . because I met you."

Rhea blinked at him, and he pressed on. "When we left the Community, I knew he would send someone after me. That's why I wanted to be far away from everyone, so they wouldn't know where to look. Raven found me during our week beyond the Wall. We're lucky it was her and not someone worse. She told me how things stood with Adder and what I would have to do. He was done waiting—it had been seven years, and he was coming in one way or another. If you had just wanted to stay in that clearing with me . . . but you didn't. And we went back, and I had to open the gates, or more people would have died. But Adder didn't hurt . . . almost anyone. Most people came peacefully, and they're all fine. And they're living beyond the Wall, like I always said we could do!" Brooks took her hands. "You can come back with me and see everyone! You'll love our camp, and you loved it when we lived beyond the Wall. No one will ever tell us that we can't be together there."

"What do you mean?"

"What?"

"What do you mean 'Adder didn't hurt *almost* anyone'?"

Brooks froze. His hands stiffened in hers. "Rhea," he said nervously. "Your . . . your father . . . he wouldn't listen to Adder . . . Adder wanted to set an example."

Rhea's face crumpled as she dissolved into tears. Brooks tried to hold her but she beat him repeatedly, her fists barely landing blows at all, until she became limp in his arms and sobbed into his chest.

"I got him, Rhea," Brooks was saying. "Adder's gone now—he's gone, he's gone. Raven and I took care of him."

Rhea pushed herself into a seated position. "If you had never opened the gate, he would still be alive."

"I know," Brooks whispered, his eyes down. "I know, I'm sorry."

Rhea sniffed.

"But don't you see what this means?" Brooks said in a rush. "I'm a leader now, me and Raven, and we'll take care of all of our people, and we'll keep everyone safe! It's not like in the Communities—out here, everyone votes on everything. If the people don't like us, they vote us out right away and someone new comes along to lead. It didn't work that way with Adder because he decided he was better than everyone else and scared them into following him, but we're setting up our own rules to make sure no one can ever do that again. Everyone gets a say and gets to choose all the rules now that we're in charge! There are lots of us out here. Lots of people are so happy to be done with the Community, and you can be a leader like you always wanted."

"Who is Raven?"

"She's a girl from my camp. She's alright."

"If you and Raven are the leaders, how could I ever be one?"

Brooks laughed. "We'll just show everyone how wonderful you are, and everyone will vote for you over me."

"You never listen! You never learn!" Rhea yelled suddenly. Brooks winced. "The Communities are the only way that anything actually works! You all live out here, making choices like animals, and you end up with murderers like Spark! We can't pick our leaders—they need to be chosen by the tests. It's the natural way to live. We can't be together because the tests didn't decide that we should be! That means that we're not matched!"

"I told you, the tests aren't real! You were going to be wed to Gael because he wanted you, not because the tests said so!"

"You're lying! You always lie!"

"I am not! We're not all murderers! Spark was Adder's man, not mine."

"He was armed! In Communities, we don't have a need for weapons!"

"Yes, you do! It's just that only certain people are trusted with them—your Defenders and the Council and even your own Nurse. Do you know why people like me weren't permitted to have weapons?"

"Because you could have used them against people in charge!"

"Exactly," Brooks spoke slowly, as though trying to break things down for her like she didn't understand. "If the people were able to overthrow the Council, they would have had to ensure that the people were happy and well taken care of. Without the means to defend themselves, the Council could do whatever they wanted, and the people stayed helpless."

"People don't need help inside a Community! The Council and the Defenders keep them safe!"

"And what if someone who was a bad Defender, or a bad Leader, came along and hurt the people?"

"That would never happen!"

"How do you know?"

"We have *rules* in the Community! Out here, you don't have any rules. Out here, anyone can do whatever they want!"

"Including us! Don't you see? Don't you feel that freedom?"

"Freedom is poison. People are too stupid to make their own decisions!"

"Oh, yeah? Aren't your precious Communities run by people?"

"It's not the same! The Leaders know, and the tests know!"

"No, the Leaders *control*. The tests are just a curtain for them to hide behind!"

"They are not! These decisions, who you wed, your occupation, and how many children you have . . . they're too important of decisions to be left up to the will of people!"

"Do you hear yourself? Who *you* wed? What *your* occupation is? *Your* children? You should be in control of your own life!"

"If we left people in control of their own lives, the world would end!"

Brooks threw his head back and laughed. It was an awful, humorless sound that echoed eerily around the clearing.

"The world would end!" Brooks repeated incredulously. "Can you even open your mouth without spewing the unverified teachings they shoved down your throat? I remember that lesson: 'You can't have another portion of meat because we're conserving the Community, which is essential to saving the whole world. It's not that cold out—put out your fire so that we can save the world! No, we need to toss that extra child out to the Outcasts as soon as it comes of age because you weren't supposed to have twins, and now the population is too high. Let's save the world!' How long has your Community predicted the end of the world? Were you ever right? You believe that you could end the world? You believe that how much you eat or how big your dwelling is or how many children you have matters to the world? Do you even know how big the world is? That people exist all around it, making their own decisions and impacting the world in ways that you, in your own tiny life, never could!"

"You're wrong! The Communities are all that there is!"

"There is so much more!"

"You don't know anything!"

"*You* don't know anything!"

And suddenly they were kissing as though it was the last time.

Rhea clung to Brooks, not wanting to break apart. Kissing him was blissful—every worry in her mind floated away. How could there be anything more important? What did it matter where they lived or what they had to do, as long as they were together? They kissed hard, roughly, as though trying to vent their anger and frustration with each other, with the world in which they lived.

Rhea broke away. Somehow, they had found their way to the ground next to her fire. Brooks leaned closer to continue the kiss, but she put up a hand and pushed him away.

"We can't do this."

Brooks laughed. It was one of the most beautiful and irritating things about him. Brooks often laughed when she wanted to be serious. He was scarcely in control of his emotions at any point in time, whereas she knew to guard hers. She knew the penalty of disobedience and was reminded of it by her brand each day.

"Stop laughing," Rhea snapped, but Brooks ignored her.

"You just don't understand how this works, Rhea. This is *love*."

Rhea glared at him. She had never been taught the word or concept of "love," although Brooks had whispered it to her before. She had no way of knowing if he was making this word up or not. If it wasn't beneficial to her Community, why would she need to know what it was?

"You didn't know what love was, did you? Of all the things that they forced you to memorize in that school, love wasn't one of them."

"It doesn't matter. If I don't know what it is, it is because it doesn't help a Community function and is therefore a distraction from fairness and efficiency."

"Oh, it is," Brooks confirmed. "Love isn't fair, it isn't efficient. It's wild and unexpected. It's stupid and crazy."

"There is no point to it, then."

"It's the only thing that there is a point to." He took her face in his and stared hard into her eyes. "There's no point to life without you. There's no reason for me to do anything unless it is for you."

Rhea shook her head. "We . . . we never should have gone away together."

"No," Brooks agreed, "but we did. And now you know what love is, because you love me."

"I am not stupid or crazy!"

"Of course you are." Brooks laughed again. Rhea wanted to hit him.

"I am going to find a new Community."

"You're going to abandon everyone you have ever known in order to be ruled over by someone new? You have no idea what they might require of you." Brooks's smile had melted away.

"It's a *Community*! It's *safe*!"

"You're safe with me!"

"I am not safe with you—there are no rules out here! Everyone does what they want. Look at that man your people sent to kill me!"

"I am in charge of them now, me and Raven. No one is going to hurt you."

"That's not good enough! I need . . . I need a society that works. There is only one way that this *works*."

"If you come with me, you can live in a society. It might be a society where no one tells you what your occupation will be, what you're allowed to eat or how much, where or how you should live, or who you need to be with, but it does work. No one will hurt you there, and you'll be able to protect yourself if anyone tries. I'll protect you. I'm in charge, but I'm not leading like Adder did. You had to do everything he said when he was leading, but he's gone now."

"And what if someone else decides they want to lead and they kill you?"

Brooks let out a scream of frustration. "That's not how it works now! You just don't get it! Because you've made up your mind, you won't listen to me! You won't concede for even a second that you might be wrong!"

"If you really love me," Rhea said, setting her jaw, "you'll come with me."

Brooks shook his head, mouthing wordlessly as he tried to put together a reply. "You're going to make me be enslaved to be with you?"

"It's not enslavement, it's civilization!"

"If we go to a Community, they might decide that we aren't compatible."

"We . . . we're not compatible, Brooks."

"How can you say that? Don't you understand what you feel for me?"

"You don't know what I feel!"

Brooks kissed her again. *I'll pull away*, Rhea thought. *I'll make him see reason . . . just . . . not yet.*

⌒

They didn't talk about their future for the rest of the night. In fact, they barely spoke at all. There was nothing to say, and neither of them wanted to fight anymore. Rhea cried, her face buried in Brooks's chest. He was silent for once as he stroked her hair. She thought that maybe Brooks cried, too, but she didn't know. Every kiss, each caress felt like he was worshiping her. The world melted away, sounds and smells drifting far away as they rose above and beyond them together, so deeply engrossed in one another that nothing else existed.

Dawn rose too early. Rhea sat up and looked down at Brooks. He looked impossibly beautiful in the soft early morning light, his curls splayed behind him, and his eyes closed. *When did he fall asleep?* Rhea stood up, staring down at him, and tears stung her eyes once more. She pressed a hand to her chest, trying to stem the pain. It felt as though her heart was tearing in two. Was this love? Is this what Brooks had meant? Why couldn't she just stay here, curled up in his arms? She wanted to lie back down with him, kiss him awake, feel his arms wrap around her. It would be the easiest and most natural thing to do. Rhea shook her head. She knew what she wanted to do, but it simply wasn't the right thing to do. The right thing to do was never the thing she wanted to do. It never had been, and it never would be.

Rhea walked to her horse. She had almost forgotten it the night before, but it was still there. She saddled it, swung up, and slowly rode away. She desperately listened for signs that Brooks was following her but heard nothing.

Rhea wound her way through the woods, not going in any particular direction, only hoping that she wasn't walking in circles.

Eventually, Rhea realized that she was walking along a path. There was certainly a section of the forest that looked worn, as though several pairs of hooves and feet had trampled on it. She sped up, her heart quickening. She would be able to tell the Community about the Outcasts, and they could come and help. They would provide her with Defenders and bring all of the Outcasts into a Community, and she would be reunited with everyone. Except her father.

Rage rose up within her as she thought of the brutal savages who had brought about his death. It was Brooks's fault, but it also wasn't. It was the fault of the loosely defined society that lived beyond Walls and did as they pleased. Brooks didn't want to choose a Community. That was fine—there were probably more Communities than there were Outcasts. They could overpower the Outcasts, bring them into Communities, and teach them how to behave. Perhaps this whole notion of having different Communities all around was ridiculous anyway. Why not one Community with large Wall and everyone in order, working together? But, she wondered, why would they need Walls without the Outcasts? Walls were designed to keep them out . . . but it seemed necessary somehow to have them around Communities. It would be easier to regulate the proper behavior.

Rhea looked up, quite startled. She had wandered to the very edge of the forest and was staring at a Community, the likes of which she had never seen.

The Walls surrounding this Community were not the simple logs that had adorned hers. They were dark metal bars, twisted, huge, and ugly. It looked as though a grotesque plant had erupted from the earth to surround the Community. Rhea couldn't fit through any of the irregularly spaced bars. She had been so desperate to find the next Community, but there was something about that metal Wall that filled her with dread. She couldn't see much beyond the Wall, but through the slats between the bars she saw a sprawling dirty-looking Community with low dwellings.

The dwellings are short to keep people from getting too close to the top of the Wall, Rhea thought. It was a terrifying thought, one that shouldn't have belonged to her. She pulled back on the reins of her horse and it took several steps backwards, neighing softly in protest.

"Enjoying the view?" a voice behind her asked. Rhea turned in the saddle and stared wildly behind her. A young man, hardly older than her, held a crossbow with an arrow pointed directly at her. His clothes were like nothing she had ever seen before, black and soft looking. He smiled easily.

"Oh, honey," he whispered, "you have no idea how lost you are, do you?"

Rhea felt chills race from her ankles up her spine. There was something about this man that reminded her of the one who had been sent to kill her. That cold overconfidence, the condescending yet hungry way that he looked at her, like a wolf eyeing a rabbit.

"I do apologize," Rhea said, trying to sound braver than she felt. "I am lost. I will continue on my way."

The man smiled wider. "You will dismount, or I will kill you."

Rhea shivered. It must have been a miracle that she had survived this long, with so many death threats recently. She slowly slid out of the saddle and landed shakily on her feet. "You're afraid," the man observed. Rhea glared at him; she was hardly in the mood to be toyed with. "You should be," the man went on when she didn't reply. "Once you go beyond that Wall, you will never come out again. Move."

CHAPTER 14
LEADING

Brooks woke up, sat up, and swore loudly. Sunlight covered him in a warm blanket, and Rhea was gone. He cursed himself, wishing he hadn't fallen asleep. He had been lulled into such a state of relaxation by her closeness the night before that sleep had embraced him in a way it usually didn't. He quickly stood and rubbed sleep from his eyes. He squinted around and spotted her tracks, and farther on, her horse's. He hurried after them, fear rising within him.

Someone must have come along and carried her off, he thought despite how preposterous it sounded, even to him. Of course no one had carried her off. She had run. She had run again. Away from him, away from any future they had together.

Brooks swore several times more under his breath as he ran, watching her tracks. After a few minutes, his breath started tearing at his lungs as he panted. Living within a Community had softened and weakened him, but he ran on. Panic seized him the longer he ran, sunlight dancing through the trees, a stream bubbling as he passed it, birds, deer, and who knew what else hurrying away from him as he crashed through the underbrush.

His mind traced the maps of Communities that he had found. He knew where the closest one was. *If she is already there* . . . But he mustn't think that.

Brooks ran on and on, chest heaving, arms pumping, bile in the back of his throat. Finally, he saw the path. He gingerly stepped off of it, slowed down, and mastered his breathing, leaning against a tree.

When he stopped panting, he began to climb. He wormed his way through the branches, stepping lightly from one tree to the next until he could see the clearing ahead.

Communities were all the same. They tore down the trees around themselves to build dwellings and Walls. Rhea was foolish enough to think that this was done as an act to keep others out, rather than to keep people like herself in and void of alternatives. This Community had more sophisticated buildings than Rhea's had. They were low and long, made of stone and mortar instead of wood. And surrounding it, like a massive cage, was a twisted metal Wall. It was bent, ugly, and rusted with sharp spikes adorning the top.

Brooks shook his head, examining the structure for points of weakness. There was a small gate, and the Wall would be easy enough to climb—the metal provided countless handholds and footholds—but Brooks wondered if that was the point of the Wall. *Try to climb in, or climb out, and see what happens.* Yes, getting in could be easy, but getting out would be impossible. It truly wasn't that hard, Brooks reflected, to control other people. A controlled environment and a reasonable amount of fear and consent from others was all that it took. How easy it was to designate a little section of earth as a community, give a select few powers, and convince everyone that all would be lost without them in charge.

Footsteps shattered the peaceful noises of the forest. They were gentle, but Brooks heard them and shrank back into the branches, carefully looking down to see who was coming.

A patrol of three men crossed underneath, bows slung across their shoulders and blades at their hips. Brooks gently eased himself forward until he was lying on his stomach, peering down. They walked carefully, stopping every few feet to listen, glancing around, searching. Brooks assumed that they were searching for anyone wandering too close to the Community, wanting to keep Outcasts away or perhaps find any escapees and bring them back quickly . . . . or dispose of them quietly.

"Let's go," one of them said. "It's almost breakfast time, and Dex caught that one girl today."

"He'll be rewarded for her," the second said. "She's young. Should be useful for something." Brooks stiffened.

"If they can't make use of her, I will," the first added. They all laughed.

"Enough," said the third man, and the first two clamped their mouths shut.

Effortless control, Brooks thought.

"We must finish our shift. It is our duty."

"It is our duty," the other two repeated on command. Brooks snorted softly with laughter. The third man looked up sharply, staring close to where Brooks was, but Brooks was hidden deeply enough in shadow that he was easily missed. The three men moved slowly on. Brooks released his breath, staring hungrily through the branches at the Community. Rhea was there. Who knew what she would be forced to do—what she would willingly do.

Brooks couldn't breach the Community today. He would have to gather more supplies, study the Community, make a plan, and come back to save Rhea once again. Brooks swiftly left the tree, dropping deftly from the lowest branch to his feet.

"Don't move!" someone yelled. Brooks ignored the order and whirled around, his bow and an arrow flying to his hand as he turned. He had the bow cocked and aimed just as the source of the shout came into view—a fourth man. One that he had not seen from the tree. He also had his bow cocked, but his was a crossbow.

"You're slow, Resident," Brooks sneered. "An Outcast would have shot me by now."

"You're worth more to me alive than dead," he answered. Brooks thought they were about the same age. The man was taller than Brooks. He wore fine black clothes and boots the likes of which Brooks had only ever seen on Adder.

"I wish that I could say the same. Where are your little cronies?"

"They only slow me down," the man answered. "Are you alone out here?"

"Like I would tell you," Brooks said, laughing lightly. He had always figured the best way to die would be to die laughing. "Drop the bow."

"You will drop the bow and come with me."

"Nope. You'll have to shoot me. Do you think you're faster than me?"

"A crossbow is faster than a bow."

"Maybe, but can you make my death immediate? Can you pull the trigger and dart out of the way before my arrow finds you?" The man twisted his mouth, and Brooks smiled. "I didn't think so. Wouldn't you rather be home right now, enjoying your breakfast? Eating right out of the hand of the maniac that runs that place?" He jerked his head toward the Community.

"Are you looking for your girlfriend?" the man asked suddenly. Brooks stiffened. "Ah, you are. I don't know how useful she'll be, but we're always looking for new metal workers. If she's no good at that, the population is a little low right now. Could do with some new breeding."

Brooks loosed his arrow and quickly dove to the forest floor to avoid an incoming arrow. His hasty drive had impacted his aim, and his arrow landed in a tree trunk after only grazing the man's leg. The man screamed and loosed his own arrow wildly, missing Brooks by several feet. Brooks knocked back his own arrow and grinned. "My arrow might be slower than yours, but it really makes up for it in the reload, doesn't it?" He leaned closer to the man. "Stay away from my girl and tell her that I will be back for her soon."

The man tried to spit on Brooks, but the Outcast stepped back and retreated, the sound of hurried footsteps filling his ears as the other guards finally burst through the trees yelling.

Brooks sprinted back through the woods, retracting his steps back to where he had met Rhea the night before. There, he found Spark's body and searched it, relieving him of his spare weapons. He then turned back for his people.

Brooks had argued with Raven the day before, directly after they had killed Adder while Brooks grabbed supplies and readied himself to go after Rhea. "You're in charge now," she had said. "You can't just go running off after that idiot."

"She's not an idiot, and you can handle things here."

"Of course I can handle things here," she snapped. "That's not the point. What if you come back and I've decided I can do this without you?"

"Then I wish you luck," Brooks said. "You don't want to share power with me, anyway."

"Damn right I don't, but that's not how things work. The people will be more comfortable with us both, and they'll have to kill us both to get rid of us."

"I'd like to change that rule about killing the existing leaders to get new ones. How about just a vote?"

"A vote? A bit medieval, isn't it?"

"And less bloody."

"Fine, I'll draft some new rules, and you and me can decide on them when you come back. *If* you come back."

"Draft some new rules, and when I come back, the people can all vote on them."

"Not a bad idea . . . should keep the people happy for a bit. Maybe they can even make up some rules themselves."

"Good idea. The whole point is to keep them happy."

"She won't come back with you," Raven said, grinning slightly. "And that's if you manage to head off the hunters sent after her."

"She will," Brooks countered confidently. "She loves me."

"She doesn't know what love is."

"You don't have to know what love is to feel it." He stopped filling his quiver with arrows long enough to look at Raven. "Nothing else matters but Rhea. I won't let them kill her."

Raven let out a long, dramatic sigh. "You're so weak. One of my lovers dumps me, I get a new one."

Brooks grinned, knowing that she was consenting to letting him go. "Don't do anything stupid while I'm gone."

"One of us has to have a brain."

Brooks nodded and ran, ran until he found Rhea's trail, followed it to her campsite, and saved her.

~

Brooks walked through the day and then through the night, not caring that it was cold or that his insides were gnawing at him with hunger. He finally emerged at his own campsite as dawn started sliding through the trees, turning the camp orange and pink. Sounds of greeting met him. He continued to the leader's fire, where Raven was sitting. His people were nocturnal and would not turn in for the night until after the sun had risen. Brooks sank down next to her, and she handed him a bowl full of venison stew from the fire. "Well?" Raven asked.

"She ran to the next Community."

"Which one?"

"The metal one."

Raven snorted. "That's that, then."

"No."

"No?"

"No, it's not."

"You men are so stupid."

"You women are so cold."

"Eh, that might just be me."

"Could be."

"What's the plan, then?"

"Haven't you ever wondered," Brooks said, "why we're always the ones running and hiding, waiting for the next attack, the next raid, when there are more of us than there are of them? Have you ever wondered why Adder was always so terrified to just attack them?"

"He always said he didn't want to risk injuring the women or the children, especially his. That's why he sent in spies when he could."

"He lied."

"Probably."

"He was afraid to attack them, and he only sent in people he thought of as a threat but was too afraid to kill off."

"Like you?"

"Think about it—I was his son. I don't remember this wife of his, or his daughter. He said they were stolen right after I was born and sent me after them as soon as I was old enough. But he never gave me a description of them. He acted like they were the most important thing, but he didn't mind all that much that it took me seven years to undo a lock."

"Yeah, so?"

"So, he wanted to expand his followers, but was too much of a coward to actually storm in. He had no idea what they might have beyond the Walls. He lived to survive, running anytime they came close, sending away anyone that might take over from him eventually. They always assume that sons will take over for their fathers in leadership, even though no one says it."

"What do you want to do, then, oh great leader?" Raven asked sarcastically.

"Oh, I'd like to expand our numbers, too. We can set up a space beyond their Walls, one that they will whisper of in fear and never dare to attack."

"You want to setup a civilization, in one spot, without Walls?" she said in mock admiration, not believing such a thing was even possible.

"Of course. Walls are their way of creating control. We don't need to control our people."

"You would be surprised. How are we going to keep them in line without Walls, or something to fear?"

"Common decency?"

"You must be joking."

"We've always had rules; they're just not complicated. They know how to follow them."

"The only rules we've always had that you and I would keep are to take care of yourself and not hurt anyone else."

"Seems simple enough to me. We'll pick a spot and build a real society. A proper one, with dwellings that they won't have to hide in or move."

"Sounds like a dream."

"Hopefully it will to them, too."

"But they'll be too scared . . . they're used to moving around and living in fear. You'll be changing things on them too radically."

"No, they're craving stability. And they'll be looking for revenge on the raids. Have they been bad since I've been gone?"

"We're still planning on moving around and living in fear, aren't we?"

"But once they have a home, they'll want to defend it, not run away."

"You have a point there. How will they get their revenge?"

"We'll go on the attack in a way Adder never did."

"You're willing to sacrifice our best fighters to get your little girl-friend back?"

"We're not like Adder. They'll have the option to say no, but they won't. They're sick of the Communities—they want to end the raids. Just because the Community I lived in was full of mostly scared and weak Residents doesn't mean they all are. Also, it's in our nature to fight. Adder has kept our best fighters on too tight of a leash."

"All right . . . so when do you want to pitch the idea to them?"

"Soon as I wake up," Brooks said before he stumbled into his new hut, bowl of stew in hand.

⌒

The sun was sinking when Brooks called for his new followers to gather around his fire. They looked nervous, glancing around warily, suspicious of an attack. Lila stood close to Brooks and watched him with something like reverence in her eyes. Raven managed to catch her eye and let out a low growl from deep within her throat until Lila looked away. Brooks stifled a laugh.

"Here's what I'm thinking," he addressed the gathering crowd. "We can't live like this anymore."

"What's wrong with the way we live?" shouted a voice. Brooks squinted into the crowd; it was Thorn. He was a few years older than Brooks, and quite a bit bigger.

"For starters, we're not cowards. But we're acting like it." Grumbles of dissent echoed around the semicircle. "Why should we be the ones running and hiding? There are more of us than there are of them; we're the ones who can think for ourselves. We're stronger, faster, and better fighters. With the right resources, we could develop better weapons. Why do they get to have a place to live, while we trek around like animals?" Brooks paused, making careful eye contact with each member he could see. "Right now, everything is backwards. They're the predator and we're the prey. But I know them. I lived with them, and they fear us. They fear our freedom, our ideas." Brooks grinned at Gael quivering at the corner of the circle, unsure as to whether he belonged. "Isn't that right?" he asked. Gael flushed and dropped his gaze.

"Yes, it is!" Lila spoke up suddenly. "I was born and raised in a Community, and it was like being a servant. They wouldn't let us think or speak for ourselves. As soon as we were old enough, they stuffed us into school to teach us to think the way they wanted us to.

They picked our jobs and who we were to wed. But Brooks"—she cast him a glowing look—"he set us free." Lila looked at all of the faces around her. "This isn't like what I am used to. I don't understand the rules yet . . . I don't know what I am supposed to do or how to act."

"There ain't rules here!" someone shouted, and several people laughed. Lila smiled.

"There, I did what I was told and waited to die. Out here, you don't have to wait for anything. If you want it"—she locked eyes with Brooks—"you work for it . . . and then you get it. Or maybe you don't, but at least you can try. Why not try to have a real place to live? You—no, *we* have nothing to fear from them."

"Hear, hear!" a voice shouted, and a few people applauded.

"Why not?" someone else said. "Nothing wrong with setting up a real camp, one that doesn't move."

"What will stop you from letting us leave? What if you want to turn us into one of them Community prisons?" Thorn yelled.

Brooks laughed. "You think anyone in their right mind would escape a place like that and decide to go back?" he asked, trying not to think of Rhea.

"Seems to work out pretty well for the few pulling the strings behind those Walls," Thorn shot back. Brooks cast a glance at Gael, but he had melted back into the trees.

"That's not how we do things. You got a problem with me, or with Raven, you call a meeting and let everyone vote it out." Brooks looked around. "Anyone want to fight us? Anyone want to raise their hands and vote us out? Maybe vote Thorn in?"

Not a single hand was raised. Brooks reflected on how well Adder had kept everyone in line through his unique brand of fear. Only a few poor souls had ever tried to fight Adder, and no one had ever suggested voting him out. Brooks wondered vaguely if any of his followers had ever considered voting before at all. Where had *he* even learned about voting? Was it a vague memory of how things had worked when Adder first took over? Brooks couldn't remember.

"I support you, boy!" Moss shouted, raising a hand to point at Raven. "But we haven't had a woman in charge befo—" Raven's knife flew through the greasy strands of hair forming a curtain between Moss's ear and shoulder and landed with a *thunk* in a tree behind him before he could even finish his sentence.

"If you want to go toe to toe with me, Moss, step up." Moss didn't move, his mouth hanging slightly open. "It's like Brook said," Raven continued. "We killed Adder together, so we're in charge now. If you don't like it, vote for someone else. We only killed Adder because we had to—he wouldn't have allowed himself to be voted out. That's why he had to die. This isn't a prison; everyone's voice matters the same here. So, step up, or shut up!" No one moved.

"Fine," Raven continued. "If you want to come with us to find a good place for camp with good resources now that we have leaders who won't move us around every time they have a new grudge, go pack your things. We'll move out tomorrow morning. We're not staying up all night like a bunch of racoons anymore. We have nothing to fear from the light." Raven grabbed Brooks's hand and tugged him away from the circle, ending the meeting.

"You're too gentle with them," she muttered as she pulled him into his dwelling, which used to belong to Adder.

"You know, you catch more flies with honey and all that."

"You can catch the most flies with horseshit," Raven grumbled, flopping down in front of his fire. "So, where are we going?"

"Mountains." Brooks sat beside her. "We can butt right up against them, near a river. There should be one that flows from the top, and lots of plants and game nearby. We can fell the trees and build real homes, maybe even a school."

"And a smithy?"

"Well . . . yes, that, too."

"And what then?"

"Start training soldiers to come fight with me."

"Demolishing the Communities?"

"Well, one in particular."

"You're so pathetic. There are other women, you know."

"There's only one like her."

"That's not true. We could knock off any number of Communities tomorrow and you'd find another brain-dead blonde in an instant."

"She's not brain-dead . . . she just doesn't know any better."

"I would know better even if I was born into one of those prisons. You would know better, too."

"Would we? We only know that this kind of life exists because we're in it. When you're born into servitude, do you really know any different?"

"Of course you do! Servitude is a choice."

"It is not."

"There is *always* a choice."

"You mean you would choose death before living in a Community?"

"Of course I would! No one is going to tell me what to do." She glared at him hard. "No one," she repeated as she sat up on her knees and leaned forward, grabbing Brooks by his curls and pulling his face to hers. She kissed forcefully, so different from Rhea. Raven was crude and aggressive; Rhea was delicate, sweet.

Brooks kissed her hungrily, willing it to mean something, anything. They broke apart a moment later and Raven sighed. "I was hoping that we could have an understanding," she said in a very businesslike way. "I know you have no interest in killing me, I have no interest in killing you. Neither of us has any interest in each other . . . not long-term, anyway."

Brooks grinned. "You can't do any better than me, huh?"

"Don't be ridiculous!" Raven snapped. "I am a queen of the forest; I can have whatever and whoever I want. But why waste time pretending that I have any interest in someone? You can't have Rhea now, and I see nothing of interest in our measly followers at the moment. Why not?"

"Because you're not Rhea," Brooks said.

Raven laughed. "Even though I'm better?"

"Yeah."

"Even though it would mean nothing?"

"You're right about that."

Raven gave him a searching look. "You're going to end up broken and useless by the time this thing is done."

"Love does that."

"Love is a fairytale."

"For you," Brooks countered.

"Suppose I'll go look through our latest crop of followers to see if one looks good," Raven sighed, striding out of his dwelling.

~

They set out at first light with Brooks and Raven in the front, their followers trailing behind them like a long line of ducklings. As they walked, Brooks thought hard about what they were leaving behind and what lay before them. Brooks remembered being at camp when he was young. It had moved around constantly, with Adder sending people to infiltrate Communities whenever a violent mood struck him. Brooks had run, happy and wild, with the other children. Every now and then an adult would catch them and force them to learn their numbers or alphabet, steadily increasing their education as they mastered the last task and eventually moving on to stories about their own history, reading, writing, and arithmetic. Arithmetic had been key because trading was so common. You wouldn't understand if you were being conned unless you were smart enough to add, subtract, and know value.

Logic was the most powerful tool Brooks had mastered. The children in Rhea's Community might have spoken sweeter and read better, but logic was the only weapon that Brooks had had against the indoctrination of Rhea's Community. Logic had allowed him to ask "Why?"—a question he decided should be asked whenever someone was demanding something of him, and a question that was actively discouraged within the Community. He would never ask Rhea "Why?" but he would do anything to take care of her and love her with everything he was worth. When the Council made demands of him and the other "Residents," though, he examined their motivations and found that they only really had one: power.

People wanted power, Brooks decided, and once they had it, they didn't want to part with it. They wanted more. At first, Brooks thought it was ridiculous that the Council bothered to dictate who their Residents married, where they lived, what they did, how many children they had, and what and how much they ate, but by the time he left, everything made sense to him. Rhea's Community was founded on the idea that all decisions were too important to be made by common people, so those in charge took over every single one. If they would have left any—even trivial decisions, such as allowing parents to name their own children—the Residents would have wanted more. Instead, they took over each decision and made it the norm, which made people more compliant and willing to give up more of their freedoms. Brooks didn't know for sure, but he assumed that things had started out slowly.

The Council, or whoever was first in charge, likely hadn't had much trouble persuading people to build Walls around themselves to keep out the dangerous "Outcasts" after the war. It would only be too easy to delegate tasks and occupations according to what the Community needed. Their numbers would have been small, and it would have been easy to convince people that they would need to populate their little Community. Food would have been in short supply, and convincing people that some needed more than others would not have been too difficult. After all, wasn't it just so lovely to have a safe place to live?

By the time Brooks had entered the Community, the system of food distribution was efficient, and Brooks was assured that he was being given the correct amount of nutrition according to what his body needed. What did it matter that he always went to sleep with his stomach aching from hunger when a nice nutritionist said he was getting enough? He assumed that once those in charge had accomplished these tasks, the next step would have been to take these starved, scared, and war-torn people and assure them that they didn't need a single worldly possession that was theirs. Having things was not fair, after all, if everyone else didn't have the exact same thing— Council members excluded, of course. They shoved families out of their dwellings, kept the best ones for themselves, and shuffled people around like property according to their family size. Small families or single people didn't "need" as much space, the same way that Brooks didn't "need" as much food as Rhea.

Brooks guessed that the final freedom that those in charge took away was the ability to choose a partner. He supposed it could have come about in many different ways, but the theory he liked best was that one of the early Council members had wanted someone who scorned him, like Gael and Rhea. He couldn't handle the humiliation of being rejected and devised the "tests" to bring her to him, thus forcing Residents to fall in line in every way possible. Freedom, once given away, was never given back. In fact, people became comfortable with parting with the things and the people they once loved with enough repetition. Brooks could only guess what the Council would have taken from their Residents next.

Life beyond the Walls had been wildly different for Brooks. Growing up, Brooks had known that Adder was his father, along with plenty of other children, but it hadn't mattered. Brooks wasn't considered above any of his fellow children. Children measured leadership abilities by who could run the fastest, spit the farthest, and bring down the biggest game with a bow.

Adder had stepped into the role of leader in the aftermath of a horrific raid from some long-forgotten Community that killed many members of the camp. Even more had been dragged off beyond Walls for no one knew what purpose. Adder had started with speeches of sweet revenge, and they had flocked to him, desperate for security.

He had declared that his wife and daughter had been carried away in the raid and spent countless hours scheming, plotting against the Communities. Brooks didn't remember if Adder had truly had a wife, and he also knew Adder had plenty of other women and children within the camp. Adder had dragged their camp to the first Community he could find and attacked. It has been a massacre, with their already dwindling numbers taking more heavy losses. The Communities had thick Walls, were in the middle of clearings, and had weapons that the Outcasts simply didn't. Adder quickly changed tactics, sending in spies to infiltrate. It worked a few times, with the Communities accepting these Outcasts who came on their knees and crying about seeking a better life. But a few times the spies never returned, and when Adder sent men to carefully check to see what had become of them, they reported back that the spy's bodies could be seen on display at the top of the Walls.

That was when Adder had created a new plan: send in children. He had assumed, rightly so, that children could more easily infiltrate the camps, start a large fire to begin chaos and fear as well as signal that the gates were about to open, and ensure that the gates were open for an attack. Brooks's childhood had changed dramatically then. He and the other children in the camp had been forced to study the limited information they had on their Communities, as well as his basic reading, writing, and arithmetic to ready him for education within a Community. He needed to appear smart enough to be seen as useful, but not so smart that they would gain greater fear from the Outcasts.

Brooks had watched as one by one, many of his friends went beyond the Walls. Some of them never came back, but many of them executed their missions and were rewarded once they returned. Brooks had watched them be applauded, lifted onto shoulders, and given choice cuts of meat that they hadn't had to hunt and raspberry wine they hadn't had to ferment. Adder had kept the cause alive in this way, celebrating the victories and always entering the Community himself once the fighting was over.

Morale had been high when Brooks had left, but it didn't seem so when he returned seven years later. Seven years in a seemingly endless war had put a strain on them. The children were dirtier and the adults, more haggard, their cheeks hollow and their bellies flat. While Outcasts took responsibility for their own food and health, Adder's reign had prioritized revenge over well-being. Outcasts were expected to train and be ready to fight at any moment, had to move constantly—regardless of game trails—and were unable to plant. They were both hungry and angry, pleased to see Adder dead, but Brooks and Raven's reign could end any day if they pushed everyone too hard. They needed to make swift time to a prime place to live where everyone could feel safe, or else they risked being voted out.

Brooks thought of the commonsense rules that he needed to implement. He remembered murder and thievery had always been against the rules in Outcast camps, but that self-defense was encouraged. He knew that his people enjoyed being able to take care of themselves and their families, choosing what and when to eat or building their own shelter. Anyone could ask anyone for help if they needed it. No one had to make demands or take from his people for them to be kind, they simply were. Brooks reflected on the importance of enhancing his Outcast's lives, not using them to enhance his. *Being in charge should mean making sacrifices, not demands.* If they could find a safe and fruitful place to live, they could start farming, breeding animals to eat instead of hunting them, and giving the children a real education.

If they could find a proper place to live.

Each day the morning dawned a little later and a little colder with a fine mist frosting the trees. Slow autumn drizzles lazily drifted down from fat grey clouds and kept their clothes and moods damp. Brooks started longing wistfully for a dwelling, wanting a reprieve from the rain. He pushed his people a little less, taking more breaks and demanding the best hunters and gatherers work harder and harder to feed the protesting mouths. Lila tried to stick close to him, especially when

Raven was busy. Brooks treated her with polite indifference, hoping that she would get the hint. She didn't.

On the fifth day, Brooks stopped. Raven stopped beside him. "What?" she snapped.

"Here."

"Here what?"

"We're here."

Raven looked around. They had reached the base of the mountain. The earth around them gently sloped upward until it sharply met a wall of rock that would prevent attacks on one side. The trees were dense, several branches meeting together to block out the sunlight. A river ran down from the mountain and created a waterfall that cascaded into a pool among the trees. Brooks peered behind the waterfall to find a deep cave that wormed its way into plunging darkness. The water from the mountain was freezing, but children splashed happily into the pool and squealed with joy. Brooks smiled. This was a place that they could turn into a home. A real home, one that didn't come under attack each day. Brooks smiled at Raven, who grinned back.

"I guess this is home," Raven assented. She flopped onto the bank of the pool and pulled off her boots to dangle her feet in the water.

Brooks looked around at his people, waiting for his next order. "This is home!" he declared. Many cheered and eagerly started unpacking their meager belongings, building fires, and gathering water. Brooks turned to find himself face-to-face with Lila.

"We're going to stay here?" she asked.

"Yeah," he said. "Seems like a good place."

"You're a very good leader," she said, casting Gael a dirty look. He stood at the edge of camp, looking as though he was waiting for someone to tell him what to do. "He would have been a disaster."

"How do you know that? The tests did choose him."

Lila rolled her eyes at him. "Come on, Brooks. You're not an idiot. You know our Community was rigged."

"Remind me what was going to happen to you?"

"The same thing that happened to all the women. I was going to wed an idiot I didn't pick, work a useless job to keep life comfortable for the council, and pop out drooling offspring when I was told."

"Some would say that was your duty to your people."

Lila shook her head. "I deserve more. These are my people now." She gestured around her. "You're all much smarter."

"I don't know about that. You had a system in place that worked for you." Brooks said sarcastically.

"It worked for the oligarchs in charge."

Brooks laughed. "That's not a word they taught you in the Community."

"No," Lila agreed, "I learned that here. I always knew what it was, but they wouldn't let us name it." She turned away abruptly and stalked her way to the waterfall.

Several hours later, Brooks and Raven knelt at the edge of the cave, torches raised high, trying to pierce through the gloom.

"This is stupid," Raven declared. "Why can't we just go in?"

"Because that would be a very stupid thing to do," Brooks said. "Anything could be in there."

"Like what?"

"Someone capable of having a rational conversation?"

"Hysterical. I want to go."

"You can't always do whatever you want, Raven."

"Maybe *you* can't."

Brooks rolled his eyes. Keeping Raven alive wasn't easy, but he needed her. If everything went according to plan, he would soon be waging war on an impenetrable Community, and she would be left in charge. Brooks was abrupt, rash, and quick to laugh, but Raven was far worse. She was rapidly turning into an annoying sibling that he had never asked for.

"We can search the caves in the morning," Brooks decided, standing up. "We should rest. It's been a long march." He ducked around the waterfall and stiffened.

"What?" Raven asked, joining him.

"Shhh . . ." Brooks hissed, listening hard. There it was again—the softest footfall. No one could move through the trees silently, regardless of their skill. A rustle slithered through the underbrush. A soft bed of leaves crunched ever so slightly. A boot scraped over a rock.

Raven slowly drew her knife from her belt, careful not to make a noise. Brooks glanced at it, realizing what a poor weapon it was, what poor weapons they all had. He dropped his torch into the pool before drawing his own knife in his left hand and his axe in his right. He nodded at Raven, and they quickly set off in opposite directions, nudging their people awake with a boot, shaking them, and clamping a quick hand over their mouths to muffle a gasp or a scream. "We're under attack," they each whispered.

The fires had burned down to smoldering coals and the moon and stars were dark. A warm glow from the dying fires scarcely illuminated their little camp. Brooks's people quickly threw dancing shadows around as they started scrambling to their feet, reaching for their weapons, hurrying in crouched positions to put their backs against the wall of rock. *Our weapons might not be much, but at least we have something,* Brooks thought, remembering the rules against weapons within Communities.

Movement at the edge of the camp caught his eye—Lila was being quietly dragged away. She squirmed and tugged at the large hand clamped over her mouth, but he was much bigger than her.

"WE'RE UNDER ATTACK!" Brooks screamed, causing several people to jump and the attack to finally erupt from the trees. They were clothed in nearly flawless camouflage, and they had crept closer than Brooks had realized. One sprang to life from the tree trunk directly in front of him, bringing a long dark blade up to meet Brooks's throat. Brooks blocked the blade and brought his axe down, but his counterattack was deflected easily. Brooks stamped a foot into the man's knee and heard him yell in pain, then hastily brought his knife up under the man's chin, feeling it meet flesh. The man screamed louder than ever and fell. The man dragging Lila had melted into the darkness, Brooks hurrying after him.

Lila finally freed her mouth and screamed for all that she was worth, scratching and biting her attacker frantically. Brooks crashed through the brush loudly behind them as he sprinted after.

"Don't move!" the man shouted, whirling around and pressing a black blade to Lila's neck. "I'll kill her like it was nothing."

Brooks froze, his eyes searching Lila's. He saw trust that he didn't deserve and knew what to do. Gingerly adjusting the axe in his hand, he hurled it with all his might.

He missed. But as the man whirled away from the axe, Lila squirmed out of his arms. She ran past Brooks, heading straight back for camp, while Brooks charged at the man, knife in hand, and a wordless scream escaped him. He bowled over the man, kneeing him, throwing an elbow in his face, and punching every inch that he could reach. He had forgotten to use his knife; he had forgotten who he was, who the man might be, what they were doing. Blind rage filled him as he realized these men had come to hurt his people. With Rhea locked away in a prison, they were all he had.

The man went limp under him. Brooks collapsed next to him, shaking. What was the point of all of this? Why couldn't they have one night in their new home in peace? He quickly wiped his face, blood mixing with the sweat. He was a leader. He couldn't let his people see him like this—they would be looking to him for guidance now. Steeling himself, he grasped the limp man under the arms and dragged him back into camp.

It wasn't as bad as it might have been.

But it was bad.

Seven of the attackers lay dead, three killed by Raven, one by Brooks, and the other three by two of the hunters who Brooks had rechristened Guardians and vetted to ensure there wasn't a Spark among them. Four of their own young women and six children had been carried off. Brooks shook with anger, examining the bodies.

Their camouflage was eerie; it had allowed them to blend in perfectly with the shadows and textures of the forest. Most of them had carried several dark weapons, from short swords to tiny push daggers, which wouldn't shine in the moonlight.

"They're assassins," Raven declared.

"No," Brooks said. "They're kidnappers."

"Why?" Raven asked. "Why would they want us?"

Brooks turned over the kidnapper he had beaten and saw he was still alive. "We'll find out soon."

Brooks and Raven wound their way from one revived fire to another. They grasped shaking hands, handed out weapons to the few that didn't have any, bandaged small wounds, and promised revenge. None of their people were seriously hurt or dead, but their newfound feeling of safety was shattered.

Brooks watched Raven, a surprisingly tender expression adorning her face, wiping away the angry tears of one boy. "They took Mom," he cried, his small hands curling into fists.

"I know," Raven said. "We'll get her back."

"You don't know that!" the boy yelled suddenly. "We never get anyone back!"

"Enough!" Raven snapped. "You want to cry or are you going to step up?" The boy pressed his lips together. "That's better. You have brothers and sisters who need you now. You don't get to fall apart. I've told you that we'll get your mother back—have I ever lied to you?" The boy shook his head, his lips still pressed tightly together and unshed tears in his eyes. "Then believe me, we'll get her back. That's my job. Your job is to take care of your family. Now go do it." The boy turned away and walked steadily back to his little cluster of siblings. Raven watched him go proudly. *Children grow up too fast*, Brooks reflected, *inside of the Communities and now outside of them, too*.

Brooks finally reached Lila. She sat alone on a fallen log, staring at the fire with blank brown eyes. A long red cut on her throat slowly dripped blood onto the dirty collar of her shirt.

"Lila?" Brooks said, sitting next to her. She jumped and looked up, a smile brightening her face.

"Brooks," she answered. "Thank you for saving me again."

"Again? When did I save you?"

"When you burned down the prison I was born in and again tonight."

"I didn't do that to save anyone."

"Of course you did," Lila insisted. Brooks didn't answer but gently pressed a clean cloth to Lila's wound. She watched him for a long moment while he avoided her gaze. "Brooks, the best thing that ever happened to me was when you came over the Wall. I've been patient, I've waited for you . . . I assumed that once the tests came back, we would be matched. But it didn't happen. Then you burned everything down, and you made it possible again."

"Lila, don't," Brooks warned. He had taken everything that he could tonight. The adrenaline that had coursed so strongly through him during the attack was fading quickly, leaving behind anger, exhaustion, and a sadness he had scarcely ever known. He was seventeen, as far as he was aware, yet everyone he knew was counting on him. The girl he loved was imprisoned, he had no idea what he was doing, and he was trying to create a free society, never having seen what one actually looked like.

Lila put her hand on his. "You broke me out, and you made everything that I had never been allowed to dream of possible."

"I'm in love with Rhea."

"Then where is she?" Lila demanded, throwing her arms wide. "If you two are so in love, why isn't she here with you?"

"She's in trouble. Another Community took her."

"No, Brooks, Rhea ran away. She doesn't know how to think for herself. You two can't be together, because she can't survive out here!"

"You don't know her!"

"No, *you* don't know her." Lila shook her head. "I really thought . . . I've waited my entire life for something good to happen to me. I always figured, growing up, that I would get to be the exception, that I would be able to wed someone that I loved."

"Yeah, so did I," Brooks snapped, unable to help himself.

Lila looked down. "You aren't in love. You're obsessed, and obsessions eat you alive. They slowly take over each part of your life until you have nothing, and no one, left." She stood up and strode deeper into the camp.

⁓

The icy water hit the kidnapper directly in the face, and he woke with a spluttering gasp. "Wha—" he started, staring around him. It was very dark, but a bright ray of sunlight shone on him in a hot sliver that burned his eyes. He couldn't tell where he was, but he was on a stone floor, his hands and feet bound with strips of fabric. He struggled into a sitting position, his head spinning.

"I have questions," a man's voice said. The sliver of light was blocked as the man stood and towered over him, his face shrouded in darkness.

"What . . . what do you want from me?"

"Very, very little. Who are you?"

"I . . . I'm Noah," the kidnapper said, cringing. His head hurt so badly. Everything hurt so badly.

"No, who are you? Who are your people?"

"I . . . I'm not telling you anything!" Noah said, trying to sound braver than he felt. A weight suddenly dropped on him from above and he jumped. Someone had landed on him and thrust a knife under his throat—he felt a small trickle of blood sliding down his throat into his shirt. He yelled in fear and shock, trying to shake off this new terror.

A girl with dark hair sat astride him. He could just make out her face in the gloom. "This is Raven," the man said. "She will cut you once every time she thinks you are lying, or you refuse to tell us what we want to know. Her cuts will get gradually more . . . *serious* the longer this takes."

"I . . . I come from Community 98." Noah was shaking, terrified, not daring to meet Raven's eyes.

"You are well trained to sneak around."

"We do not sneak!" Noah protested, unable to help himself.

"What would you call it?"

"There are Outcasts—they're savage, sick and violent. We save who we can! We give people a purpose!"

"Why do you target women and children?"

"We need women and children. We have too few to maintain our needed population."

"Our women are savage, but good enough to turn into breeding factories to meet your population requirements?" Raven hissed. "I wonder, have you ever had too *high* of a population before?"

"N–n . . . yes," Noah stammered.

"Ah, what did you do then?"

"Not . . . not every person is needed. They do not need to stay behind the Walls."

"You cast them out? When you don't need someone, you send them out into the wild, without any means to care for themselves?" Brooks asked.

"They . . . if they aren't what we need . . . aren't benefitting the Community . . . if they refuse their education, or they break the rules—"

Raven screamed, her scream echoing through the caves and re-sounding back upon her until many Ravens seemed to be screaming at once.

"Don't, Raven!" Brooks snapped.

"You hear him? The way they see people as worthless, the way they use them! Just enough people behind the Wall to rule over, to keep under their heel, but not enough for a rebellion! How can you stand it?" she raged, turning to face Brooks.

"If he's dead," Brooks said evenly, "how will he lead us to his Community?"

CHAPTER 15
COMMUNITY ONE

R hea gasped in a great lungful of air, her head emerging from the hot water. She was shaking hard, her wet hair plastered to her head.

Everything was over. Everything and everyone she loved was far beyond her reach; she would never have a purpose to follow again. She was utterly and completely alone, trapped in a prison that she had walked willingly into. A hard brush scrapped against her skin, sloughing off layers of dirt, sweat, and skin. Rhea had tried to cover herself, had attempted to refuse, but it didn't matter. It was as though she wasn't human here. She was a tool, a cog, something to be used and discarded. And it was only her first day.

⌒

Upon entering the Community, she had observed that the buildings, the people, *everything* was immaculate. Streets wound their way like great veins between the large dwellings, most of which were made of stone. The people all moved quickly, working hard and sweating as they cleaned the streets, cared for the animals, or made large blades of metal. There were watchtowers that lined the Walls and Defenders everywhere, like giant insects swarming over the people. They carried weapons and whips, wheeling them freely over bent backs. Even children didn't seem to play but only worked and cleaned alongside the adults. The Community slopped upward to the largest dwelling, a beautiful and terrible stone thing with an extra Wall around it.

Rhea had scarcely had time to take in the horror around her, to see the crooked backs of Residents resigned to their fate, the dull hopelessness in their eyes, when the Defender marching her along pushed her into a bathhouse. He had kept up a constant stream of threats their entire way, explaining that she was nothing in his eyes and the horrors she was about to face. When they entered the bathhouse, Rhea shrank back, but he pushed her forward. She had never had to use a bathhouse before; being the daughter of a Leader had had its privileges. *But there is nothing wrong with that, of course. It is necessary that leaders and their families have privileges*, she reminded herself. The house was hot and damp, with several tubs staged all the way down the house.

"What's this?" a thin woman asked as they entered. She was the only one in the bathhouse.

"New one," the Defender grunted.

"I got her," she said.

The Defender snorted. "You do not."

"Eh? Didn't I say I did?"

"I'm not to let her out of my sight until she's been looked over by the Master."

"Eh? Who told you that?"

"Those are the rules."

"No they ain't. You ain't allowed in here. Get out!" The Defender slowly uncoiled his whip from around his belt.

"You're going to fight me on this? Like your life means anything?"

"You go ahead. Beat an old woman for following the rules, see how the Master likes that."

"She doesn't need to know."

"You sure she won't find out? You sure she won't find out you hangin' around my bathhouse when I told you to get out?"

The Defender and the woman stared at each other for a long moment, then he turned on his heel and marched to the door. "I'm right out here," he said sharply before slamming it behind him.

"Thank you," Rhea said, relief coursing through her. *A friend, and an ally.* She didn't think the same a moment later when the old lady slapped her.

"We ain't friends. You think I'm sticking up for you? You know what would happen if I started letting them Defender s in here? Someone would snitch on me for breaking the rules, and my back would be striped! Easier to face one of 'em than all of 'em." Rhea could hardly understand what the old woman was saying, she was so shaken. The old woman's face was hard and lined, deeply tanned, her hands red and chapped from hours of washing. Rhea just stood there with her hand over her cheek, tears stinging her eyes and blurring her vision. It was all too much. She couldn't do this anymore. There was an entirely new set of rules here and she would never learn, never keep up. She would end up whipped and dead.

"Shut up," the woman warned her. Rhea bit her lip. "Get in here," she commanded, gesturing toward a large tub.

"Will . . . will you leave?" Rhea asked.

The woman laughed. "Privacy is a privilege you don't get in many places these days. Get in the tub."

Despite the scalding water, Rhea shook violently. The old woman washed her hair and scraped her hard with the brush until her skin was an angry pink.

"Guess you been bad," the woman said, touching her brand. Rhea flinched away. "Guess you know what it's like in these places."

"Wha . . . what do you mean?" Rhea asked.

"These prisons."

"You mean . . . you mean Communities?"

"Oh, you're one of *those*."

"One of what?"

"One of those what needs other people to tell them what to do."

"No . . . I'm not."

"Where were you before they caught you?"

"I was in a Community. Outcasts attacked and burned it to the ground."

"Why didn't you go with them?"

"What?"

"With the Outcasts. Our Defender s wouldn't have got you if you were with 'em scary Outcasts."

"I . . . they attacked us."

"No, girl. They freed you."

"They . . ." Rhea put her head in her hands. "What's going to happen to me here?"

The old lady shrugged. "Nothin' too bad . . . probably. Our population is right at that sweet spot where there are enough of us to boss around, but not too many for a revolution. I'd reckon you'd make a pretty good Defender , you buyin' into what they're shovelin' and all that, but you got that brand, so they won't trust you. I guess blade-smithin' could use an extra pair of bands, as could the farmers and the cleaners. You better make sure you're good at whatever they tell you to be good at. Learnin' comes hard here."

"They . . . they'll assign me to whatever job they want me to do?"

"'Course. What else would they do with you? Let you pick?" The old lady laughed.

"No," Rhea replied, stung. "In my Community we take tests to determine our aptitudes."

The old lady laughed harder than ever. "That's the best bit I heard all year!" she declared.

"It's not a joke!" Rhea snapped.

"How do you know them tests did anything?"

"Why would they give them to us if they didn't do anything?"

"To keep you stupid, sounds like to me. Sure worked, too."

"I'm not stupid!"

"You got a man back at your Community?"

"I . . . I was assigned to one, yes. But the Outcasts came before we were able to wed."

"Uh-huh. You love this man?" There it was again—that word that Brooks had used. Rhea twisted her mouth, unsure how to respond.

"Poor baby," the old lady chuckled. "They never let you learn what love is, did they?"

Rhea didn't answer. "How long have you been here?" she asked instead.

"Years, girl. There's no gettin' out of here. Wish them Outcasts would come rescue me."

"Were you born here?"

"You see how old I am? You think I was born after all of this was made?"

"Communities weren't made; they've existed for centuries," Rhea said automatically.

"I remember when this was all one place," the old woman said dreamily, her eyes glazing over. "I was real young, but I remember. Then we had that war. Some people wanted to turn everything into . . . like one big Community, with everyone under control. Telling everyone what to do, where to live, and how many kids to have, I think, is how it started. They were saying they'd cracked the code to happiness itself and that if we didn't go along, we'd be destroying the world. They said it would end in a few years if we didn't do exactly what they said.

"They decided next that we had too many people. They started discouraging people from bein' married, discouraging people from havin' kids, started talkin' like kids were a great burden. Half the people loved it; bein' told what to do would be easier than tryin' to figure out what to do themselves. There was finally a right answer for every question: Who am I? What should I do? But half the people didn't like it so much. They wanted to choose these things. You can't have it both ways. You can't have half a people sayin' they'll follow the rules and half sayin' they won't, and so those in charge got worried the ones who didn't want to follow would start convincing the ones that did that freedom was the answer instead of order. So, everyone started killing each other over it.

"After that, everyone was scattered around, didn't know what to do. No one in charge, since we'd taken out all the leaders on both sides. There were so few of us left, they got their smaller population wish, all right. In times like that, power goes to the first person who steps up and takes it. Trouble was, more than one person stepped up. Turns out lots of people want power. It was easy, too easy, to convince the followers to go behind some Walls, lock everyone else out, and start following some new rules. After a generation, it was all anyone knew. These 'Outcasts,' as you call them, are just the people who decided they didn't wanna be locked up. I didn't wanna be locked up, but my ma did. She brought me here, Community One. Died not long after trying to get free. But once you give your freedom away to someone else, they won't never give it back to you."

Rhea sat stunned and defeated in the cooling water. What this woman was saying didn't make sense. Communities were the natural state of being. They existed because they were the correct way to live—to ensure each person was properly taken care of, that the population was consistent, that partners and occupations were rightly matched. Someone had to be in charge of it! People were inherently selfish. If they were left alone to decide for themselves, they would only focus on what they wanted, on their own needs, and ignore the needs of the Community. What if they chose an occupation that they performed poorly at? Or chose to not have children? Or selected a partner who was not an ideal fit? Would they simply leave their occupation? Grow old without having a child? Choose a different partner? Rhea shook her head, once again wishing that she could dislodge the doubt that crept in like the darkness that followed the sunset into the corners of her mind, making her question everything she had been taught.

"Did you wed?" she asked the old woman.

"I did, eventually. They didn't care about me too much until the population dropped too low. Then they informed me that I would be given a man. I was living with the other single women, and him with the men. They can't have us procreating without their permission, see? They keep us apart and guarded. We all know each other—we all been here forever—but this man was still practically a stranger to me. But they stuck us in a dwelling together all the same."

"And you procreated?"

"No."

"What do you mean no?"

"Couldn't. After a while, they assumed somethin' was wrong with one of us, so they decided to move him into a different house with a new woman. They had no problem meetin' the requirements—I think it was two children at the time. Right as I was startin' to like being wed, started to think this could be love, they took him away from me. He died years ago, but his woman and children are still around."

Rhea wondered what it would be like, being wed to Brooks before seeing him taken away from her and presented to someone else. She shuddered. She wanted to say something, but there was nothing to say. It would be wrong to express sympathy toward this woman, as her story reflected consistence to what was best for the Community.

"You're clean enough," the woman said. Rhea stood and dried herself, then dressed in the light-grey pants, shirt, and soft shoes that the woman presented her. She dried her hair with her towel and combed the curls with her fingers, dragging it over her right shoulder to hide the disobedient brand. The old woman watched her fussing, a small smile playing around her mouth.

"Thank you," Rhea said, "for . . . for sharing your wisdom." She thought that sounded very polite, even though she didn't fully believe what the woman had said. The woman did not respond. "I am Rhea. Will you please tell me your name?"

"Resident Number Twenty-Seven."

⁓

Rhea opened the door to the bathhouse and almost walked into her Defender as he was hurrying toward the door. There was a white bandage wrapped around one of his legs. "There you are," he snarled. "What took so long?" Rhea did not bother to respond, knowing that whatever she said would further anger him. She had the daunting suspicion that she would be keeping her mouth shut more and more, relying on silence rather than polite words to save herself. She dropped her eyes to the ground and attempted to look ashamed.

"Come on," he said, grabbing her arm and marching her back into the street. She walked meekly beside him, fussing with her hair to stop the wind from blowing it aside and revealing her shame. As they walked, Rhea took in the countless buildings and Residents bustling around, all in different-colored uniforms. "Why does everyone wear different colors?" Rhea asked quietly.

"They wear colors based on their occupation. The darker the color, the more prestigious the position." The Defender adjusted his own black uniform proudly. "Those of us privileged enough to work directly with the Master wear black. She wears white, and no one else."

"What is your . . . your Resident number?" Rhea asked him.

The Defender laughed. "I don't have a number; I have a name. I'm a member of the Master's guard, which makes me a person, worthy of a name."

"Oh," she whispered.

"My name is Dex, and you might as well learn it. I wonder if they'll put us together." The Defender cast a sideways glance at her. "I don't have a woman yet. They're sure to give me one soon."

Rhea suppressed another shudder with difficulty. She supposed that this Defender might not have even been the worst candidate that she might face in the near future. He seemed rather simple to understand; he had an unhealthy view of himself and wanted power over other people. Rhea didn't desire to be a person that he could control, and goodness knows she was easy enough to control. She suddenly longed for Gael. She had stood up to him and defended herself against him, and she was certain that she could have learned to handle him. She was supposed to wed Gael. That's what the tests had said.

"Where are we going?" Rhea asked.

"The Master likes to take a look at the people we capture, see if they're quality or not and decide what to do with them. Sometimes she likes to take her time, sometimes she decides right away."

Rhea looked up at the large dwelling again. It looked more menacing with every step they took. The top of it was full of pointed spikes, seeming to brandish them at the sky, threatening to slice it open.

The dwellings became larger and nicer the closer to the Master's dwelling they got. The clothing became darker as well, and the population of children appeared to increase. *Perhaps the most elite in the Community are allowed to have more children?* Rhea shrugged off this thought; it was ridiculous. There were not "more elite" people in a true Community—everyone was equal. Although, as she took in the increasing beauty of the Community, Rhea had to wonder what it would be like to live in such a beautiful dwelling. What would it be like to pick out her own dwelling, live there with Brooks, and create as many children as they wanted? She could choose her own occupation, maybe even change it if she wanted to.

The Defender yanked Rhea to a halt, and she looked up at a large gate. There was another metal Wall around the largest of the dwellings with two Defenders on either side. The gate was pulled open from the inside and Rhea and Dex marched through it. The Master's dwelling looked even larger the closer that Rhea got. She had never seen so many floors in a dwelling before, and it was made of beautiful stone instead of the wood she was used to seeing. If her Community had been made of stone, Brooks would never have been able to burn it to the ground.

Dex and Rhea crossed a courtyard filled with more Defenders talking and laughing in small groups. They finally reached an enormous wooden door and Dex pushed it open. Rhea gasped as Dex sniggered. The inside of the dwelling was absolutely beautiful. The floor and walls were dark stone, there were large windows letting in weak sunlight, and warm fires burned in large fireplaces. Dex dragged

Rhea down a hallway, trying to hurry her along now. Rhea couldn't take it all in; there was too much beauty. There were clear and colorful panes in the windows, large contraptions with candles burning in them hanging from the ceiling, and something that made Rhea stop in her tracks. Dex pulled on her arm, but she didn't budge. Her eyes had locked on to something that she had never even imagined. She was gazing, transfixed, at an image of a woman. It was like a drawing but filled with colors. Her hair was long and dark, matching her eyes. She looked cold and angry. Dex sidled up next to Rhea.

"Haven't you seen a painting before?"

"Is that what it's called?" Rhea stretched out a hand to touch it. She gently traced a finger over it, feeling the texture change on different parts of the *painting.* "What is the purpose of it?"

"I don't think it has one. It just sits there."

"Why would someone make it if it didn't have a purpose?"

"I think the Master wanted it."

Rhea shivered, looking into the dark eyes. "Everything that happened in my Community was done for a specific purpose. There wasn't time for idle tasks like this," Rhea said, condescension threading her voice.

"Maybe you just didn't have anyone who was talented enough to make this," Dex sneered.

"Talented?"

"It means naturally good at something."

"You mean 'proficient.'"

"You're pathetic." Dex laughed. "You really believe anything anyone tells you, don't you?" He grabbed her hair and pulled it away from her brand to examine it more closely. Rhea tried to pull back, but his fingers wound their way tightly into her hair, and he shoved her hard against the wall. "What did you do to earn that?" Rhea tried not answering again, her eyes cast down, but Dex shook her hard. "Answer me!" he snapped.

"I . . . I broke the rules," Rhea said quietly.

"Which rule?"

Rhea had to think about that one for a minute. "I . . . I don't think it was a specific rule. It wasn't something that was written. I . . . I stopped them from casting out someone."

"Oh? What happened to him?"

"He . . . he ended up choosing to be an Outcast anyway."

Dex suddenly stepped back from Rhea. "What does he look like?"

"He . . . he has curly brown hair and blue eyes."

Dex gave Rhea a hard, angry look. "Come on," he said, grabbing her arm once more. "We've kept the Master waiting long enough."

Dex marched her to a large door and knocked. "Enter," someone said from within. They entered. Rhea faltered looking at the Master— the woman from the painting. She was sitting at a large desk with papers scattered around it. Behind her, the walls were lined with books, more than Rhea had ever seen before. The desk was beautiful, wooden, carved, and stained dark. A fire crackled in a grate despite the heat of the day. Sunshine poured through the windows and bathed the woman in watery golden light.

The Master herself fixed Rhea with the most intense gaze she'd ever witnessed. The woman was old, even older than Resident Twenty-Seven, but she didn't look as old. She looked strong and well taken care of. Her dark eyes pinned Rhea in place. "A new one?" she asked Dex.

"Yes, Master," he said, suddenly polite in her presence.

"Where are you from?" she asked Rhea.

"Community 215." Rhea clenched her fists to stop them from shaking.

"What's that on your neck?"

Rhea had forgotten to curtain her hair back over her brand. "It . . . it's a brand," she whispered.

"I see. You broke the rules?"

"Y . . . yes."

"I see."

"I . . . I will not break the rules here."

"No," the Master said, "you will not." She stood and took a few quick strides to stand in front of Rhea. She was tall and moved with effortless grace. "Dex, get out." Dex turned and stalked out of the room, looking slightly annoyed. "Do you understand the history of the Communities?"

"The . . . the history?"

"After the war," the Master said, walking to the bookshelves and taking down a thick volume. "My husband had an idea. Do you know what a husband is?"

"No."

"He was the man that I married."

"Married?" Rhea asked, uncertain.

The Master rolled her eyes. "Wed. He was the man that I wed."

"Oh."

"Even I can forget the words that I chose for you people to use. As I was saying, Adder, my husband, believed that the correct way to live was to allow people to have choices. They could choose whatever they wanted to do, when they wanted to do it, and they would simply have to live with the consequences of their actions. I saw a different world after the war. I created this," she said, holding her arms out wide. "I created a large Community. It was once much larger, but I found that the population was too large to control correctly, and Adder came looking for me. He burned my Community to the ground, but I escaped and started again.

"I chose a select few to lead my Community and gave them a set of rules and instructions. Then I left to start new Communities. I had learned that too many people in one place was problematic. People have dangerous minds. Large populations eventually discovered that there were more of them than there were of me, even though I surrounded myself with Defenders. We were outnumbered." The Master tilted her head, studying Rhea. Rhea could feel the expression on her face, a frozen mask of terror.

"Oh, child. You believed, didn't you?" She laughed. "There are few things that exist that were not made by man. There were once great thinkers of this world who contemplated deep concepts, such as our purpose in life, freedom, and death. But these people died out long ago. There is not a benefit today to deep thinking. There is not a benefit to competition, or to invention. It is not how I run my world."

"Why are you telling me this?" Rhea whispered.

"You are afraid," the Master said. "Fear is worthless. I can see you; I can see that you are moronic, a true follower. You do as you are told." She raised her eyebrows. "Do you agree?"

"Yes . . . Master."

She laughed again. "I have learned so much about the true nature of people as I have created Communities and Adder kept burning them. I found the perfect population size needed to keep utter control. I made up everything that they and their children would need to learn in order to serve me correctly. I even convinced people that there was no need for weapons within Communities! Why would they need them when I protect them? There are no enemies within our Walls; only the Outcasts are to be feared. I, of course, made that up, too. People need something to unite against, and the Outcasts were perfect candidates. I convinced people that I knew what they should do, who they should . . . what did I call it? *Wed.* How many children they really wanted. There are, of course, a few with dissenting opinions. It doesn't matter; they are isolated from the masses, social outcasts. I often step in and stop my people from hurting them. I show mercy."

Rhea was trembling, tears rolling silently down her face. *Brooks was right. Brooks was right about everything.* Brooks had burned down her Community, which hadn't truly been where she was meant to be. She might have believed that it was a beautiful, loving, support-ive Community, but it all had been invented, made up by this woman who had decided that she was going to be in charge of everyone. Population control wasn't about ensuring everyone was taken care of. Weapon bans weren't because leaders were concerned about people hurting each other—they simply wanted to take care of themselves. Was her test real? Was Brooks right about that as well? Rhea thought about how she had felt while they were together, how the world had melted away and only the two of them existed. Could any test manifest or define something so pure, so natural?

"You evidently know the rules well," the woman before her was saying. "Tell me more about your brand—it is very interesting. I never instructed anyone to use branding as a punishment."

Rhea opened her mouth, wanting to politely explain the story, but anger poured from her like steam out of a kettle. "You didn't instruct them to brand?" Rhea asked, her eyes locking on the Master's. "Are you surprised? Not pleased with your grand experiment? Did your minions develop their own ideas, their own brains?" Rhea suddenly turned away and started pacing up and down the study.

"You put a family in charge of my Community. I assume they ensured that they were always selected to be Leaders—until they thought people started to get suspicious, and then they selected my father to lead. I was to wed the next Leader, who knew this history that you're telling me, who selected me to wed when he had no right to. They said the tests would decide what our occupation was and who we would wed, but that was all a lie, wasn't it? Gael got to choose me because his family had the power, and you gave it to them. It . . . if I could have chosen . . ." Rhea swallowed hard. The lump in her throat was so painful that she couldn't speak anymore.

"I remember Community 215," the Master said, almost dreamily. "I have almost lost count of how many Communities there are, or how many there have been. Countless have been burned by Adder with his bloodthirsty Outcasts, or by other Masters who have sought to challenge me. It was too much work to attempt to control the Communities from afar, and too dangerous to risk traveling to them to check in with Adder hunting me. I started establishing them, ordering them to be built when our population became too great, throwing some rules at them, putting those in charge who had proven their loyalty, and moving on. Creating Communities kept the Outcasts population somewhat in check. I left a very good family in charge of Community 215, gave them a rule book and a copy of a test. I have stopped doing the tests, myself. I only needed them at the start of this Community to obtain buy-in from people who remembered life before the war. After that, it was all a matter of teaching children the rules and the best ways to serve me. The philosophy of the classroom becomes the philosophy of government, after all.

"Once everyone understood that this was the natural way of being, I got rid of the tests. It was tedious, trying to keep them all straight. Those who were worthy of my favor would simply get what and who they wanted. Everyone would take the test for appearance's sake, of course, and those who were not worthy of my favor would actually *need* the results to dictate what and who they would spend their days doing. However, if someone matched well with someone who was already taken by one who had curried favor with me, I would have to randomly match followers together. It was tedious."

"Why do you care who people wed?" Rhea snarled, her hands curled into fists. "You could let them decide."

"If I allowed my people to choose one thing, they would inevitably want to make *more* choices, then be unhappy with them. Deep down, people don't want to decide. It is much easier for them to listen when I instruct them where to live, what and how much to eat, where to work, who to wed, what to wear, and whatever else I care to think of. Eventually, they become used to it, and they don't even remember what it was like to own anything. There are no personal possessions within my Communities, except for mine. I own everything and everyone you see. Why allow people to make their own choices when I am simply better at it? I am smarter than my idiot minions. I mean, look at how they have given everything up simply because I instructed them to!"

"Yes, and then you change your mind, and you take even more away from them. You took away Resident Twenty-Seven's partner."

"Oh, yes, I take as readily as I give." The Master waved her hand dismissively. "Her husband came to me and explained that she had dangerous ideas, and I rewarded him."

"Dangerous ideas?"

"She was talking about a rebellion."

"A rebellion?"

"It is truly amazing how my power has impacted your vocabulary. A rebellion is when a group of people attempts to overthrow their leader."

"You would deserve it!"

"You are not in a position to say what I do or do not deserve—only I can decide that. I am the only person with any power. I am the only thing that stands between you and the apocalypse."

"No one in the other Communities even knows who you are."

"Of course they don't—not anymore. If each of the Communities knew me, I would be in greater danger. They can rebel against their own little leaders; I am very happy here. There are just enough people to take care of my every need, and not so many that I cannot have complete control. It has the highest and strongest Walls, and it is truly beautiful."

"This place is awful," Rhea scoffed. "Your people all hate you! You are one problematic Resident away from them . . . them . . . rebelling you!"

"That is what I am wondering," the Master said, tipping her head thoughtfully to one side. "That is why I am telling you all of this."

"What?"

"I am going to give you something that you have never been given before: a choice."

"Will you let me go?"

"Go? Where would you go? There is nothing out there for you."

Rhea thought of Brooks who she had left sleeping in the grass, his curls splayed around his head and his beautiful eyes closed.

"If you aren't going to offer me the choice of leaving, what are you offering me?"

"You are being offered a chance to have a life that everyone wants. I would like for you to take over from me. My daughter . . . tragically, she did not adapt well to being here. She missed her father and didn't understand what I was building for her. As you have nothing and no one, and you have grown up in a different Community, I believe you might be an ideal candidate to someday lead Community One."

Rhea shook her head. "I don't understand you. How do I know you're not making all of this up? It's not what I learned growing up at all—it doesn't make any sense! I was told that the Communities are designed for us, for people. It's the natural way to live, with people helping each other."

"There is a difference between choosing to help each other and understanding that the natural way of being is to serve the superior being in a society. Did you really help each other in your little Community? Or did everyone work and sacrifice to make one or a few persons' lives better?"

"What makes you a superior being?" Rhea snapped, choosing to ignore the rest.

"Perhaps you aren't what I'm looking for," the Master sighed, anger threading her voice. "You're perhaps too delusional, too submerged in the simulation that I created to understand that a world exists beyond the shadows on the cave wall."

Rhea bit her lip, her hands curling into fists. "No," she said finally.

"No?"

"No."

"What do you mean no?"

"No, I don't want any part of this. I want to go to my Community," Rhea said. "Please, just let me go."

"You don't have a Community. Everything that you have ever known was not real—it was created by me!" The Master walked to the window and looked out at her world.

What it must be like, looking down on people from such a height, taking from them, delegating what they deserved, who they deserved.

Rhea closed her eyes. Intense pressure seemed to be forcing her into the rich, soft flooring, pushing her breath from her lungs, causing her knees to tremble. She couldn't stand this anymore; she couldn't stand having to make choices. She longed for her old Community, for her father, her Nurse, and her Teacher . . . and Brooks.

"You're pathetic," the woman hissed. Rhea opened her tear-filled eyes, releasing fat tears onto her cheeks, to find the Master directly in front of her. "There is nothing left for you, no one left for you. You're a child—a weak child. I'll design a life for you. You'll do everything that I say."

"No!" Rhea said, her voice stronger now. "If I refuse, you'll have to cast me out of the Community."

"That's not how things work here," the Master said, a smile stretching her face into a malevolent mask. "Here you obey, or you die."

CHAPTER 16
OBEYING

Rhea's hands bled onto the rough stone. She quickly dipped her brush back into the hot water and scrubbed off the blood before it set into the stone, but each movement sent another little river of blood down onto the floor. Rhea chased the crimson off of the stone, swearing under her breath, her knees and back aching, her stomach growling. Her hair fell forward to hide her tears. No one here cared if she bled. No one cared if she cried. No one cared if she died.

Her days were long, hard, and repetitive. Each day someone walked along the streets at dawn, banging on doors and ringing a loud bell, yelling for Residents to wake up. Rhea would groan with her eyes still shut tight, savoring that one second where she woke and didn't remember where she was before her day started. She lived in a long low hut with fifteen other women. The other women were mostly older widowers, but three were Rhea's age, and she wondered vaguely why they hadn't been permitted to wed. Other dwellings held single young people who were housed according to their age and waiting to be matched and wed, but it was common knowledge that those in Rhea's dwelling would not be permitted to. Perhaps the Master had just decided they couldn't because they had offended her in some way, as Rhea had done.

She had ordered Rhea from her grand dwelling on that day, and Dex had marched her down to the women's hut. The hut was stone, like everything in Community One, so that Adder would have a harder time burning it if he came to call, which Rhea knew he wouldn't.

Adder was dead. Brooks and Raven had killed him. Rhea wondered if she should tell the Master, but quickly decided it was safer for her to believe her husband was somewhere out there still looking for her. She deserved to know what fear was.

Inside Rhea's shared hut was a cooking stove, a washroom, and rows upon rows of beds for the women to sleep on. The women had shown Rhea a bed that was open, right under one of the windows, and she had curled up on the hard mattress and cried. They threw new grey clothes at her to show her new station, but she didn't move. One of them made a plate of food and left it by her, but she hadn't touched it, and eventually the woman had taken it away and eaten it herself. Rhea cried, letting her tears fall into the mattress until it was damp. Her shoulders shook, and her breath only came in sobs well into the night. At last, she finally fell asleep and dreamed of Brooks.

He was standing in their meadow, his arms open, waiting for her to run to him. She gasped and laughed, unable to believe that he was here—he was so close. She ran, her arms pumping wildly, but when she reached Brooks, she found that he was the Master, her face a cold smile. Rhea screamed, drawing back her fist, and punched her, but her smile never faded.

Rhea gasped and sat up in bed, dripping wet. Resident Twenty-Seven had thrown water on her. "Up," she said curtly.

"No," Rhea said, her voice weak. "I'm done."

"You think they care? You ready to see what someone can do to you when they have total control over you?" the woman asked. "Get up, One."

"One?"

"That's what Dex said the Master named you. Don't think we've ever had a One before—usually she wants people to have bigger numbers. Guess she's been savin' it for you."

Rhea slowly sat up, her head spinning. She licked her lips. "Here," Twenty-Seven said, handing Rhea a cup of water. She downed it and climbed shakily into her new clothes.

"What do I have to do?"

"Dex said Master wants you at her house."

"She . . . she wants me there?"

"Suppose so. You best start walking—it's a long way."

Rhea had left her new dwelling to follow a little knot of Residents winding their way up to the Master's in the chilly early morning light. Fall was crisp in the air. Rhea puffed out her cheeks to see her breath billow like white smoke before her, dancing in the air before dissolving into nothing.

Rhea's dwelling was on the outskirts of the Community, right up against the metal Wall. The dwellings became more and more beautiful the closer to the Master's she drew. People with lower stations, like her, lived in the smallest dwellings, while those who had favor with the Master lived in large, beautiful stone dwellings. The people that Rhea walked with had large, haunted eyes. Their hands were red and raw, and their feet dragged while they walked. Rhea tried making eye contact with several of them, wanting to find out more, wishing someone would tell her something about this bizarre place, but they were careful not to catch hers or anyone else's eye. Rhea remembered what the Master had said about Twenty-Seven's partner informing her that she was planning a rebellion. In a society where you could not even trust who you were wed to, people would be bound to guard themselves to a heartbreaking degree. *How tragic, to see someone in charge of a society exploit their people instead of protecting their people.* Even the way that she spoke of them dripped with condescension.

The crowd around Rhea shrank as people reached their occupations. She watched smithies and seamstresses, cooks and cleaners, farmers and carpenters filter their ways into various stone buildings. Close to the Master's dwelling was a large building with small children milling about outside. As Rhea passed, she saw several of the children point at her.

"That's one of the Outcasts!" one small girl said to her friend. "The Master saved her."

"I heard the Outcasts all have red eyes!" her friend said.

"No," a little boy chimed in. "They have horns!"

"Don't be stupid!" another boy yelled. "They look just like us— that's how they lure you into a trap! If evil people looked scary, no one would ever fall for their tricks!"

Rhea stopped, watching the children argue. She wanted to smack them. She wanted to cry, to stomp her foot and yell that they didn't know anything about Outcasts, that Brooks was an Outcast and that he was kind and beautiful and funny. Just then, a hand gently grasped her arm and pulled her away from the children. She jumped and looked around to see a man about her age smiling gently at her.

"Children don't know anything, especially here," he said quietly.

"No," she agreed, "they don't." She glanced down at his hand. "Are you permitted to touch me?"

"Yes, I am," he said, although he released her as he said it. "I'm a Defender. We're kind of allowed to do what we want, but we also have to follow each rule. It's an interesting balance." He smiled. His hair was light brown and short while his eyes were wide and dark. "Shall we walk to work, then?"

Rhea nodded and continued on her journey, the Defender keeping pace with her. "How are you liking our Community, One?"

"I have already dealt with the Defenders here," Rhea said pointedly. "I would prefer not to do so again."

"I suppose you met Dex?"

"Yes."

"Not all of us are like Dex."

"I do not know you."

"You could."

"I would prefer not to." Talking with him was fast and easy, almost like talking with Brooks. Although, she had never been afraid of Brooks, and she was afraid of this Defender with his sweet smile.

They walked together to the Master's gate, and he showed her the side door through which she could enter for work each day. She followed a little queue of other Residents through the door and the Defender said, "Enjoy your first day, One," before turning from her and strutting across the yard to join the other Defenders.

"You stay away from those Defender boys, One," a small woman whispered to Rhea. "They do something against the rules, and you'll be the one punished for it."

"I know," Rhea sighed. She followed the woman up a set of stone steps and into a larger room filled with washing basins, brushes, brooms, and other things that Rhea couldn't name. A finely dressed man waited for them, a long list of jobs in his hand. He began the day by yelling that they were all late, and wouldn't they be sorry that they had dawdled on their way into work this morning, because he had jobs that would take all day. He then pointed at each of them and screamed what they would have to do that day. Rhea was put in charge of scrubbing the floors. She filled a bucket with hot water from a large boiling kettle on the fire, put a hunk of soap in it, and set to work.

Rhea scrubbed the floors until her hands bled, until the floors were spotless, until her knees screamed in protest, and while she scrubbed, she thought only of the Master and what she had done. The lives that she had stolen and twisted. Rhea scrubbed with vengeance, her stomach grumbling with hunger, for several hours until she was fetched to come back into the large room and eat. She swallowed thin stew and a hunk of bread while wishing for more, thinking longingly of the greasy rabbits that Brooks had caught and cooked for her, and then went back to work.

Work ended a few hours after the sun went down. When Rhea limped down the stairs to the side door, the same Defender was waiting for her.

On and on it went. Again and again Rhea rose, dressed, and went to work, her Defender at her side. Again and again she scrubbed the stone floor, the stone walls, the clothes, dishes, and pans, anything that the Master wanted. Finally, exhausted and starving, she would walk to her dwelling with her Defender, eat silently with the other women, and fall onto her bed.

She knew that the Master had sent the Defender to watch her for signs of weakness, wanting her to break. She had wanted to. She had come so very close to breaking, but she wouldn't do it. Rhea had to find a way out, and she knew the only way out was through her, one way or another. She figured that the Master made Residents work too hard to have the energy for a rebellion. Rebellion was a word that she repeated over and over again in her head, a word with a sharp and sweet taste. *Rebellion.*

Days trickled by with agonizing slowness, aging into weeks. Rhea felt herself deteriorating slowly, becoming gaunt and hard like the people around her, dragging herself grudgingly through life. The air crisped as winter approached, adding a biting sting to the constant ache in her chapped hands.

One particularly cold morning, Rhea walked beside her Defender to work, contemplating how much she missed Brooks, and abruptly noticed a scuttle outside of the schoolyard. The children were arranged in neat lines and teachers and Defenders walked amongst them, pointing at various children. Rhea stopped, staring. The Master was walking along the lines of children, bending low to speak to one, tilting her head, as she contemplated another.

"What is she doing?" Rhea asked her Defender.

"Oh, today's the day she decides their future."

"Their future?"

"Well, yeah. She talks to their teachers and meets the children and decides what their occupation will be."

"But . . . they're not seventeen."

"No," her Defender agreed.

"How can she possibly pick their occupation when they are so young?"

"The classrooms can get a little crowded, so she chooses their professions and gets them to work as young as possible. The smartest children get to stay in school."

Rhea shook her head, looking at the young children. They couldn't have been older than eight. "They're too young to go to work."

"Not here," her Defender said, his voice low. "We've had younger start working here, especially if we need something."

"Like what?"

"I was six when I started working as a bladesmith."

Rhea looked at him. She had never seen eyes so dark. "How did you become a Defender, then?"

"It's . . . it's a rare thing for someone's occupation to change. She usually hand selects Defenders at a very young age, and they start training immediately. It's not just physical training; there's a unique education that goes along with being a Defender. But in my case, she made an exception."

Rhea stared at him. "Did you ask her to make you a Defender?"

"No," he said, a hint of anger bubbling to the surface.

"What is your name?" Rhea asked. She had become so used to thinking of him as "her Defender" that she had never contemplated that he could be trapped here every bit as much as she was.

"It used to be Storm."

Rhea blinked at him as she processed his reply. "You're . . . you're from out there? You're an Outcast?"

The Defender bent closer to her. "You have no idea what she has done," he hissed. His light smile and tone had vanished, and his eyes burned into hers. Rhea blinked and looked back at the school. The Master was gazing at her, a small smile playing around her mouth.

"Meet me tonight?" Rhea breathed.

"Yes."

They turned and marched on their way to work without saying another word.

Rhea listened carefully for the breathing around her to become slow and steady before she crept out of bed and slipped through the door. Storm was already waiting for her. He took her arm and guided her carefully through the maze of streets, sticking to the shadows. He finally stopped near a niche right against the Wall, where the metal was so tightly clustered together that it made a small cave in the Wall. Storm ducked into the niche and Rhea followed. They sat side by side, smashed together.

"So?" Storm asked.

"So what?" Rhea said.

"Why did you want to meet me?"

"Isn't it obvious?" Rhea snapped. "I want information!"

"Information? On what?"

"The Master, of course!"

He laughed. "You think I have information on her?"

"You . . . you sounded so bitter earlier today."

"I am bitter."

"What did she do to you?"

"It was during a population crisis. There weren't enough people to maintain this place. She sent out a few groups of Defenders, and one of them found where my family and I were hiding. We were a part of a small band of Outcasts, but we had left them when the raids started."

"Raids?"

"People in Communities kept raiding us, stealing people. Mostly women and children."

"From Community One?"

"No."

"What?"

"You do know that there are other Communities, right?"

"Of course I do."

"And that other Communities can also have population crises?"

"I suppose so."

"And would be willing to do anything to protect their way of life?"

"No, no, no. My Community would have never done anything like that!"

"How do you know? How do you know you weren't a baby who was stolen from somewhere?"

"I was born in my Community!"

"You're positive about that?"

Rhea shook her head, once again trying to dislodge the horrible thoughts that cloyed at the edges of her mind. Everything that she had ever known had been a lie—why not this too?

"I don't know," Rhea snapped. "I don't know anything anymore!" Her head sank into her hands. "The way I grew up made sense— everything was fine! Our children went to school, we received our occupations and our partners . . . everyone was well!"

"Were people happy?"

"Happiness is irrelevant. People were . . . everyone had uniform lives. Happiness isn't fair, because some people can end up happier than others."

"So, you didn't even care about people being happy?"

"It wasn't relevant to anyone!"

"How do you know?"

Rhea bit her lip. There wasn't an answer for that. Happiness wasn't something that Residents talked about in her Community. Population, occupations, what the Council said the well-being of the Community was—those were things that mattered. The concerns of individualism, competition, acts of kindness, or happiness were all just selfish concepts. They didn't serve the needs of the Council. Furthermore, it wasn't fair if one Resident was happy if everyone couldn't be equally as happy. Right? There were things more important than happiness or this love that Brooks kept talking about such as . . . such as *what*?

"I don't know," Rhea confessed, raising her head. "I just know that being there was better than being here."

"I believe that," Storm said.

"Where is your family now? Did they escape the Defenders?"

"No. They asked the Defenders to kill them."

"They what?"

"They said they would rather die than lose their freedom."

"Freedom?"

"Yes, they would rather die than not be free."

"That's ridiculous!"

"Is it?" Rhea couldn't think of anything to say. "The Defenders brought them here. The Master asked each of us if we would pledge to live our lives for her. I said yes; my mother and father and my sisters said no. She executed them."

"I . . . I didn't know that she—"

"There is a thin layer of civility that blankets the savagery of our dear Community One."

"I . . . I am sorry."

"As am I," Storm said, sounding far away. "I was only four at the time. I cried and begged the Master for my life, which she gave me. She sent me to school, decided I was too stupid to stay there, and made me into a bladesmith. I worked there for years, honing my craft. It wasn't easy to do. We were permitted to make weapons, but never test them. The common people cannot know how to *use* weapons; we're only permitted to make them for those worthy enough to wield them."

"How did you become a Defender?"

"I broke the rules. I started testing what I made. Knives, swords, axes, crossbows—it didn't matter. I taught myself how to use them. Any weapon was better than nothing at all. I started to feel powerful, like I could control my own future. She knew. I don't know how she knew; I don't know who could have seen me practicing, but it didn't matter. She called me up to her palace and offered me everything and anything that I could ever want. Did I want the best food? Done. The best house? Yes. A nice cushy job? Of course. To select my mate? Obviously."

"You took her offer?" Rhea asked, incredulous.

"I took the offer, and I lived like . . . like *her* for a while. I had everything I ever wanted, and I was just eighteen. But my chosen mate wasn't so happy. Nothing would make her happy. She kept going on and on about leaving, about making our own lives beyond the Wall. She hadn't been as fortunate as me growing up; she was born here in Community One. Children are taken into school at two years—indoctrination has to start young. They eventually forget who their parents are, who their siblings are, although the Master keeps a careful record. Our bond to our families was stronger than our bond to her, so she took the children out of their family dwellings and put them in schools that they couldn't leave.

"My partner was taught her entire life that the Master was everything, that nothing existed beyond these Walls but savagery, pain, and suffering. She was allowed to stay in school until age ten, then she was deemed unintelligent enough to continue and given an occupation. She worked as a seamstress after that in the Master's own house, altering clothes with other workers. She measured the Master countless times but wasn't permitted to speak or to meet her eyes."

"There's . . . nothing like that ever happened in my Community."

"And you know about every single person suffering in your Community, do you?" Storm snapped. "After she and I wed, she started telling me about everything that she had been through. We were hopelessly in love; I had gotten so lucky. The woman I picked had actually picked me in turn. I told her what actually exists outside of these Walls, and my partner, Resident 7098, got an idea. She was close to the Master on almost a weekly basis. She would take her out, and we would run."

He buried his face in his hands, his shoulders shaking. "I don't . . . I don't know how she knew . . ." he whispered. "But she did. And the only thing I have ever loved since I was a child was taken from me."

Rhea couldn't breathe. It was impossible for so much tragedy to exist in one place. For Storm to have lost everyone . . . for Resident

Twenty-Seven and all of the other unloved women in her dwelling to live as social outcasts . . . for Brooks to have been so very close and for her to have walked away . . .

"I can't do this anymore," Rhea cried. "I can't . . . it's all too much!"

"You don't understand what too much is!" Storm snapped.

"No . . . I don't. But I've had enough."

"We all have."

"No, you haven't," Rhea shot back. "You all claim that you've had enough, but none of you are actually doing anything about it!"

"What can we possibly do? She has everything! She has Defenders—"

"Not all of the Defenders," Rhea pointed out.

"It's not just that! Plenty of people here live wonderful lives, the way that I did. Without her in charge, there's nothing for them. They've treated the people beneath them so badly that a rebellion would mean their death as much as hers."

"Rebellion . . . the Master said that Resident Twenty-Seven had been planning a rebellion, too. If enough people want to have a rebellion, it cannot possibly be that difficult to create one."

"Yes, it is. She will kill all of us," Storm said matter-of-factly.

"She cannot kill *all* of us! There are more in our class than there are in hers!"

"We don't have weapons!"

"Weapons can be made—you made them!"

"Quality weapons take quality material and time."

"So? Steal the quality material and make the quality time."

"You don't understand. She will kill everyone." His voice was flat, defeated.

"You said that it was better to die than to not be free!" Rhea hissed, her voice shaking with anger. "And if we cannot be free, we will still be making a choice. We will be choosing to die—not because she wants us to, but because one way or another, we will break her hold on us!"

Storm shook his head, smiling. "You haven't even been here that long. You haven't suffered enough to be talking like this."

Rhea felt her back stiffen uncomfortably. "If you would rather live your life as a coward, be my guest."

"Don't get all offended. I'm just wondering what's in this for you. How did you get here?""That's my business."

"No, it's my business, too, if you want me to trust you."

Rhea looked at him, weighing her options. She couldn't think of a single lie to tell; she had never learned how to lie. "My Community was burned to the ground by someone I thought was . . . unique."

"You loved him?"

"Love is not a word that I am familiar with."

"Are you sure?"

She didn't respond. "He was an Outcast, but I protected him. He waited until the time was right before burning everything to the ground."

"You think he used you." It wasn't a question.

"He didn't understand that the way we lived . . . it was the only way."

Storm snorted. "You think that your way of life was so different from ours."

"It was!"

"How do you know?"

"Because I was there!"

"I see. So, you were allowed to pick your occupation?"

"We were assigned occupations according to our attributes."

"Sure. What about your partners? Could you pick those?" Rhea twisted her lip. "Your house? Could you pick that? What about how many children you have? What you eat? What you wear?"

"It wasn't like *this*," she said stiffly.

"What do you want?" Storm asked. "Why go through all of this?"

"No one has ever asked me what I want before."

"Sounds about right, given your hometown."

"I want him."

"Who? Your Outcast?"

"Yes."

"What happened to him?"

"He asked me to go with him, but I refused. I came here instead. I don't know . . . if I saw him now, I know I would turn and run the other way. He ruined everything. But he . . . I need to see him again." Rhea looked away from Storm. "What do you want?" she asked.

"Only to kill the Master."

And so, the rebellion began.

CHAPTER 17
THE REEDUCATION COMMUNITY

Brooks peered through the thick leaves crowning a bush and watched. He had scarcely seen a more heavily armed Community; the Walls were wooden, like Rhea's had been, and adorned with several watchtowers and a ledge along the top for Defenders to walk along. The Defenders were armed with bows or crossbows, and there were always at least thirty of them on duty. The dwellings in the Community were low, too low for Brooks to see them over the Wall. The gate remained tightly closed at all times.

"Well?" Raven asked impatiently. She wanted to storm the Community, damn the consequences. Planning was not her strong suit.

Brooks sighed in response. While he had previously thought that Adder's painstaking process of implanting followers into Communities to open the gate and start the fires had been tedious, he now understood his thought process. Communities were chaotic, filled with Defenders and Residents who were worse than useless in a fight, but the Walls were rather impenetrable. Communities stood in large clearings, rendering stealthy attacks impossible.

"Well?" Raven asked again.

"Is that it?" Brooks asked the would-be-kidnapper Noah.

"Yes," Noah said. He was shaking hard; Brooks had scarcely ever met anyone so afraid.

"Then let's go," Raven said.

"The goal here is *rescue*," Brooks snapped at Raven. "Not following some Raven plan and getting us all killed." He had tried to persuade her to stay at their new home and help turn it into a safe place to live, but unsurprisingly, she had refused.

"Your goal is making us die here of old age," Raven said, rolling her eyes.

"When was the last time you heard of someone dying from old age?"

"Never."

"We can make it a possibility, eventually." That would really be something. If they could stop the raids and kidnappings, maybe they could work to make old age a possibility for their people.

"I thought the goal here was to get our people back."

"It is."

"Are you hoping to use your mind powers to get them back?"

Brooks twisted around to look at the trees above them. "Maybe," he said, grinning.

The catapult was a hideous thing, a twisted wooden monster. "It's not going to work," Raven said, her arms folded.

"It will work," Brooks insisted, trying to shove the pinpricks of doubt away. He had never seen a catapult before. He had heard that once, innovations and inventions had been things that people would strive for. They would focus on not merely just surviving but thriving within a society. Ambition had been rewarded. Now, Brooks's people and other Outcasts were focused on surviving one more year, one more week, one more day. Communities deliberately punished innovation and ambition. Those in charge had everything that they could want. If their people had the gall to start thinking, to grow their abilities and their intelligence, they likely would come to the conclusion that there was no reason for them to serve their Leaders' every whim. They might even create ways to make their own freedom. Brooks was forcing himself and his people to innovate out of a desperate need to do so. No one was coming—no one was going to save their people or punish those who had taken them. The only rules that existed within Communities were the ones created by those in charge. If they said to go abduct Brooks and Raven's people, no one would believe there was anything wrong with it.

"We can't test it," Raven insisted.

"Sure we can. Hop in!" Brooks sniggered.

"Not everything is a joke, Brooks."

"Not with you, Raven."

Building the catapult had been incredibly tedious, difficult work. They had hidden behind a layer of trees so they could work without the noise of their hammers reaching the Community. Now, they would have to use a system of pullies and logs to drag it to the clearing under the cover of darkness, load it with a rock large enough to damage the gate, and fire. It wasn't a sophisticated plan, but Brooks saw a spark of determination in his men and women that he had never seen before. For years they had sent their children into the Communities, never to know if they would return, carry out their missions, or become a stranger behind those Walls. They were finally taking charge, choosing when and where to attack, and they were ready for a real fight.

"When are we finally going to use this thing?" Raven demanded.

"Dawn."

⁓

It started with the light from the stars fading, blending slowly into the deep sky behind them as it lightened one shade of blue at a time. The sky blushed as the sun warmed it, and Brooks nodded at Raven. She grasped a large rope on the catapult, then pulled it hard. Brooks watched as a large rock sailed through the air, headed toward the gate of the Community, and fell several yards short. Screams erupted from the Community, and Raven's accusing gaze found Brooks.

"It didn't hit them!" she screamed.

"Pull!" Brooks bellowed, shoving her aside. His strongest followers grabbed their ropes and pulled hard. "Pull!" he yelled again.
"Pull!" They finally broke through the last trees and presented the
doom of the Communities as the sun broke over the horizon. "Load!"
Brooks shouted, and another rock was placed into the catapult. "Fire!"

Nothing happened. He looked around to find Raven. She stood
in the edges of the trees, her eyes narrowed as she glared at him. He
launched himself toward her rope and pulled. The rock sailed through
the air and hit the top of the gate. Wood splintered, and the gate
shuddered.

"Reload!" Books shouted, and another rock was dragged into the
catapult. Brooks pulled the rope again and again, watching the gate
shudder and splinter, chunks of wood soaring through the air. *We
should have brought fire*, Brooks thought.

"We can make it over that!" he yelled at his fighters. "Let's go!"
Axes, swords, and bows leapt into hands and they charged, shout-
ing incoherent cries of war. A few arrows whistled through the air
and rained feebly down on them. Brooks changed directions as he ran
several times, hoping to throw off the Community archers.

Their defense was feeble, to the point of being laughable. Brooks
and his followers easily climbed over the crumbling remains of the
Wall and looked around. Chaos had once again shrouded a Community.
People cried and screamed, running practically in circles looking for
something, anything, that they could use to defend themselves. But
defense was impossible; their Leaders elected only a select few worthy enough of holding weapons due to fear of revolt. Brooks stood,
axe in hand and breathing hard, waiting for the Defenders to attack.
No one charged. He looked up at the Wall where the Defenders had
been shooting from. Arrows were trained on them from above, each
bowstring pulled tight and waiting to be released.

"Come on!" Brooks bellowed. "What are you waiting for?" The
Defenders looked at each other uncertainly.

"What's happening?" Lila whispered at Brooks's shoulder.

"They . . . I think they need orders to fire once we're over the Wall." He laughed. It was ridiculous—ludicrous. These absolute idiots had stormed their way into his camp, abducted his people, and now stood there with their faces pale and their arms shaking, waiting for an order.

"Lower your weapons!" Brooks yelled. The Defenders blinked before slowly pointing their arrows at the ground. "Drop them!" The Defenders dropped their bows. "Lila, pick them up," Brooks ordered, and she scurried to do so.

"This is bizarre!" one of his other followers muttered.

"What a sorry excuse for a society, not even willing to protect themselves."

"I was hoping for a real fight."

"I was, too," Brooks agreed. He looked around. The Residents were starting to huddle forward, looking curiously at the newcomers. "This Community has fallen!" Brooks shouted. "If anyone doesn't like that, step forward now and fight us!" No one moved. The Residents looked hungry and weak, their eyes hollow and exhausted, full of a haunted quality Brooks had scarcely ever seen before.

"All right, then," Brooks said. "We're here to find people who . . . who used to be Outcasts and who were stolen to be a part of this . . . Community. Know anyone like that?" The Residents looked around at each other, and every hand slowly went up.

⌒

Brooks sat on a tree stump outside of the Community Walls—or what was left of it—shaking hard. This had been one of the longest days of his life. Captured Residents had collapsed, sobbing, into his and his people's arms. The horrific treatment they described seemed to seep into him, infecting him with a deep sadness he had never before known. They hadn't encountered a true "Community"; they had liberated a camp of sorts where Outcasts were taken to be conditioned before being placed into a real Community.

Everyone was separated according to their gender, age, and level of education. It wasn't education that Brooks was familiar with. It wasn't about reading and writing and math; this education was about saying and, more importantly, thinking the correct things. When an Outcast was captured, they were scrubbed clean, given a uniform, and placed into the lowest level of education for their grade level. At daybreak, they were given a meager breakfast, taken to a classroom, and taught the rules of being a part of a Community. They weren't permitted to speak to each other or to ask questions. After classroom instruction, they were forced to do any number of physical tasks until dinner. Exhausted, they would finally fall into bed, but every few hours they were woken up for seemingly no reason but to keep them as tired as possible. And on and on it went.

When a Resident proved that they were starting to believe the teachings of the camp, they would move them to a different building and present them with new "privileges," such as allowing them to sleep through the night or eating better food. Once a Resident had truly been reeducated and didn't see themselves as an Outcast anymore but as a Resident of a Community, they were finally permitted to leave and be taken to a real Community.

The camp was filled with small low wooden buildings. Hard dirt paths wound around the Community, and everything about it was dismal and depressing. If an Outcast came in with any personal possessions, they were burned. Even the smallest children were not permitted toys or dolls. Mothers, fathers, and siblings were taught that those titles meant nothing, that a child wasn't theirs but a member of something bigger now. The very foundation of what it meant to be human was stripped away from them. They didn't have a purpose unless it was to serve the society that had been built around them. Hopelessness hung like a physical sink over the entire camp.

"They don't think like us at all," Sky, a woman Brooks had never met before, told him. "They don't believe we have any purpose besides serving them. We didn't have a choice over anything here. Even stupid things, like what we wore or what we ate or how much, they thought they knew better." She looked down at the ground, toying with the grey hem of her skirt. "My man . . . he got sick a few days after we were stolen. They took him away, said it was because he would infect us all. They never told me where they took him . . . but I know he's gone. They tried to . . . make me happy about it. Said they were protecting me." Tears streamed down her face. "They told me if my little boy started to get sick, I should tell them about it so they could protect me from him, too. They think I need protecting from my own little boy."

The people here were forced into various "occupation" trainings and classes. They were taught that they hadn't been "stolen," but "rescued" by superior people who cared about them and knew what was best for them. They were encouraged to keep each other accountable and tell a Defender if someone was speaking "offensively" or had "dangerous ideas." Defenders routinely broke into their huts and searched their meager belongings. No one knew what they were looking for, and they didn't dare to ask any questions. Daily, there were announcements regarding the outside world—the dangers and the savages beyond the Walls who were waiting for the slightest sign of weakness. They were told that they were vital to helping society survive, that they needed to help Communities, that Outcasts had committed unthinkable atrocities that they now had to make up for.

"They said I was a bad person . . . that I needed to work hard and do exactly as they said to make up for everything I've done," a child whispered to Brooks. "But I didn't know what I had done."

Brooks and his people recovered most of those who were stolen, but a select few had already been sent off to Communities. It seemed that three nearby Communities used the camp to condition Residents before bringing them "home." Some people moved on quickly, and some stayed in the camp for years due to "adjustment problems." Brooks and his people had interrogated the Defenders and asked for their Leaders. Afterwards, a small group of elderly people were presented to them.

"We're not in charge here!" one of them insisted. "We only do what we're told." The Leaders of the Communities that they filtered people to had provided the camp with a thick rule book and instructions. Brooks ordered the Leaders to be put under Defender to stand trial when they got back to the Outcast camp. Several of the people who had been stolen eyed the leaders vindictively.

"We will be responsible for deciding their fate," Brooks had reassured them, "and you will have a say, but it isn't right to take that say away from others that they have impacted back at our home. Leave them alone." There were only slightly resentful murmurs of assent at that.

Raven sat next to Brooks on his tree stump. "Well?"

"Well what?"

"What do we do now?"

"Why are you asking me?"

"Because you're in charge."

"I thought we were both in charge."

"You knocked me over during the attack."

"You were moving too slowly."

"That means I'm done."

"You're done?"

"No one will respect me after you took over, Brooks."

Brooks buried his face in his hands. "You and your drama. Are you done? You want to quit? Maybe start a cute little camp like this one, where people will be afraid of you, do whatever you say?" Raven drew back her fist and struck out at his face, but he slipped the blow and grabbed her hand, twisting it hard until she whirled around, and he thrust her arm behind her, pinning it to her back. He threaded his other arm around her throat and pulled her close. "You done?" he hissed.

She struggled for a minute, then breathed, "Fine," and he released her.

"Look around you!" Brooks snarled at her. "You see this? You think I want to be here, dealing with this? Rhea could be in a place worse than this right now!"

"She is all you care about!"

"Yes, she is."

"You're never going to be a leader until you put your feelings aside and let her go."

"Then *you* lead!"

"They don't follow me—they follow you!"

"You think taking down Adder made us fit to lead these people?" Brooks snapped. "If you want their respect, you need to earn it. You don't know any of the new names. Do you know what they want from you? What they need from you? Have you spoken to them?"

"That's not how Adder did things, Brooks."

"And look how he ended up. He got what he deserved. Do you want that to be what we deserve?"

"Our people wouldn't attack us."

"Our people have seen and experienced terror, relief, tyranny, freedom, and everything in between. Don't underestimate them. If I ever turn into Adder, I hope they have the respect for themselves and each other to stop me."

Raven shook her head. "I don't take orders well, so I don't want to follow anyone. But I've never cared if people like me, either."

"People don't have to like you to follow you. They have to respect you."

"What's the difference?"

"It doesn't matter if they want to spend time with you. In fact, they likely don't! They have more important things to worry about than liking you, like feeding their families and keeping them safe. They don't care about your feelings; they care about how you're improving their lives."

"How have we improved their lives?"

"Look at that." Brooks pointed back at the camp they had liberated.

Reunited families and friends embraced. Someone had brought down a deer and slabs of meat were being cooked on open fires. There was ease, laughter, and conversation. Even a few of the camp Defenders were shifting eagerly at the edge of the fires, hoping to be included. "Many of them have their loved ones back. They have something to live for, something that they care about."

"You did that," Raven said. "We didn't even get to fight. I didn't get to do anything."

"If you don't want to be a leader, I'm not going to make you," Brooks said. "It's not my job to make you feel included. If you want to be a leader, good. I need you. But you need to stop being so selfish and self-centered. This isn't about you; it's about our people. We have work to do."

Raven folded her arms. "If I decide to stay and we keep leading together, what are we going to do next?"

Brooks looked to the west, where the sun was sinking back under the trees. Rhea was out there, needing him. Thinking about her made him ache with longing. Being away from her was like being without air—he couldn't breathe. But close by were other Communities filled with his people, more who had been stolen. They had the catapult, they had the time, and even better, they had people with more anger and venom coursing through them than was natural. "We keep going," Brooks stated. "We go home, we regroup, and we keep taking down tyrants."

Raven grinned. "So, we just go to war?"

Brooks looked at the camp. He had explored it carefully earlier, taken in the starving people who were told they had plenty to eat and to stop being so selfish, the dingy huts people lived in while the elderly Leaders had rich dwellings, and the conditioning and brainwashing. "We're already at war," Brooks said. "It's just that no one told us yet."

"What was that thing you said about being a leader?"

"People don't work for their leaders. Leaders work for their people."

CHAPTER 18
REBELLION

"I want the story," Rhea demanded in a low whisper.

"You want the what?"

"The story." She had finally cornered Resident Twenty-Seven in their dwelling. It was bath day, and the other women were still gone. Bath day was mandatory, but Rhea had rushed for the chance to speak with Twenty-Seven, who worked in the bathhouse and was able to bathe before anyone else. Rhea's hair was still wet. "I want the whole story of how this happened."

"I told you the day you arrived," Resident Twenty-Seven snapped. "Why you wanna hear it again?"

"You didn't tell me everything."

"'Course I didn't. You didn't wanna hear it."

"I want to hear it now."

"Why? You gonna turn me over to the Master?"

"No. I need your help killing her," Rhea stated evenly. Resident Twenty-Seven blinked at her, then grinned. "You startin' to hate that manual labor? Startin' to think you're special, deserve more than you're gettin'?"

"No!" Rhea snapped. "It's not like that."

"Sure, it is," Resident Twenty-Seven taunted. "You used to be a princess back at your Community, and now you're nothin' and you can't stand it."

"I don't know what a 'princess' is," Rhea said stiffly.

"No, I don't think you do." She grinned. "Alright, I'll tell you."

She sat at the scrubbed wooden table, splaying her rough, worn hands out in front of her. "There were always two simple ideas in our world. One said that our purpose was to take care of ourselves and the people we love, and the other, that our purpose was to serve others."

"Yes, and serving others is the correct way to live."

"You ain't listening. Serving others wasn't about takin' care of each other; it was about serving people who decided they were better than anyone else."

"How would anyone ever get someone else to believe that they were better than everyone else?"

"Money and power."

"What's that?"

"Ways that people were controlled. Everyone wanted 'em, and once they had 'em, they didn't wanna give 'em up. They believed they were better than everyone else, and they saw the rest of us as being people who were just here to serve them. To make 'em things, give 'em more money and power, worship 'em, and all the while thank 'em for what they were doin' to us. Power was supposed to have its limits, and they had rules they were supposed to follow. But when they stopped followin' the rules, there was no one to stop them. Sure, people got mad and some tried to stand up to 'em, but gaining power is hard. They broke rules, lied, and sabotaged anyone who got in their way."

"Didn't the people get mad? Didn't they see what was happening?"

"Some of 'em did. But as soon as they started to stand up, people in charge could still find fault with them, tell everyone they had done somethin' awful, and lock 'em up."

"What did the people in power want?"

"More power, I suppose."

"They already had it," Rhea pointed out.

"Sure."

"They wanted more?"

"I guess so."

"So, what happened?"

"People decided they'd had enough—somethin' finally pushed them over the edge. People got a lot of bend, but when they snap, there ain't no goin' back."

"So, the people started a rebellion."

"It had been done lots of times over the course of history. Power only goes so far when there are more of us than there are of them. It started with people in power explaining that people didn't need so many things, that they were getting greedy, wanting to pick where they lived and what they owned. Times were gettin' harder and harder, and instead of trying to fix it, people were saying we needed to just adjust our expectations. Instead of saying it was their fault for livin' like kings while the rest of us panicked over food, they whined that we were evil for wanting our own things and that going without things like food would be good for the world. You would have loved it."

Rhea ignored her jab. "And that's when the war started?"

"Yes, I think both sides were ready for it. The ones in power didn't see a point to people who didn't agree with them. Lockin' 'em up one at a time was hard. Might as well stamp them out. They said we were evil if we wouldn't go along with what they wanted, like they got to choose what evil is."

"There were people who fought for those in power?"

"Part of being in power is telling people what to do, you know. And plenty of people thought it was a great idea."

"And who won?"

"Depends on who you ask. I would guess that our Master would say she won. The casualties were devastating."

"The Outcasts might say that they won, if they don't have to follow the rules that they fought against."

"I would say so."

"So, I suppose rebellions are possible?"

"Yeah."

"Want to start one?" Rhea asked. Resident Twenty-Seven grinned.

Rhea hurried through the maze of streets to meet Storm, her heart in her throat and cold sweat trickling down her face. Her breath fogged in the frigid air before her and she suddenly held it, terrified that a Defender would see the plume and spot her. Footsteps thundered in her direction, and she slipped quickly into a door frame. She held her hot breath, pressing her freezing hands over her nose and mouth. Two Defenders hurried past her, and she slipped back onto the street and continued. She finally reached the niche in the Wall and squeezed herself into the space.

"Hey," Storm breathed, his warm breath rushing over her.

"Hello," Rhea whispered.

"Well?" he demanded.

"Four."

"Four?"

"Four."

"Four isn't enough."

"It's the best I could do," Rhea insisted. "They're all terrified. Apparently, the last time you people had a rebellion, the Master publicly executed everyone who even *heard* about it. Not everyone who was a part of it—everyone who *heard* about it."

"I remember. It wasn't a brief execution."

"You all remember," Rhea snapped. "That's why no one will talk about it now."

"Four is still something. How many is that total?"

"Including us? Six."

"I think there might be another Defender who would be in."

"Is it safe to ask him?"

"It's not safe to ask anyone. You know that. You know the risks."

"I know the risks, but I'm willing to take them."

"You weren't at that last execution."

"You were, and you still want to do this, don't you?"

"Yes, but the worst thing that can happen to me is that I will be with my family again."

"Your . . . your family is dead."

"I know that, Rhea."

"You . . . you can't see dead people."

"I will when I die."

"Nothing happens when you die."

"Is that what they taught you?"

"Of course!"

"How would you know that nothing happens when you die? You've never died."

Rhea didn't have an answer for that. "Because . . . I was taught."

"At some point during this rebellion process, you're going to have to learn to critically examine what you learned."

"My Community was not like this place," Rhea said defensively.

"Sure, it wasn't," Storm muttered.

"We always do this," Rhea snapped. "The point isn't us agreeing—it's us taking down the Master!"

"You're right. We're not going to get the numbers to do this."

"You're giving up?"

Even in the darkness of their niche, Rhea saw Storm roll his eyes. "Don't be stupid, I don't give up," he said. "We just need to change our strategy."

"How? How can we possibly take this system down without more people?" Rhea was starting to feel desperate again. Their plan had too many holes in it, too many flaws. She had assumed that all of the Residents in Community One would be chomping at the bit to rebel, but now she knew that it was more complicated than that.

"We're assuming that once we take out the Master, the people will revolt against us."

"Yes, of course."

"They won't. They don't love her."

"The people who are in her inner circle, the ones she gives all of the favors to, will fight back."

"Sure, but they aren't fighters."

"What about the Defenders?"

"Well . . . yes. That might be a bit of a problem."

"This is a ridiculous plan, Storm!"

"It's not! If we cut off the head of the snake, the body will die."

"But her Defender and some of her other people will retaliate."

"Once our people see that she is gone, they will rise up."

"We don't have any weapons."

"I'm taking care of that; it will just take time."

"You haven't thought this through. How are we even going to get to her?"

"You."

"Me?"

"Of course. She offered you a job."

"She offered me a smaller prison—one that I refused."

"Un-refuse."

"No."

"You can't just say no to this, Rhea, it's our only shot!"

"I . . . I don't know how to lie, okay? I never learned how."

"Yeah, believe it or not, outside of these Walls, the 'savages' you hate so much aren't taught how to lie, either. Once you people capture us, it's something that we're forced to do for survival."

"I never . . . why do you blame me for what happened to your family? I'm on your side! I didn't do it!"

"You blame me, and every other Outcast, for what happened to your Community."

"The problem with you people is that you think there is only one correct way of living, and it's the incorrect way!"

"We're arguing again," Storm said, sniggering.

"You started it," Rhea muttered.

She and Storm glared at each other in the darkness, each barely able to make out the outline of the other's face, then each started laughing.

Rhea stuffed her hand into her mouth, trying to stifle the noise. She couldn't remember the last time that she had laughed. She had never argued with anyone the way that she argued with Storm, except maybe for Brooks. Storm and Brooks were both Outcasts, and didn't understand her, but that was where their similarities ended. Storm was far more serious than Brooks. He played the idiot Defender well when he was in public with her, following her around with a big moronic smile adorning his face. When they were alone, he dropped the act. He was full of pain, missing his family in a way that Rhea had never learned to do. While she missed her own father, she didn't expect to ever see him again. Storm was waiting for his family.

"Fine," Rhea hissed, struggling to regain her composure and restrain her giggles. "What do I need to do?"

"Go to her and grovel. Tell her that you've seen how awful it is here . . . no, tell her you've seen how she is right about everything. How awful the *people* here are, how she sorted them correctly and how much you want to be in her favor, how you'll do anything to gain her favor, all that stuff."

"Can't you do it?"

"She's not interested in me. She picked you."

"And what do we do if she says no?"

"We figure it out."

"What if she says yes?"

"Then we will go from there."

"You're just full of ideas tonight, aren't you?"

"Yes, I am." Storm suddenly stiffened. Rhea heard it, too—footsteps drawing closer. She struggled to her feet.

"Quick!" she whispered. "We need to run!"

Storm struggled to his feet, pulled her close, and kissed her. She frowned in confusion for just a moment before the Defenders rounded the corner.

"Hey!" one of them yelled. "You're out past curfew! You'll catch it!" Storm and Rhea broke apart. "Oh," the Defender said, surprised.

"It's you, Sam." He laughed. "Guess you have good reason to be out past curfew." Rhea felt her face flush.

"What are you two doing out here?" the other Defender snapped.

"We've become close," Storm said, laughing. He had switched to his idiot persona flawlessly. Rhea stood beside him, stony, unsure what to do or how to behave.

"You know she can't be out past curfew," the second Defender said. He moved closer and the moon cast a beam across his face. It was Dex. "I'll have to talk to the Master about this."

"Oh, come on," the other Defender said. "Sam's looked the other way on plenty of things for us." Rhea glanced at Storm. Had they forced him to change his name when he became a Defender? Or just a Resident?

"Rules are rules!" Dex snapped. "And she's had it coming since she first arrived here. She hasn't conformed, she doesn't listen."

"That's what you think," Storm sniggered. The first Defender laughed while Dex's face twisted in anger.

"I'm taking you home," Dex huffed, his fingers finding Rhea's upper arm and pulling hard, dragging her in the opposite direction of her dwelling.

"Hey!" Rhea screamed, suddenly finding her voice. It cut through the silence of the night like a knife, and Dex quickly dropped her arm. "Let me go! Let me go!" she continued to yell.

"Shut up, you little idiot!" Dex snarled. He started for her again and she felt Storm close in behind her, wanting to defend her.

"He's attacking me!" Rhea screamed. "Get off, Dex!" She quickly drew back a leg and stamped on his knee, just like Brooks had taught her. Dex yelled wildly, his hands gripping his knee before closing around her throat.

"Enough!" Storm yelled. His dagger was out of his belt in an instant and gleamed silver as he thrust it into Dex's face. "Let her go."

Rhea's eyes locked with Dex's, watching him calculate. His fingers loosened and she backed up against Storm, gasping for breath.

"The Master will hear about this," Dex hissed through his teeth.

"Yes," Rhea agreed, wheezing slightly. "She will." She took Storm's hand and they wound their way quickly back to her dwelling.

"When push comes to shove, you know how to lie," Storm whispered.

"So do you."

"Sorry I kissed you."

"It's all part of our plan, isn't it?"

"Yes. Do you know how to handle the Master tomorrow?"

"You gave me an idea."

⌒

Rhea's throat was raw when she woke. There was a cracked mirror above the wash basin in her dwelling, and she walked over to it to examine the angry red mark on her neck. It wasn't bad, but she thought it would do. She pulled her hair back into a long braid, clearly displaying the bruise as well as her disobedience. She ran a finger along the brand, feeling a strange surge of courage. She had been disobedient before; she could do it again.

When she stepped out of her shared dwelling, hands immediately seized her. *Dex.* One hand tangled in her hair and the other pushed at her back. The next thing Rhea knew, her face was shoved against the side of her dwelling, the rough stone scraping her cheek.

"You feel brave now?" Dex sneered in Rhea's ear.

"I'm being attacked!" Rhea screamed. Dex shoved her face harder into the stone. "A Resident is attacking me! Help! Help!" At that, Dex released her. She looked around at the stony faces of the onlookers. "It's okay," Rhea called, taking in the looks of hatred pelted at Dex. "It was a Defender. Now I know that I'm safe." She faced Dex, a small smile playing around her mouth in spite of herself.

"You have no idea what you're doing," Dex said, lowering his voice dramatically.

"You're right about that," Rhea agreed.

"You have no idea who I am."

"Two for two."

"These people don't care about you. They're not going to protect you."

"Then why are you so afraid of them?" Rhea had rarely ever been so amused; it was almost worth goading Dex just to watch his temper rise.

"I'm not afraid of anything!" he snapped.

"Of course you're not," Rhea said through her smile. "I'm off to see the Master. Would you care to walk with me?"

Dex opened and closed his mouth several times, then took Rhea by the arm and began marching her to the Master's dwelling. "What are you doing?" he demanded. "Why do you want to go see her?"

"We have much to discuss."

"She won't be on your side. I'll tell her that you've been sneaking around with Sam."

"As you should. It is a part of your obligation as a Defender."

"You don't make any sense."

"I'm sure I don't." They walked in silence for a while. Rhea looked around, trying to observe and remember. There were countless tiny details that she had never noticed before. Did the Residents always sigh before walking in to their jobs? Did their faces always stiffen while they looked at the nicer dwellings that had been doled out by the Master?

"Why Sam?" Dex demanded. "What are you trying to get out of him?"

"I'm not using Sam."

"Everyone uses everyone."

"I don't use people."

"It's not like he's good-looking."

"No, he really isn't," Rhea agreed. It was much easier to agree with Dex than to argue with him. It was almost as though he wanted her to argue with him.

"You're crazy," Dex muttered.

"What does that mean?"

"You don't know what 'crazy' means?"

"No." Dex shook his head and rolled his eyes but didn't bother to elaborate. "In my Community," Rhea said, "all of the words that we used meant something."

"You're not even a real person. You're too brainwashed."

"What does 'brainwashed' mean?" Dex shook his head again. He stayed silent after that while he marched Rhea through the streets, but he released her arm. *He thinks I'm stupid*, Rhea reflected. *Maybe the Master will think so, too*.

She walked on with Dex to the Master's dwelling, then through her quarters to the room Rhea had entered on her very first day in Community One. Dex raised his hand to knock, but Rhea pushed open the door before he could.

"Master," Rhea said, entering the room. "I apologize for disturbing you, but I need to speak with you. It is urgent."

The Master was sitting behind her large desk, perusing papers. She raised her eyes to meet Rhea's, her eyebrows high in surprise. "No one has ever entered my chambers without knocking before," she said pointedly.

"No, I would think not," Rhea agreed.

The Master's eyes flickered toward Dex. "What do you want?"

Dex swallowed. "Master, yesterday—last night . . . I saw Resident One embracing one of your Defenders. It was Sam. She was . . ." Dex trailed off, seeing the look on the Master's face. "It was past curfew. And . . . they haven't been assigned . . . to each other."

"Interesting," she said dryly. "Is that all?"

"Yes."

"Leave." Dex knelt and then left, looking confused. "Well?" the Master asked, looking at Rhea.

"I would like to discuss my future within Community One with you."

"Would you like to discuss breaking my rules? Out past curfew, embracing—these are rules that you violated. I thought you assured me that you were obedient."

"I apologize for breaking the rules, Master, and I will gladly accept any punishment that you believe is fit for the crimes that I have committed."

"I see." The Master surveyed her closely. "You have changed since I last saw you in this office."

"Yes, Master, I have."

"What has brought about this change in you?"

"I fell in love with my Defender."

CHAPTER 19
HOME

Brooks panted hard. Situated up against the mountain, the slope up to their new home was steep. He looked up to check their progress as he walked and his mouth fell open. The most beautiful homes he had ever seen were coming into view. They varied in size, both large and small, and in type, both wooden and stone. He craned his neck to stare into the trees and found several houses nestled around the canopy. He stumbled, tripping over roots and rocks as he gazed around him. There were orchards and gardens around the homes. Some of them were close together, and many were spread apart. Children ran in all directions, chasing one another. Smoke drifted lazily out of the homes and delicious smells reached Brooks, making his mouth water.

Raven hurried to catch up with him. "How did they do all of this in just a few weeks?" she demanded, staring around. "There was no one here giving instructions."

"They didn't do it for us," Brooks beamed. "They did it for themselves. They built their own homes."

Several buildings weren't homes at all, but huts and buildings for people to trade out of. Brooks saw several animals corralled, people carrying water from the fall, some sharpening or beating weapons, and even a little group of children sitting in front of a teacher as she gestured enthusiastically, explaining something.

"You're back!" a booming voice said.

"Thunder." Brooks grinned, shaking his hand. Thunder was a

large man that Brooks remembered from his time before Adder had sent him into the Community. "You've been busy!"

"Not really," Thunder said, looking around affectionately. "We've been helping each other out, trading different things or services. We've all wanted a home for years, but Adder wouldn't have it. If we didn't depend on him, what good was he to us?" Thunder gave Brooks and Raven a large smile. His eyes traveled over the people following them, the people they had rescued from the camp who were now running in all directions, exclaiming at the ongoing construction and crying as they were reunited with friends and family. "Seems like things are different now, though."

"I don't know what kind of idiot would have been against something like this," Raven muttered, staring around.

"Adder wasn't an idiot," Brooks disagreed. "He got exactly what he wanted out of his leadership."

"But no one else did," Thunder added. "Leaders in today's world spend their time suppressing dissent, like Adder, or fostering creativity, like you kids. Sure seems like no one has time for both."

Brooks shook his head, still trying to take it all in. "What's it called?" he asked Thunder. "What's a place like this called?"

"I'd say it's a town. We got shops goin' up, we got homes, we're working on a school."

"Shops?" Brooks asked.

"Where people can get things and trade," Thunder said. Brooks shook his head in utter amazement.

"Never heard of it," Raven said.

"Lots of that to go around," Thunder chuckled. "Couple people here remember what life was like before the war, and they're working to teach us how things should be done. They're even goin' to write it all down, so the kids will grow up knowin' all that's happened. The first few homes we built weren't so good, but we learned and figured it out." He grinned even more widely. "You want to see yours?"

"Ours?"

"Yeah! We figured we'd want our leaders to have their own place, a place we could be proud of." Thunder led Brooks and Raven along a wide path through the middle of the town that had been worn through countless feet and hooves trampling it. Brooks couldn't stop shaking his head, glancing all around. In truth, there weren't that many dwellings—less than one dwelling for each family than they had so far—yet it was something amazing to see so much built. The Communities had built identical dwellings in varying sizes that Residents might live in for one year or twenty. It wasn't really a home, though, when Leaders could come through at any moment and move you; Residents didn't know the word "home."

Brooks himself had never learned about "shops." Growing up, his people had scarcely practiced farming. Perhaps a few of Adder's followers would save and plant seeds here and there or drag a goat on a rope behind themselves as Adder moved them from spot to spot, but it had looked nothing like this. He had never seen anything like this—this, he thought, was the very definition of a home.

Thunder stopped and pointed. "There ya go," he said happily.

Brooks stared in awe. Their people had gathered stones to create a beautiful home. It had two floors, lots of windows, and wooden shutters to help keep out the rain. There were two horses in a corral outside grazing on tall grass and a small, tilled garden out front. Thunder opened the large wooden door, motioning for Raven and Brooks to step inside, and Thunder showed them around each room. There was a room with a large fireplace for sitting, a kitchen, a room for washing, and upstairs, two large rooms for sleeping. The walls were the same rough stone as the outside, and the floors were thick wooden planks. A trapdoor in the sitting room floor opened into an earth cellar that Thunder explained would keep their food fresher.

Finally, Thunder led Brooks and Raven back out through the front door. The sun had started to sink, and the soft evening light illuminated the crowd of people standing out in front of their new home. Brooks and Raven stood outside their door, staring out at their people and their town. Brooks felt the light sting of tears in his eyes, and an overwhelming happiness that he hadn't felt since his last night with Rhea in the meadow.

"Thank you," Brooks said to his people. "Thank you for building our home. Thank you for building *all* of our homes." He glanced at Raven; she was radiant in her happiness. "While we were gone, we found a camp. It was where our people have been taken when they were stolen from us, and in it our people were abused and brainwashed. Those in charge were preparing them for the Communities, trying to force them to do things that they didn't want to do." Brooks pointed back to where they had come from, his voice rising and shaking with anger as he spoke. "We believe in taking care of ourselves and our neighbors, of choosing what and who we want. They don't. They believe in control.

"They believe that we're evil. They attack us, they steal our children, they beat and brainwash their own people . . . I know a lot of you have lived in a Community at one point or another. Here's the difference between us and them: if you want to leave us, you can." Brooks dropped his hand. "I am sorry to report that we failed. There are some of our people who were already reconditioned in the camp and sent off to the next Community. We weren't able to rescue them. But this isn't the end." He shook his head in anger. "I don't know what our responsibility is to these people, these *Residents* who are little more than prisoners, but I would like to make the offer to all of you to choose. Take tonight and think it over—this is not a decision to be entered into lightly. What do we do now?

"Do we stay here, in our new home, and defend it—I'm sure there will be more attacks—or do we take the fight to them? Do we go after our people? Do we free them? Do we free them all? Do we finally take the war to the Communities and finish what our grandfathers and grandmothers started?" Brooks studied the crowd around him. Several people were nodding and Raven's eyes were bright and alive, a sly smile playing around her wide mouth. "You know the way we live.

Think this over, talk to each other, and tomorrow we will debate and vote. Then, if you choose to come with us, Raven and I will lead the fight into the next Community." He swallowed hard; it was difficult to speak in front of so many people. And even more difficult to finish his speech. "What . . . what Raven and I want doesn't matter. We're here to talk about what *you* all want. We have a home now—most of us for the very first time—but there are still countless people out there who don't."

"So, the question is," Raven concluded, "do you care?"

Rhea lifted her chin and forced herself to look the Master in the eyes, her hands trembling. Sweat ran in a wet line down the side of her face. She silently dared the tyrant to read the truth in her gaze.

Brooks lifted his head proudly, listening to his people roar in approval, and tears stung his eyes. There was something so powerful about people coming together for the first time, something ridiculously beautiful about people being given a choice for the first time in their lives.

Rhea and Brooks each thought of the other as they both faced the point of no return, wondering if their paths would ever cross again.

CPSIA information can be obtained
at www.ICGtesting.com
Printed in the USA
LVHW030833210623
750296LV00002B/7